Holiday HOLIDAY Heart

Holiday Express Book 2
A Sweet Historical Holiday Romance
by
USA Today Bestselling Author
SHANNA HATFIELD

Holiday Heart
Holiday Express Series, Book 2

Copyright © 2021 by Shanna Hatfield

ISBN: 9798782502812

All rights reserved. By purchasing this publication through an authorized outlet, you have been granted the nonexclusive, nontransferable right to access and read the text of this book. No part of this publication may be reproduced, distributed, downloaded, decompiled, reverse engineered, transmitted, or stored in or introduced into any information storage and retrieval system, in any form or by any means, including photocopying, recording, or other electronic or mechanical methods, now known or hereafter invented, without the written permission of the author, except in the case of brief quotations embodied in reviews and certain other noncommercial uses permitted by copyright law. Please purchase only authorized editions.

For permission requests, please contact the author, with a subject line of "permission request" at the e-mail address below or through her website.
shanna@shannahatfield.com

This is a work of fiction. Names, characters, businesses, places, events, and incidents either are the product of the author's imagination or are used in a fictitious manner. Any resemblance to actual persons, living or dead, business establishments, or actual events is purely coincidental.

Cover Design: Covers and Cupcakes, LLC.

Published by Wholesome Hearts Publishing, LLC.
wholesomeheartspublishing@gmail.com

*To those so full of joy,
it spills onto those around them . . .*

Books by Shanna Hatfield

FICTION

<u>**CONTEMPORARY**</u>

Holiday Brides
Valentine Bride
Summer Bride
Easter Bride
Lilac Bride

Rodeo Romance
The Christmas Cowboy
Wrestlin' Christmas
Capturing Christmas
Barreling Through Christmas
Chasing Christmas
Racing Christmas
Keeping Christmas
Roping Christmas
Remembering Christmas

Grass Valley Cowboys
The Cowboy's Christmas Plan
The Cowboy's Spring Romance
The Cowboy's Summer Love
The Cowboy's Autumn Fall
The Cowboy's New Heart
The Cowboy's Last Goodbye

Summer Creek
Catching the Cowboy
Rescuing the Rancher
Protecting the Princess
Distracting the Deputy

Women of Tenacity
Heart of Clay
Heart of Hope
Heart of Love

<u>**HISTORICAL**</u>

Pendleton Petticoats
Dacey   *Lacey*
Aundy   *Bertie*
Caterina *Millie*
Ilsa   *Dally*
Marnie   *Quinn*
            Evie

Pendleton Promises
Sadie

Baker City Brides
Tad's Treasure
Crumpets and Cowpies
Thimbles and Thistles
Corsets and Cuffs
Bobbins and Boots
Lightning and Lawmen
Dumplings and Dynamite

Hearts of the War
Garden of Her Heart
Home of Her Heart
Dream of Her Heart

Hardman Holidays
The Christmas Bargain
The Christmas Token
The Christmas Calamity
The Christmas Vow
The Christmas Quandary
The Christmas Confection
The Christmas Melody
The Christmas Ring
The Christmas Wish

Chapter One

1914

Zach Coleman polished the gilded letters that spelled out "Hope" on the side of a train engine that was as familiar to him as his own hands. His father had been the one to name the engine when it was brand new and had been the first engineer to drive it on the Holiday Express line located in Eastern Oregon.

The steam engine was still running strong, even if his father hadn't driven it in years. Jace Coleman had retired from the railroad shortly after Zach's brother Noah had been born.

Although he thought his father sometimes missed the adventure of driving the train down the tracks between Holiday and Baker City, he knew his parents were happier than most and seemed to cherish each day they had together.

Zach rubbed a brass plaque denoting the company that built the engine and the year it was completed until it shone in the October light streaming in the bank of windows at the engine house, then leaned back to study his handiwork.

"Your dad would be proud," a gravelly voice said from behind him.

He looked over his shoulder at Henry Biggins, the engine house manager and head mechanic. Henry banked the coals in a firebox, preparing the fire to burn all night so the steam engine would be ready to go first thing in the morning.

Growing up, Zach had been crazy about trains and working with his hands. Thanks to his father's training, he'd learned each piece of equipment and part that went on every car of a train from the engine to the caboose. And he'd learned how to tear things apart, study how they operated, then put them back together. Generally, the equipment worked better than it had before he tinkered with it.

He'd been fifteen and desperate to get his hands on a train when Henry had agreed to let him work at the engine house after school. Eight years later, Zach was second in charge and loved his job.

It was hard to imagine how much the small town of Holiday had grown in the last decade. The tiny community had gone from having one hotel, a mercantile, and a few other businesses, to boasting a variety of businesses including four restaurants, three hotels, three general stores, two doctor's offices, and a public school.

Holiday was booming, mostly due to the gold mine and the mill located north of town. Last month alone, the mill had shipped six hundred carloads of lumber.

Zach had grown up watching the town expand into the bustling community it was today. One of which he was proud to be a resident.

"Is Betty making dumplings for dinner?" Zach asked as he gave the plaque one more rub with the rag in his hand before he jumped off the engine and began to gather his tools.

Henry grinned at him and patted his round belly. "She sure is. I can almost taste them. Mmm, mmm. There's nothing like her dumplings on a fine autumn day."

"Unless it's a nippy winter day." Zach often accompanied Henry home for lunch and enjoyed a hot meal instead of the cold sandwich his mother always packed for him.

"True, my boy. That is true," Henry said as he climbed off the engine and began his nightly routine of checking to make sure everything was turned off, banked, properly stored, and ready for the next day.

Zach used his polishing rag to clean his tools, then hung them on the hooks where they were stored each evening.

Corliss, the seventeen-year-old boy Henry had hired a few weeks ago, pushed the broom across the floor, while Tom, another mechanic who'd worked at the engine house the past three years, locked doors and closed the windows they'd opened earlier since the day had been so warm and pleasant.

"Good job, fellas. Have a nice evening," Henry said, standing at the back door, waiting for them all to exit.

Zach shrugged out of his greasy coveralls, yanked on his cap, tossed his jacket over his shoulder, then pushed his motorcycle outside. He kept it inside the engine house while he was working so no one was tempted to take it for a ride when he wasn't looking. He was the only one in town who rode one, although one of the Milton boys had been considering a purchase of a Harley Davidson. Personally, Zach preferred the Henderson model he rode but figured Andy Milton could make up his own mind about what he wanted.

"Does your mother still grimace every time you ride that thing to town?" Henry asked as Zach draped his jacket over the handlebars of the motorcycle.

"Every time."

Henry chuckled. "Cora Lee just worries about her boys. It's a wonder your sweet mama's hair hasn't turned white after raising you three hooligans."

Zach feigned an affronted look. "Jonah's the rabble-rouser. Noah's the hooligan. I'm the fair-haired child who's never done anything wrong."

The sound of Henry's laughter echoed around them as they sauntered away from the depot.

"Fair-haired child? Now that's a good one, Zach. Considering your hair is nearly black and you were, and sometimes still are, full of more mischief than the other two put together, that is a comment worth a laugh. You may have been sneakier about being caught than your brothers and gotten away with more shenanigans since you were the youngest, but you are every bit as ornery as Jonah and Noah. Every bit."

Zach shrugged and grinned at Henry when they came to an intersection and waited for a wagon headed for the express office to drive by. "Tell

Betty I said hello."

"Will do. Give your folks my best regards." Henry tipped his head to Zach, then sauntered north in the direction of the tidy little cottage where he and his wife lived.

Still grinning, Zach continued to push his motorcycle through the intersection rather than riding it, since the noise it made always drew a lot of attention and interest he didn't particularly appreciate receiving. His mother had asked him to bring home cinnamon and nutmeg for her baking, so he headed toward Roger's Mercantile. His family had been shopping there since the store had opened back in the years before Holiday had been incorporated as a town. Rupert Rogers had made money in gold mining. He used the funds to build the store and purchase stock. Then he'd married a woman named Goldie, and they'd raised a son and two daughters in the apartment above the store. As the town had grown, so had the success of the mercantile. Even with other stores in town, Roger's Mercantile remained the largest and most successful. Five years ago, Rupert had retired, and he and Goldie had moved to Portland to live near their daughters. Their son, Albert, and his wife, Helen, had taken over the store, guiding it on to more success while maintaining the friendly service so many in Holiday had come to expect.

Thoughts of the delicious baked goods his mother was sure to create with the spices and the baskets of apples he'd recently helped pick made his mouth water as he neared the town's park that had been installed two years ago.

Pathways lined with crushed gravel, artfully planted rosebushes and shrubs, and even a fountain where children splashed during the summer heat made the park a wonderful place to visit. A magnificent gazebo, the likes of which no one had seen in these parts until it had been constructed, stood in the center of the park, a testament to Holiday's growth. His father had been the one to suggest the design, based on a similar gazebo he'd once seen in his travels back East when he'd been an engineer.

Zach slowed his step and studied the gazebo as he pushed his motorcycle toward the mercantile located across the town's main street.

Painted white, the gazebo had been constructed in an octagon shape with eight sturdy pillars encircling it. The foundation was made of brick hauled up from Baker City. Between three pillars on each side, there were built-in flower boxes that burst with a profusion of flowers from spring through the autumn season, thanks to the efforts of the Holiday Women's League, of which his mother was a founding member. The north and south ends of the gazebo were left open for people to wander through, while benches lined the inside of the gazebo, inviting people to sit and rest. Latticework hung along the eaves, beneath the unique bell-shaped copper roof topped with a beautiful cupola. Arched dormers centered between the pillars always made him think of a woman's petticoats flouncing out in a scalloped ripple as she spun across a dance floor.

Amused by his fanciful thoughts, he stopped

and stared at a young woman as she studied the gazebo. Sunlight danced across her bare head, making it look as though the chestnut tresses glowed with bright embers. The dark green dress she wore perfectly fit her curvaceous form. Even from a distance, he could almost feel the energy pulsing off her as she held her hands in front of her, index fingers and thumbs positioned to make an imaginary picture frame. She tilted her head in study and continued backing up. If she'd held a camera in her hands, he would have thought she was a photographer, aligning her photograph before she captured the image.

As it was, if she didn't stop, she was likely to back right into the street and get hit by a passing automobile or wagon. Surely, she was aware of how close she was to danger.

But as she continued moving away from the gazebo, one step at a time, Zach hastily rocked his motorcycle onto the rear kickstand and took off running across the park. He hoped to reach her before she injured herself.

"Miss!" he shouted, but the woman paid him no heed as she continued edging backward. Zach glanced behind her to the street. Doc Holt drove his Model T toward her at a rapid pace while a wagon full of lumber jostled directly for her from the opposite direction.

"Miss!" he yelled louder, sprinting toward her as she stepped into the street, seemingly oblivious to the world around her.

Zach lunged forward, grabbed her around the waist, and swung around with such force, it knocked them both to the ground, a mere foot away from the wheels of the hulking lumber wagon as it rolled past them.

"Nice catch, Zach!" Ernie Elroy yelled from the wagon seat as he continued on his way. "No wonder you're so good at baseball."

Air stirred against Zach's cheek as the woman beneath him drew in a startled gasp. A soft fragrance enveloped him, a scent of delicate flowers mixed with something rich and sensual. The only word that came to mind to describe the perfume was scrumptious, and that was not a word he'd even known was in his vocabulary.

Time slowed until it nearly stood still as the woman shifted slightly. Zach became acutely aware of how well her curves, so soft and lush, fit against the angles and planes of his body as he held her wrapped in his arms. He could feel the runaway thumping of her heart as it kept time with the wildly beating tempo in his chest.

Despite how improper it was for him to be pressed against a woman he'd never met, he couldn't force himself to move away. Instead, he placed his hands flat on either side of her and pushed himself up far enough to look into her face.

A wild tumble of curls that had escaped her hairpins fell around her forehead and down to her shoulders. One springy coil rested on her cheek. Zach gently lifted it away, rubbing the silky strands between his fingers before he tucked it behind her ear. He took in a complexion his mother would have referred to as peaches and cream, even if it was dotted by freckles across her cheeks, and a thin, small nose. He noticed a scar above her left eyebrow, and a tiny, barely noticeable dimple in her stubborn chin.

Lips that did, indeed, remind him of ripe peaches, made him wonder if they'd taste as sweet. The woman's heart-shaped face gave her the appearance of a mischievous pixie. But it was her eyes that held and captivated him. He'd never seen eyes such a pale shade of green, like frost had settled over the heart of a forest glade. Unlike a frozen landscape, though, they held warmth. A great deal of warmth, and, if he wasn't mistaken, a bit of humor.

The lovely young woman was unlike any he'd ever encountered. He hesitated to end this most unexpected encounter with her, doubting he'd have a second opportunity to be this close to such a fascinating female. Unable to stop himself, he allowed his head to dip closer to her, inhaling again her luscious scent.

"Hi," he whispered, unsure why he felt the need to speak so quietly, other than to keep from breaking the spell she had seemingly cast over him.

"Hi," she replied in a hushed tone. The barest hint of a smile kicked up the right corner of her mouth, making him battle the urge to kiss her tempting lips. "Thank you for rescuing me."

"My pleasure," he said, reluctantly pushing himself off her, rolling to the side, and rising to his feet. He extended both hands to her and, when she clasped them, pulled her upright. Propriety demanded he immediately turn loose of her fingers, but he couldn't muster the will to let her go.

"I do apologize for not paying better attention." The smile she offered to him showed off teeth so white they nearly dazzled him in spite of a front tooth being slightly crooked. She tugged one hand free from his and waved it in the direction of the gazebo. "That is the most spectacular gazebo I've ever seen. I was picturing how best to draw it and got lost in my thoughts. Just when I'd landed on the precise perfection of placement, the vision changed. It's a dilly! What a sight to behold when the sun began to dip toward the horizon and sent beams of gold dancing off that glorious copper roof. Just take a gander and see if it doesn't leave you mesmerized."

Something had left him mesmerized, for certain, and it had nothing to do with the sunset or the gazebo. He tried to yank his scattered wits together long enough to extract at least one thread of conversation. "You're an artist?"

She laughed, not a silly schoolgirl laugh, but one that held the confidence of a woman. "No. I lack the talent and dedication to be an artist, but I do enjoy sketching and sometimes add splashes of color to my endeavors."

Zach realized people were staring at them and released the woman's hand before someone he knew marched over and began asking questions. His mother, sister-in-law, and all the females in the Milton family felt it was their duty to constantly be on the lookout for his potential bride.

The problem was that Zach was perfectly happy with his life the way it was. His father and grandfather had both assured him, when the right woman came along, he'd change his perspective on remaining blissfully single. Until she did, he had no intention of letting the women in his life force him into courting a girl he had no interest in pursuing. A fact that he'd reiterated frequently, even if no one listened to him.

As he studied the woman beside him, he felt something shift inside him, as though it was a moment of great importance, one he'd always remember.

"I hope I didn't hurt you." Zach knew he'd probably landed on her rather hard, but that was preferable to the woman being run over by Ernie's lumber wagon. As he looked at her, though, with the sunlight setting her hair aflame and her eyes sparkling with interest, she certainly appeared unharmed. And far too pretty for his jangled nerves to ignore.

She shook her head, causing all that wondrous hair to shimmer in the fading light. For a wickedly decadent minute, he considered how hard she might slap him if he yielded to the ever-increasing need to kiss her. Lest the desire overtake him, he took a step back. "You're sure you aren't hurt?"

"No. I'm fine, sir, and your assistance in keeping me from being seriously injured due to my negligence is appreciated." She brushed at the back of her skirt, then turned those uniquely beautiful eyes on him. "Truly, I'm grateful for your help."

"My pleasure, Miss …"

"Lennox. Lorna Lennox. I arrived in town earlier this afternoon and wanted to explore a bit before dinner. I'd barely started on my walk when I happened to see the gazebo."

"It's nice to meet you, Miss Lennox. Welcome to Holiday. I'm Zach Coleman."

"Coleman? If I have my details in order, your family has been here since before Holiday became a town."

He grinned. "That's true. Pops—he's my grandfather—moved out here when my father and uncle were young. We've been living out at Elk Creek Ranch ever since."

"Your father and uncle live there now? With your grandfather?"

Zach wanted to sidestep her question, but if she asked anyone about their family, everyone in town seemed to know the story of his uncle Jude. Might as well tell her the truth and see how she reacted to it. Over the years, he'd found the reactions of people to be a good gauge of their character.

"My father runs the ranch. My brother Noah will take over when Dad decides to slow down. Pops lives in a little house on the ranch with his wife, Ava. They married about ten years ago, and we call her Grams. As for my uncle, he died in prison when I was three."

"Oh, I'm sorry to hear about your uncle." Lorna placed a hand over his and offered a sympathetic squeeze. "But it's marvelous the rest of your family is there."

"Not quite all of my family. My oldest brother, Jonah, moved to Idaho where he and his wife ranch with her parents."

"Do you have other siblings, besides the two brothers you mentioned?"

Zach smirked. "Nope. I'm not sure my folks could have kept up with more of us. They claim Jonah, Noah, and I were a handful."

She smiled again. Zach entertained the crazy notion that it was like having sunlight poured directly into his soul.

"I imagine you were a handful," she said, "but I believe children with a little gumption are tomorrow's future."

"Then the future of Holiday is secure because I grew up with a gang of troublemakers." Zach leaned closer to her and dropped his voice. "Sadly, most of them have matured past such nonsense."

"That's both gladdening and disheartening to hear."

Before Zach could decipher what she meant, she brushed at her skirts one more time, then gave him a long glance. "I do thank you for saving me from a premature demise at the wheels of that hulking wagon."

"I'm more than happy to be of assistance. Since you are so new to town, would it be acceptable if I walk you home, just to make sure you arrive there safely?"

"Under the circumstances, I suppose that would be more than acceptable." She took a step toward the street, then looked down as though she'd just noticed the planks that covered the entire main street from a block past the church to the other end of town just beyond the marshal's office and jail.

The board-covered street was a source of pride in Holiday. When it rained, the boards kept the street from becoming a quagmire. In the summer, it helped keep down the dust. Zach had heard from his uncle R.C. that the town hoped to place boards on several more streets in the spring. As one of the town's councilmen, R.C. was usually in the know when it came to happenings in Holiday.

Zach motioned toward the motorcycle he'd left on the other side of the park. "I'll be right back," he said, loping back to where he'd left the Henderson, then pushed it up the street and around the corner to where Lorna waited.

"Is it not in an operable state?"

"Oh, it works just fine, but I try not to use it too much in town." He looked both ways before pushing the bike into the street. They crossed to the other side in front of the mercantile. He waved at Albert Rogers as he carried a box out and loaded it in old Mrs. Piedmont's automobile. She and her husband had owned the hotel in town for years, but they'd sold it last spring to a young couple who'd come west from Virginia. The Kindalls were nice people, and the hotel seemed to be doing well.

"Why don't you ride it in town?" Lorna turned to the right and continued walking, although she darted several glances at him.

"Some of the womenfolk think it's too noisy, and some of the kids come running as soon as they hear it, wanting a ride."

A teasing smile lifted her lips upward. "The children have the right idea. I think it would be a dandy treat to ride such a machine."

"Maybe one day I'll give you a ride, if you'd like."

Lorna clasped her hands beneath her chin and

beamed at him. "I'd like that very much!"

"We'll plan on it, then. Soon. In a few weeks, it will likely start to snow, and I'll have to ride a horse to town instead of this." Zach tipped his head toward the motorcycle, then looked back at her as they headed south on Holiday's Main Street. "Where do you live?"

"Our house is on Mulberry Lane, just off Milton Road."

Zach had no idea where Mulberry Lane was, but he was familiar with Milton Road. He'd spent hours and hours playing with the Milton family, for whom the street was named. Even though they weren't related, he considered R.C. and Anne Milton his uncle and aunt, and their bevy of children his cousins.

"Is it a new house?" Zach asked as they continued past the bank, then crossed the street and headed past the telephone office and a newly opened restaurant. Charles Milton and his wife, Susan, had eaten there the other day and raved about the food.

"Yes and no. It's been a project my father has worked on for a while, but he finished it in July. It just took a while for us to move everything here from our home in Philadelphia."

"I'm sure it's quite a change being here in Holiday compared to a big city like that." He couldn't begin to imagine how the small community measured up to a bustling city, but there wasn't anywhere he'd rather be than Holiday. It was home to him and always would be.

"It is a change, but I think I'm going to like it

here. It's so peaceful and quiet, and the air smells like Christmas." Lorna closed her eyes and inhaled deeply, drawing Zach's attention to her curvy figure before he glanced away.

"Funny you should mention Christmas. Our little town loves the Christmas season, and you won't find anyone who enjoys it more than my mother. She starts baking right after Thanksgiving. The men in my family do our best to eat everything as fast as she pulls it out of the oven."

Lorna laughed. "I'm picturing you and your brothers, father, and grandfather all poised around the oven, waiting for a tray of cookies fresh from the oven."

"It's happened before. If you don't believe me, ask Mamie."

"Mamie? Who's that?" Lorna's brow wrinkled slightly in confusion.

"My mother. We call her Mamie. When Jonah was little, he heard people calling her Cora Lee— that's her name, you see. He knew she was his mama, so he combined it all together and the name Mamie stuck. Even the Milton bunch refers to her as Mamie now."

"Milton bunch? As in Milton Road?"

Zach nodded as they reached a crossroads. The large Milton Feed and Seed building sitting diagonally across the street housed not just a feed store, but also a blacksmith shop, livery, and auto repair business. R.C. had purchased half a section of land not long after he and Anne had wed. The feed store was located on the end of the property nearest town. A pasture where they kept cows and horses separated it from the farmhouse and three-story barn R.C. and Anne had built a dozen years ago.

He pointed to the feed store. "Milton Feed and Seed. Everything you need for caring for animals large and small, raising a garden, maintaining an automobile, renting a horse and buggy, getting a horse shod, or having metal work completed. It's also the livery and blacksmith shop."

"Quite an enterprise," Lorna said, studying the building, then pointing down the road to the house and barn in the distance. "Is that another cupola?"

"On the barn. I'll ask Uncle R.C. if I can show it to you sometime. The barn has a big arena inside where the Milton boys show off their roping and riding skills. There's a set of steps inside that go up to the cupola, and the widow's walk has the best view around these parts."

"I'm sure it is something to see and shall look forward to exploring it at the convenience of your uncle." She appeared baffled as she turned to the left and started up Milton Road. "How are you related to the Milton family?"

"I'm not, by blood, but we spent so much time around them when we were all little, they became our aunt and uncle like my parents are to their children. There are ten of them."

"Ten children?"

"Yep. They had six boys, three girls, and then Timothy, who was a bit of a surprise to Aunt Anne. She thought she was through having children when he came along."

"I'm sure he's a special blessing to them."

Zach chuckled. "I'm not positive Uncle R.C.

would describe him that way, but it's a nice thought."

He glanced ahead of him and saw the newly constructed mansion owned by the railroad tycoon. The man had arrived in Holiday and started buying up trains and investing in mines, and had even bought a partnership in the lumber mill. Suddenly, Lorna's last name penetrated the fog that had descended on his brain the moment he'd seen her gazing at the gazebo.

"You're *that* Lennox? You're related to George Lennox?" Stunned, he stopped outside the wrought iron fence encompassing a yard that appeared to be acres in size. Everything about the yard looked precise and purposefully arranged, much like the imposing three-story brick house where Lorna now resided.

She turned to him and smiled. "Yes. George is my father. Do you know him?"

Zach couldn't tell her he'd only seen Mr. Lennox from a distance, or that he'd heard Henry complaining about the demanding, sometimes exasperating man who barked out orders and expected each one to be obeyed immediately. If rumors proved true, George Lennox was eccentric, irritable, and rich enough to buy anything he wanted or desired including the entire town of Holiday.

"I've not yet had the pleasure of meeting him," Zach said, doing his best to sound casual instead of on guard. Of course, it stood to reason the first woman to truly stir his interest had to be the daughter of a man with more money than kindness or common sense.

"Papa isn't home now, but I'll introduce you another day."

Zach highly doubted her father would allow her to consort with the likes of him, but kept his opinions to himself.

"I reckon I better head for home. Again, welcome to Holiday, Miss Lennox. In the future, you might want to be more careful about where you're walking. I'd hate to see you get hurt while you're planning the next picture you'll draw."

"Thank you, Mr. Coleman. I shall endeavor to be more aware of my surroundings. Would you care to come in for some refreshments before you venture to your home?" She pushed open the gate on the walk, then turned and gave him such a warm smile, Zach took a few steps forward before he stopped himself.

No good could possibly come from fraternizing with the daughter of the man who essentially owned the railroad, and could therefore fire him on a whim. Despite how much he wanted to spend time with Lorna, he had to turn her down.

"Maybe another time, Miss Lennox. I promised Mamie I'd run by the store and pick up some spices for her baking. I'd best get to it before the mercantile closes."

"My apologies for detaining you, sir. My deepest gratitude to you, again, for rescuing me and ensuring I made it safely home."

"You're welcome." Zach touched his fingers to his cap and turned his bike around, ready to leave. He'd only taken three steps when he stopped and glanced back over his shoulder to see Lorna watching him. "I don't know if you've heard or are even interested, but the community is holding a festival to celebrate Halloween and the end of harvest. It's this Saturday at the Grange Hall. You'll find it across the street from the church, next to the school on the other end of town. It's a costume party, so you can dress up if you like, but you don't have to."

"Oh, it sounds perfect! Thank you for the invitation. Perhaps I'll see you there."

"I'll be there." Zach grinned at her and hopped on his bike, starting it up and roaring down the street.

As he headed to the mercantile, he envisioned the type of costume Miss Lorna Lennox, heir to the Lennox empire, might wear. In spite of the voice in his head warning him to stay far away from the girl, he was glad he'd happened upon her at the park. He looked forward to seeing her again Saturday at the party.

Chapter Two

"Where on earth have you been, honey?" Cora Lee Coleman shook a spoon coated with pudding at him as Zach wiped his boots on the rug inside the kitchen door before he toed them off and hung his hat and jacket on hooks.

"I stopped to rescue a damsel in distress," he said with a cheeky grin. He dug the spices out of his jacket pocket and handed them to his mother, kissed her rosy cheek, then hurried over to the sink to wash his hands and face.

"Tell me about this damsel," Cora Lee demanded as she tossed a clean towel to him and returned to stirring the pudding that was about to bubble.

Slowly, Zach dried his hands and face, aware his mother anxiously awaited him to share his story with her. It wasn't that she was nosy, but she genuinely cared about her family and the town.

However, if he mentioned how much he'd liked meeting Lorna, he had no doubt Mamie would start hearing wedding bells ringing. For that very reason, he considered what to say to her before he admitted his attraction to Miss Lennox.

"Zachariah Coleman, you better start talking before I imagine my own details to your story. Is she a local girl? Someone we know?"

"Maybe the damsel wasn't a girl. Maybe it was a woman grown so old, she could hardly shuffle across the street and was nearly run over by one of the little rascals racing home after school." He grinned at his mother and swiped a finger through the pudding she poured into bowls. In spite of the heat threatening to burn his fingers, he licked off the sweet substance and winked at his mother when she gave him an exasperated look, one he'd seen many times over the years.

"Unless Mrs. Piedmont left her cane at home again, I can't think of who might be the damsel in need." She finished spooning the pudding into dessert bowls, then handed him the empty pan and spoon.

Zach scraped the spoon around the inside of the pan, digging up a few bites of the warm pudding. No one made it any better than Mamie.

"Maybe it was a peg-legged woman on the lam from the Ruby Palace."

Cora Lee snatched the spoon and pan away from him, waggling the spoon just inches from his nose. "And just what do you know about that … that … horrid den of iniquity?"

"Not a thing, Mamie. Not a thing, other than any mention of it gets you and Aunt Anne plenty riled."

His mother huffed and set the pan and spoon in the sink with a loud clank. "That despicable business should be run out of town for good. Anne and I have tried, along with Mrs. Ryan and several others, to see it shut down, but if it closes in one location, it just pops up in another. It's a blight on our lovely little town."

Zach refrained from telling his mother that the reason the Ruby Palace stayed in business was because some of the prominent businessmen in town made sure of it. His father and Uncle R.C. were among those who supported the women in their efforts to shut it down, but Zach doubted they'd ever have much luck. Not with miners, lumbermen, railroaders, and others bragging about how it was one of the finest brothels in the West.

"I won't be distracted, young man. Where were you really? I thought you'd be home nearly an hour ago." His mother glanced at him as she drained the water off a pot of boiled potatoes and added a generous scoop of butter before she began mashing them. He took the masher from her and pressed it into the potatoes.

She gave him a pleased smile, then turned to pull a pan of rolls from the oven. Zach breathed in the perfume of yeasty goodness, fresh and hot. His mouth watered as his mother used a fork to spread butter across the golden tops of the bread.

"I was heading to the mercantile when I noticed a woman backing toward Main Street, like she was going to step right into the street. I had to leave my motorbike on the boardwalk and race across the park. If I'd been a few seconds later, she would have been squashed like a bug under the wheels of Ernie Elroy's lumber wagon. After I so gallantly saved her life, I walked her home. Then I hurried back to the mercantile to get the spices. Are you going to bake an apple cake tomorrow? Or maybe you'll make apple fritters for breakfast? Apple oatmeal?"

"I'll bake one of your favorites, but tell me more about this woman. Was she young or old? Do you know her?"

"She was younger, and she'd just arrived in Holiday today. She said she wanted to do a little exploring and was quite taken with the gazebo. From what she shared, it sounded like she enjoys drawing and was envisioning a sunset scene with the gazebo when she backed into the street."

Cora Lee's eyes, a nearly identical shade of blue as his own, pinned him with a purposeful glare. "How young?"

Zach shrugged, wishing he'd never mentioned Lorna because his mother would latch onto the idea there was a new woman in town she hadn't yet applied her matchmaking skills to and set to work. She and Anne fancied themselves to be quite talented at pairing up couples. Admittedly, they had helped three of Anne's sons and both of his brothers find brides who made them incredibly happy.

But that didn't mean he was ready or willing to settle down, and he certainly didn't require his mother's assistance when, or if, he eventually warmed up to the idea.

"She's probably close to my age," he said quietly, pretending to focus all his attention on mashing the potatoes.

"And . . ." Cora Lee waited for him to continue.

Zach considered bolting for the safety of the bunkhouse and eating dinner with the ranch hands, but he figured his mother would just pry the details out of him later.

"She had reddish hair and greenish eyes. I think she had on a green dress."

Cora Lee expelled a frustrated breath. "Where did she live? You said you walked her home." She stared at him as she opened the oven door.

Zach took the potholders from her hands and lifted out a roasting pan. The beef roast his mother had cooked for dinner was one of his favorite meals. The meat was marinated for several days and practically fell apart at the touch of a fork. He set the pan on a dish towel on the counter, then lifted the lid on the pot still bubbling on the stove. Perfect. His mother had made red cabbage to go with the sauerbraten.

Due to her German heritage, she often prepared dishes she'd been taught to make by her mother, who'd learned from her mother, and so on, with each generation passing on recipes to the next.

With Germany involved in the Great War overseas, hostility toward Germans had begun to grow in America. Although his mother's parents had immigrated to the United States from Germany years ago, she was as American as anyone.

He didn't know if she looked German, with her blonde hair and blue eyes, and didn't care. To him, his mother was a sweet woman who loved her family, her home, and her friends, and could cook the most delicious food in the world. If anyone dared say anything disparaging to her within his hearing, they would wish they'd kept their thoughts to themselves.

"Honey?" Cora Lee prompted when he failed to respond to her question.

"Sorry, Mamie. I guess I was woolgathering." He picked up a large fork and knife, carefully moving the roast onto a platter. He sliced it while his mother scooped the cabbage into a serving bowl.

She stirred the gravy, then glanced at him as he set the meat on the table. "Thinking about that pretty girl you met today?"

"I never said she was pretty." Zach felt heat rush up his neck, and his ears burned as they did any time he was embarrassed.

"No, you didn't, but from the way your whole face just turned red, I'm sure she is. Now, where does she live?"

"You know that great big house everyone has been talking about for the past two years? The one on Milton Road near Uncle R.C.'s store?"

"The mansion?"

Zach nodded as he set plates on the table. "That's the one. She lives there. Lorna Lennox is her name. Her father is George, the railroad tycoon."

Cora Lee stared at him a moment. "Lorna is a lovely name." His mother handed him the bowl of cabbage. "Why don't you clang the triangle on the porch so your father will know supper is ready."

Caught off guard by his mother's sudden change of subject, he wondered if she'd let the matter drop or only wait to ask him more questions later.

His father came in for supper, and the three of them sat down to eat. Sometimes his grandfather and Ava joined them. Once in a while, Noah and his family came over from their house to share the meal. Other times, it was quiet, like tonight. Normally, Zach didn't mind the peacefulness at the end of a day, but tonight, it made him nervous.

Or perhaps it was his mother and her incessant questioning as he helped set the food on the table that put him on edge.

It wasn't until she'd served the warm pudding with shortbread cookies that she brought up his adventure with Miss Lennox.

"You'll never guess who Zach met today," Cora Lee said, smiling at his father.

Jace wiped his mouth on his napkin, looked at Cora Lee, then turned to Zach. "I reckon I won't guess, so you two better tell me."

"He met George Lennox's daughter." Cora Lee winked at Zach, then took a bite of her pudding.

"Is that so? Does she look like her father? Like a barrel that sprouted limbs and a head?"

Zach chuckled and shook his head. "Not exactly, Dad. She seemed nice."

"That's good. She been in town long?" Jace asked.

"No. From what she said, she just arrived today. It sounded like she's planning to stay. She mentioned moving everything from their home in Philadelphia."

"Hmm. Well, I hope she likes living here in Holiday. It will be a big change from city life, for sure. Perhaps there are some young people around who can make her feel at home." Jace gave him a knowing glance before he dug a spoonful of pudding from his bowl.

"Perhaps," Zach agreed. "I did make mention of the party Saturday."

"Oh, that's wonderful!" Cora Lee smiled, clearly pleased by this tidbit of information. "I hope she'll come."

"If she does, it will be an easy way for her to meet a lot of folks from Holiday."

"That it will." Jace gave Zach another thoughtful look. "Remind me what costume you plan to wear."

"I was thinking about wearing a clean pair of coveralls and a silly hat."

His parents looked at each other and shook their heads.

"Why don't you go as a cowboy, honey?"

Zach sighed. "I dress that way whenever I'm not working at the engine house, Mamie. It's nothing different."

"Oh, but you look so handsome in your hat and boots. You should borrow that old duster Pops has from his younger days."

"Maybe I'll do that."

"And maybe you'll catch the eye of a pretty girl," his mother said, offering him a teasing smile.

He didn't bother telling his mother he had no interest or intention of catching anyone's eye. Not unless the peepers happened to be the color of frost on a deep forest lake.

Chapter Three

"A woman who pretends indifference to her appearance is sadly lacking in good sense. It is simply not enough to be a kind and caring person: you must do your best to always appear attractive and pleasant. There is no excuse to do otherwise."

Miss Mulberry's Advice for Today's Young Woman

"Oh, Miss! What would your father say?"

Lorna looked in the mirror at the woman who had been her nanny from the day she was born. Dodi Truman had been as faithful a servant as any that had ever cared for a child. Many times, Dodi had been like a mother to her, especially after Lorna's own mother had passed. When Lorna had outgrown the need for a nanny, Dodi had stayed on as her companion, serving as a chaperone, guardian, and sometimes confidante when she wasn't helping oversee the running of the Lennox household.

She tossed Dodi a saucy grin. "He won't say anything since he's out of town for another week. Father won't know I ever dressed this way."

"But, Lorna, are you sure it's safe and proper for you to go gallivanting off to this gathering? You don't know anyone, and I just don't feel right about your attending it unchaperoned."

Lorna spun around and grabbed Dodi's hands. "Then come with me. You can dress up as a witch or the belle of the ball."

Dodi shook her head. "You know I don't care for costumes or loud gatherings, but I'll go like I am and scowl the whole time if you'd like me to be there with you. I can pretend to be a strict and stern schoolmarm."

Lorna pulled on the wig Dodi had helped her make from yellow yarn. She poked in a few pins to hold it in place, then looked at Dodi again. "You were a strict schoolmarm so that won't count as a costume."

Dodi scowled and settled a floppy straw hat over the wig. Maude Barnes, the cook, and Marcus, her husband, and the Lennox groundskeeper, helped age the hat Lorna had purchased at the mercantile that morning. From the smears of dirt embedded on the crown and the frayed edge, she wondered what the couple had done to make it look so worn.

A giggle escaped as she envisioned Marcus stomping on the hat, pretending it was her father. Lorna knew George Lennox could be a tyrant and thoroughly impossible at times, but she loved him in spite of his faults.

"What is so amusing?" Dodi asked as she crammed more stuffing down the back of Lorna's costume.

"This." Lorna pointed to the full-length cherry

mirror that showed off her hastily assembled scarecrow costume. "I look ridiculous, and I love it!"

Dodi smiled. "You do look rather silly. I suppose, since no one knows you, it will do no harm for you to attend this party alone. Just promise you'll be home by bedtime."

"I promise, Dodi." Lorna spun around and kissed the woman's cheek before she grabbed another pillow and jammed it down the front of her shirt. She didn't know where Marcus had acquired the worn flannel shirt and bibbed overalls, but they were perfect for her costume. She thought a scarecrow was an ingenious way to attend the party and meet people from the community, all while keeping her identity a secret.

Tomorrow, she would attend church services with Dodi, Maude, and Marcus and make a proper introduction into the Holiday community.

Tonight, though, was about having fun. And that was exactly what she intended to do. With the overstuffed overalls and the mask made of paper and paste that Maude had helped her create, no one would be able to tell if she was a man, woman, or child.

She just hoped that Zach Coleman would be there. After all, he was the one who mentioned the party, and she was glad that he had. Already, she greatly missed her friends and home in Philadelphia. The Halloween gathering would provide a welcome distraction, one she hoped that would bring her an evening of joy and frivolity. Aside from the gaiety of the gathering, she looked forward to seeing again the handsome man who'd walked her home.

The past two nights, since the evening he'd kept her from stepping in front of the lumber wagon, she'd hardly been able to sleep, taunted by dreams of him. One moment, she'd been envisioning a painting of the marvelous gazebo with the sun behind it, making the roof look like a molten river of copper. The next, she'd felt someone grab her waist and swing her around. In spite of Zach landing on top of her, he'd somehow managed to cushion her fall with his arms.

Startled more than anything, she'd sucked in a gasp of air and wondered what sort of strange place with such forward men her father had decided to call their new home.

Then Zach had pushed himself up and looked into her face and she felt the world as she knew it shift. And rather than feel off-kilter, everything had suddenly felt so right. As though this was the place, the very moment, that she was meant to be in, and Zach was the man with whom she was intended to experience it.

Lorna knew such thoughts were ludicrous, but they filled her mind just the same. Zach had looked at her with deep blue eyes fringed with the darkest, thickest eyelashes she'd ever seen. A shadow of stubble darkened his cheeks and chin. A thin, barely visible scar ran from the corner of his right eye a few inches down toward his ear. Some might have said his nose was just slightly too big, but it was straight, as were his teeth, clearly visible when he offered her a crooked, altogether endearing smile.

Her gaze had fastened on his mouth, the lower lip fuller than the top. A peculiar longing to kiss it nearly overtook her before she yanked her thoughts in line.

She'd felt his heart pounding against hers, as though they'd both started beating in unison the moment they'd connected. If it hadn't seemed so inexplicably preposterous, she might have considered the encounter the most magical moment of her life.

As it was, she'd been unable to stop thinking about Zach. Lest she give away her interest to Dodi and Maude, she had avoided any mention of him. The two women were convinced she was doomed to be a spinster, not because of her looks or her manners, but because she was far too independent for the liking of most men.

However, Zach Coleman wasn't like any man she'd ever met. All the males she knew, her father included, would have berated her for not paying any attention to what she was doing at the park. But not Zach. He'd inquired about her welfare, walked her home, then merely cautioned her to be more careful without attempting to make her feel like an idiot.

Oh, how she hoped to see him at the party. What would be his costume of choice? A prince? A skeleton? Perhaps a knight of old since he had come to her rescue.

Lorna slipped on her mask, and Dodi tied the ribbons that would hold it in place behind her head, covering the ends with the yarn wig.

"You look amazing!" Dodi leaned around Lorna and smiled at her reflection in the mirror. "If there is a prize for best costume, you should win."

"As always, you are too sweet and kind to me, Dodi. I'm sure there will be many spectacular costumes. With such short notice of the festivities, I think we did well with this one. Thank you for your help. It is most appreciated."

"You're welcome, darling girl." Dodi took a red bandana from Lorna's dressing table and snapped it in the air, then tucked it so it hung partially out of a front pocket of the overalls. "Don't forget your gloves. Those delicate hands will give away the fact that you are a female."

"And pampered," Lorna added, tugging on a pair of leather gloves she used on the rare occasions she helped Marcus in the gardens at home. She'd loved working in the roses and hoped the cuttings they'd shipped earlier in the fall would take root and thrive here in Holiday. The flowers had been one of her mother's great joys, and Lorna was determined to keep at least one of her mother's rosebushes alive.

"You forgot spoiled," Dodi teased as Lorna snatched up several coins and tucked them deep into a pocket, then clomped her way to the door in a pair of old boots Marcus had unearthed from goodness only knew where. They were a few sizes too big, so Dodi had stuffed the toes with cotton.

"Can you see with that mask on to make it down the stairs?" Dodi asked, reaching out to help her.

"I can. I have to squint a little, but I can see." Lorna trooped down the stairs, then loosened her joints and dipped her knees while flailing her arms as she walked off the last step. Marcus and Maude waited in the foyer and applauded at her antics.

"You look both scary and delightful," Maude said, giving her arm an affectionate pat. "Have a grand time, Miss Lorna."

"I intend to. Are you absolutely certain the three of you won't join me?"

"We're too stodgy for such goings-on," Maude said, then looked to her husband and Dodi for agreement.

The other two nodded. Marcus pulled open the door, and they all stepped outside onto the porch. "It's no trouble at all to drive you there, Miss Lorna. I'd feel better about you not walking by yourself on a night like tonight."

"If you're sure it's no bother, you could drive me to the church. The party is held across the street. As for my return trip home, I'm sure I can make friends with someone and have them walk with me. If nothing else, I'll find a telephone and call should I need a ride."

Marcus hurried down the steps and around to the carriage house where the automobiles and buggies were parked. It didn't take long before he pulled up at the end of the walk in her father's Oldsmobile.

"Here you are, now," Marcus said, getting out and walking around to open the back door of the car for her.

"I think I'd better sit up front, in case anyone sees us. That way it will look more like two fellas out for a drive, don't you think?" Lorna slid onto the front seat before Marcus had time to answer.

He jogged back around the car and put it in gear.

"Enjoy your evening!" Lorna waved to Maude and Dodi, then placed one hand on top of her hat to keep it from blowing off.

"Want me to go slower?" Marcus asked as he turned down Milton Road heading into town.

"No. I can hold it in place. I do so appreciate the ride, Marcus. It's not like Holiday is very large, but it is a little frightening to wander around in the dark on Halloween in an unfamiliar town."

"And a young lady like you shouldn't be out without a chaperone. I still can't believe Dodi is allowing you to go unattended, but I suppose it's safe enough at the Grange Hall."

"I'm sure it will be a memorable event. If I do require any assistance, I'll telephone."

"Provided you can find one. I heard at the post office they've only had the telephone system since August, and electricity since April."

"We're quite fortunate a small out-of-the-way place like this has any modern conveniences at all."

Marcus nodded. "That we are. I still haven't landed on the reason your father wanted to move to Holiday. I thought this was to be your summer home. It's such a shame we lost your mother before the house was finished. She would have loved it here."

Lorna felt the familiar sting of tears at the mention of her mother. Noel Lennox had been a bright, shining light in all of their lives. Then she'd taken sick not long after Lorna's father had begun building the house here in Holiday. Within weeks,

Noel had been confined to her bed. In another month, she was gone, drawing her last breath as she slept. Lorna knew her father had been devastated by the loss, as had all of them.

Originally, her father had been building the house in Holiday as a place for them to get away from the big city during the summer months. Lorna didn't know the details of all his business holdings, but she was aware of his investments in mines and a lumber mill in the Holiday area. He'd also purchased the Holiday Express line, including the engines and train cars. After her mother passed away, her father seemed intent on making the house in Holiday their permanent home. Not that she could blame him. Far too many memories lingered at the house in Philadelphia.

Although she would miss many, many things about the city and her life there, she was ready for a new beginning. The gathering this evening would provide her with a chance to step into her future with a great deal of anonymity.

"Stop right up there please, Marcus," Lorna said, pointing to a side street between the church and what appeared to be a dress shop. Lorna looked forward to investigating the shop another day. A beautiful hat of dark green wool on display in the window would look splendid with the new winter gown that was being shipped from her favorite dressmaker.

Marcus turned down the side street and stopped the car. "I can walk you to the door," he offered.

Lorna hopped out, tugging her hat down more firmly on her head. "I'll be fine, Marcus, but thank you. I hope you and Maude have a nice evening."

"We will. Goodnight, Miss Lorna."

Lorna waved at him, then ran across the street. What freedom! No petticoats or corsets or long skirts hampering her every move. The recent style of hobble skirts was one she particularly loathed. With the narrow opening at the bottom of the skirt, it made it nearly impossible to walk. She'd refused to partake in what others considered the height of fashion, much preferring skirts that at least allowed her to walk with a normal stride, or as normal as one could walk when dressed like an elegant lady.

As she hurried across the lot where wagons and automobiles parked behind the church, she felt a twinge of envy for the male species. How fantastic it must be to wear pants all the time. She intended to enjoy every moment of being able to stretch her legs out as far as she wanted.

The hum of happy voices greeted her as she crossed the street and walked toward the open doors of the Grange Hall. Several groups of people, all dressed in colorful costumes, ambled toward the entrance.

It appeared as though Dodi's worries were for naught. Judging by the varied height of the people, many were children, which meant it would be a safe event.

Lorna politely stood to the side and waited as a group of four women, all dressed like witches, preceded her into the building. She strode inside, following the witches through the entry, and entered a big open room decorated with paper streamers, pumpkins, stalks of corn, and bundles of wheat. The smell of cinnamon and apples wafted through the room, along with the sounds of laughter and friendly chatter.

With what she hoped were long, lanky steps, she made her way to the far end of the room where two older women dressed as circus clowns ladled hot cider into cups.

"Help yourself," one of them said, setting a cup in front of Lorna and motioning to a table laden with cookies, cakes, pies, candy, and sandwiches. Lorna chose a sugar cookie with raisins placed on top in the shape of a scary face and broke off a little piece, tucking it into her mouth beneath her mask. She picked up the cider and carefully took a sip.

"Good," she said, making her voice sound as deep as possible.

The two women gave her a curious look, then went back to serving others who lined up for treats.

Lorna moved out of the way and found a corner where she could observe those milling around the room. She watched a family of six, all wearing black with bones painted on their clothes, wander inside.

There were people dressed like farmers and bumpkins, and even a few like pumpkins. Someone had made an elaborate chicken costume out of feathers. A man dressed like a slab of bacon was being teased by someone in a pig costume.

"How fun. How utterly delightfully fun," Lorna muttered to herself as she nibbled on her cookie and sipped the cider.

She wondered what sort of costume Zach might wear and if she'd be able to recognize him. Her gaze scanned the room again. A group arrived and was greeted warmly by others. There was no missing the handsome cowboy who shook hands with someone dressed like a goblin. To her, it seemed as though every female in the building was suddenly aware of the cowboy's presence as all eyes turned to him. A rakish growth of stubble covered the cheeks of his tanned face, but she recognized that crooked smile and those beautiful blue eyes. Zach. He was here!

Lorna shifted so she had a better view of him, studying him from the cowboy hat pushed back on his head to the silk paisley neckerchief knotted around his throat. He wore a long canvas duster with blue jeans, dusty boots, and spurs.

"You forget to put on a costume, Zach?" she heard someone holler at him, and several people laughed.

"Leave him be, Noah," said a lovely middle-aged woman with eyes the same shade of blue as Zach's. Lorna assumed she had to be his mother, his beloved Mamie. The woman reached out with the fan she held in one hand and smacked the arm of a man dressed like a train engineer. The engineer held a strong resemblance to Zach, only his hair was much lighter and he was slightly shorter.

A young woman in a gypsy costume stepped next to Noah, holding the hands of a little boy dressed as a chimney sweep and a little girl in a fairy costume.

"Be nice to your brother or no treats for you, husband," the gypsy warned.

"Daddy, you better be good. You likes treats,"

the little fairy said, making the adults around her laugh. A man who looked like an older version of Zach picked up the fairy and kissed her cheek. "That's setting him straight, Tilly."

"May I have a cookie, Gampa?" Tilly asked, hugging the older man.

"Yes, you may. How about you come along, Hayes, and we'll all get something to eat." The man held out his hand to the boy, who eagerly clasped two of his fingers, then began skipping toward the food table.

Enchanted by Zach's family, Lorna leaned against the wall, unable to pull her gaze away from the cowboy who'd captured her interest.

Back in Philadelphia, Lorna had been popular among her friends and had more men coming to call than she wanted to think about. Granted, most of them were far more interested in her father's fortune than in her, but there were a few boys she'd liked and a few men she'd briefly considered suitable companions.

But not one of them had drawn her like Zach. She hardly knew anything about him, other than he was attractive and kind and seemed gentle and fun. The moment their hands had connected when he'd helped her to her feet at the park, she'd felt something spark between them. Something she'd never experienced. Something that made her think there was something different, something special, about Zach.

She had yet to name what it was, but she had time. After all, they'd only met a few days ago, and she would be in Holiday for the foreseeable future.

Lorna watched as several young women engaged in a frivolous game that involved each of them going into a closet with a small candle, a mirror, an apple, and a knife. The girls were supposed to peel the apple all in one piece. If they succeeded, they could look in the mirror. Supposedly, the image of their true love would be revealed.

When one young miss who had acted rather snobbishly toward several of the boys in attendance flounced out of the closet with a big scowl on her otherwise pretty face, Lorna wondered if she'd seen her own reflection in the mirror, for it certainly seemed she treasured herself most of all.

Chagrined she was already being judgmental, Lorna sent up a prayer for forgiveness. She watched as another young woman entered the closet. When she came out, she tossed a moon-eyed glance in Zach's direction.

Lorna held back a snort of disbelief. That was the seventh girl—or was it eighth—who came out of the closet and gave Zach a besotted look.

Bored with the game, Lorna returned to the refreshment table and helped herself to a piece of apple cake. She retreated to a shadowed corner to eat it. The cake was moist and bursting with flavor. In an unladylike fashion, she devoured every crumb, then glanced around, finding no one paying her any mind.

Several more games were played, like charades, and Lorna participated in a few. Musicians began to play and a spot was cleared for dancers. She noticed Zach's parents were among those sweeping across the floor. Noah bowed to his wife, and she gave her airy gypsy skirts a jaunty swish as he swung her into a fast-paced reel.

Those who didn't engage in the dance tapped their toes or clapped their hands. Lorna longed to dance and wanted to join in, but she didn't feel she could, not if she wanted to maintain her disguise as a man.

A few of the men in attendance had greeted her and engaged her in conversation about crops, cattle, and the railroad. Although she knew next to nothing about the first two topics, she could converse at length about the railroad.

She watched as Zach surveyed the room, as though he searched for someone. He'd done that a few times that she'd noticed. The part of her given to vanity hoped he'd been looking for her, but he most likely had already forgotten she existed.

Two identical girls in their teens dressed in fringed buckskin costumes rushed over to Zach and began tugging on his hands. He laughed and twirled them both around, then handed them off to two males who had to be their brothers.

When the boys started to step away from the girls, a hulking man moved behind one of them and nudged him forward. "It won't kill you to dance with your sister, Burt."

"It might, Dad!" the boy called on a laugh as he swung his sister in the lively dance.

Zach grabbed the hand of a young woman who looked so much like the twins, there was no doubt they were sisters. All of them were beautiful. Together, Zach and the woman who was dressed in a gown that put Lorna in mind of styles popular a hundred years ago, held to a lively step as they danced around the floor. They looked happy as they kept time to the music.

Lorna loved seeing the way these families interacted, with teasing warmth and true affection. She'd always wondered what it would be like to have siblings, and still thought it would be grand to have a brother or sister. That would never happen, but perhaps someday, when she wed, she'd have siblings through her husband's family.

If they happened to be the Coleman family, she wouldn't be opposed at all. In spite of the way Noah and Zach seemed to take great joy in tormenting each other, anyone could see they cared deeply for their family.

The musicians stopped playing, and a man dressed in a prison outfit of black and white stripes stepped in front of them and cleared his throat.

"Mrs. Piedmont baked the Halloween cake, and it's time to dig in. All you single folks out there, come on and get a slice. Remember, if you find a ring, you're the next to wed. The coin means you'll be wealthy. The button is prized since you'll meet your true love. If you find the key, pack your bag and buy a train ticket because adventure is in your future. And if you find the thimble, don't fret, it's just a game and doesn't mean you'll really be a spinster."

Several of the younger people rushed over to where the women serving refreshments waited with a large cake that had been cut into small slices.

Lorna thought about ignoring the proceedings

and heading home, but she found herself getting in line behind two of the witches she'd followed inside earlier. It didn't take long before a small plate was placed in her hands and she stared at the slice of fruit cake. She took a bite, cautious as she chewed in case she bit into something.

The flavor of the cake was not nearly as good as the apple cake she'd eaten earlier, but she took another bite. Still nothing.

Across the room, one of the witches squealed and held up a gold ring.

"Look at that! Miss Clara Hampton found the ring. She's in the market for a groom, boys!" The man who'd done the announcing earlier spoke in a teasing tone.

A tall young man with wide shoulders and a brawny physique marched over to her and pulled her against his side. "Nobody better get any ideas. Clara is mine!"

"James Milton, she is not a slab of beef," said a woman with a slight British accent as she stepped in front of him. She bore a strong resemblance to the young man. Lorna was sure the woman had to be his mother, as well as the mother of the identical twins. "You can't go around acting like a thundering cavedweller."

"Sure, he can, Mrs. Milton." The pretty witch snuggled against James' broad chest, making the crowd laugh.

"I dare say it's a good thing you two are getting married in a few weeks," Mrs. Milton said, before smiling at Clara and walking away.

Lorna was pleased the couple were about to

exchange nuptials. They seemed quite in love as they stood with arms wrapped around each other, enjoying the proceedings. One by one, the other hidden trinkets were found in the pieces of cake. The coin went to a young man dressed as a beggar. The key went to a woman in a nurse's uniform. One of the witches let out a cry of dismay when she found the thimble and rushed from the room.

Poor girl. No one wanted to think in terms of spending life all alone. No one.

Lorna forked another bite of the cake and bit into something hard. She licked it clean then looked at the red button she held in her fingers.

"Who found the button?" someone asked.

"Where is the button?" another person questioned.

"Yes! Who is about to find true love?"

Reluctantly, Lorna raised her hand in the air, holding the button between her thumb and index finger.

The man dressed in prisoner attire waggled his hand toward her. "Oh, look at that. Mr. Scarecrow is gonna fall in love."

The crowd cheered and clapped; then the musicians started playing, and the dancing resumed.

Not for a minute did Lorna believe a button found during a silly game would lead her heart to find the man she would wed. Yet, when she glanced across the room and found Zach observing her, her heart skipped a beat and her palms grew damp. She shoved the button into her pocket and slouched against the wall, hoping he hadn't figured out who she was.

The musicians played several more songs before the man in the prison costume took charge again.

"Before the evening winds to a close, it's time for the costume contest!"

Cheers erupted and soon Lorna was clapping with the rest of them as they awarded prizes to several youngsters. She liked that there were different age groups receiving prizes so more of the children had an opportunity to win something. Then they started on the adult costumes. Prizes were given to the women in several categories including the most creative costume, won by the chicken. The scariest went to a woman who appeared to have horns growing out of a skull face and claws for hands. The most authentic costume was awarded to Noah's wife, who'd sat at a table for a while and offered to read fortunes from a crystal ball which was actually a crystal bowl turned upside down. More prizes were awarded to men in the same categories as the women. The fellow dressed as bacon won the creative category. Zach was teased about having the most authentic, even if it was clothes he frequently wore, but the award went instead to a man who greatly resembled Teddy Roosevelt.

"Now for our grand prize of the evening, come on up here Mr. Scarecrow!"

Lorna looked around to see if someone else had on a scarecrow costume, but everyone seemed to be focused on her.

With a loose-limbed gait and arms swinging like they were about to become unfastened from her shoulders, she went forward and accepted the grand prize. The basket was filled with a variety of goods from several businesses in town. Lorna felt guilty accepting it since she could easily purchase anything she wanted and had a feeling there were many at the event who lacked funds to buy what they needed.

She held the basket in her arms, lowered her voice, and focused on a spot at the back of the room. "Thank you all for this honor, and for a nice evening." Quickly dipping her head, she walked out of the center of attention.

"One last dance, folks; then it's time to head for home."

Rather than wait and watch the final dance of the evening, Lorna kept walking when she reached the doorway. She hurried outside and had just crossed the street when she felt a hand on her arm.

Her first instinct was to scream, but she swallowed her fear and stopped, turning to find a particularly good-looking cowboy smiling at her.

"Mr. Scarecrow, if I'm not completely mistaken, your identity beneath that mask is someone I met a few days ago by the name of Miss Lennox." He bent his knees slightly, trying to see inside the slits of her mask to view her eyes. "Am I right?"

Lorna did her best to make her voice sound masculine and rough, and irritated. "I ought to plow my fist into your pie hole," she growled, mimicking something she'd once overheard at one of the train depots while she waited for her father.

Zach's eyes widened and he took a step back.

He opened his mouth and snapped it shut twice. He cleared his throat and held up his hands in a placating motion. "My apologies, sir. I mistook you for someone else."

One giggle erupted from her followed by another. Zach frowned and moved closer to her. "Miss Lennox?"

"It's me, Mr. Coleman. I'm sorry for teasing you."

He removed his hat and ran his fingers through his thick, dark hair. "You sure had me fooled for a minute."

Lorna glanced across the street to where partygoers left the Grange Hall. Some of them were singing "In My Merry Oldsmobile," as they filed outside. From her impression, the community of Holiday seemed fun and jovial and welcoming. In the brief conversations she'd had, no one was overtly nosy when she'd avoided questions that might have revealed her identity. For that, she was grateful.

"Do you think I fooled the others?"

Zach nodded. "Completely. I heard Uncle R.C. tell his son Rance you seemed to know a great deal about the operations of the railroad. They all think you're one of your father's employees."

Lorna shrugged and turned to walk to the end of the block. "I suppose that's true enough. Sometimes I help clean up father's desk and straighten his files."

Zach kept step with her until they reached the intersection. He glanced back to where his parents spoke with the Milton family. "Did you come alone?"

"Yes, but please don't tell anyone. Dodi, she's my, well … she used to be my nanny and now is a companion of sorts. Anyway, she didn't think it would make a good impression if I attended by myself, but I so wanted to participate in the party." Lorna smiled, then realized how stupid that was because Zach couldn't see her face behind the mask. "I had a delightful time. Your family is wonderful."

"They can be," Zach said, glancing from her to the departing partygoers. He grabbed onto her hand and gave it a light squeeze. "I don't think you should walk home alone. If you wait just a moment, I'll go with you. I'll let my folks know where I'm going so they don't leave without me. Although I've done it in the past, I don't particularly look forward to walking home in the dark tonight."

"You don't have to accompany me, Mr. Coleman. I'm sure I'll be fine." To prove her point, Lorna took a few steps but found herself pulled to a stop when Zach continued to hold onto her hand.

"Please. Let me walk you home. I won't rest tonight, worrying about you, if you don't allow me to accompany you. If you'd feel better about it, I could ask Mamie and Dad to come along."

"I don't want to be any bother."

"You won't be. Just wait here a moment. Promise?"

"I'll wait." Lorna watched as Zach rushed back to where his parents laughed at something R.C. Milton said. The sound of Zach's spurs jingling as he moved made her smile, wondering if he really did dress like that much of the time. The other day, when he'd kept the wagon from smashing her, he'd had on a pair of denims and a plaid cotton shirt with sleeves rolled halfway to his elbows, along with a cap she'd seen other motorcycle riders wear.

He hadn't looked anything like a rancher or cowboy then, but from what she'd heard tonight, and what her father had told her when he'd mentioned some of the residents of the town, the Coleman family owned Elk Creek Ranch where they raised Angus cattle descended from those Grant Coleman had originally shipped in from Scotland. Her father had heard they made a tidy profit selling beef to the lumber mill and the mines in the area.

Regardless of their finances, she thought they seemed like good, kind people. The sort of people she'd like to get to know better.

Zach said something to his father; then they both looked in her direction. The older man nodded and thumped Zach on the shoulder. He strode to the church lot where several autos and wagons were parked and started one of the automobiles. It didn't take long until he pulled up next to her and stopped.

"An International Harvester Auto-Buggy," she said, admiring the vehicle with large buggy-like wheels and two rows of seats. "I've not ridden in one of these before."

"Then you'd best hop in, Mr. Scarecrow." Zach gave her a broad grin and his teeth flashed in the moonlight. He took the prize basket from her and set it in the back, then waited as she climbed in.

Lorna didn't know when she'd seen a man who

looked more ruggedly appealing and quickly concluded she never had. Zach Coleman was one of a kind. One she wanted to know, to call her friend.

"Your parents don't mind waiting?" she asked as he drove around the corner and headed down Birch Road. It would intersect with Milton Road a short distance from her home.

"Nah. They'll go home with Uncle R.C. and Aunt Anne. I'll pick them up there."

"Is your Aunt Anne the lovely woman with the British accent?"

Zach nodded. "That's her. Aren't the twins just the spitting image of her?"

"I don't know about spitting, but they certainly do resemble their mother. So does James. I take it the other boys were in attendance too?"

Zach nodded. "All but Mike. He had a sick horse he was tending to this evening, but his wife was there with their baby. She was dressed up as a strawberry."

"The wife or the baby?"

"The baby. Gwen would look a little odd dressed like a berry, but then I guess most of us don't look like ourselves this evening." Zach gave her a pointed look as he turned left on Milton Road. "That's quite a costume. How'd you manage to make it on short notice?"

"Dodi helped, as did Maude and Marcus. Maude is our cook, and Marcus takes care of the grounds and does a hundred other things. He and Maude are married, and I've known them and Dodi all my life."

"It's nice they all moved out here, so you have

familiar faces in a strange new place."

Lorna had been so grateful the three faithful employees had decided to travel with her to Oregon. Her father had given them a choice of remaining in Philadelphia at the house there or embarking on a new adventure in Holiday. Much to her everlasting pleasure, they'd decided to come to Holiday. She couldn't help but wonder if the promise of traveling in luxury in her father's private train car had prompted their decision, but she knew they'd come because they were dedicated to her family and were the closest thing she had to grandparents.

"It is nice," Lorna agreed as Zach turned into the drive and pulled the car around by the carriage house.

"May I walk you to the door?" Zach asked as the auto rolled to a stop.

"I'll be fine, Mr. Coleman, but thank you so much for the ride. I truly appreciate it."

"My pleasure, Mr. Scarecrow. If you happen to see Miss Lennox, let her know I look forward to seeing her at church tomorrow. Services begin at half-past ten." He reached back for the basket and held it out to her.

"I'll be sure to tell her," Lorna said, sliding out of the car. "Perhaps you know someone who could benefit from that basket."

"I do, and that's kind of you to offer it. I'll drop it off on my way to Uncle R.C.'s house." Zach put the car in gear and drove away with a wave.

Lorna expelled a long breath, watching until he disappeared at the end of the drive when he turned onto the road. She turned and fairly skipped into the house, holding a red button in her hand and wondering if magic truly was afoot.

Chapter Four

Zach contemplated how much trouble he'd be in if he popped Andy Milton in the nose right there in the church vestibule.

The idiot had been fawning over Lorna far longer than was necessary and definitely more than Zach appreciated. Even if Andy was his best friend, and regardless of their parents and Pastor Ryan watching, he battled the urge to pummel him.

Finally, Andy's brother Burt elbowed his way in and bowed over Lorna's hand, kissing the back of her gloved fingers.

"It's a pleasure to meet you, Miss Lennox. Please don't judge all of us by my brother. He's so homely and dimwitted, he has to try and catch a girl before they have a chance to escape."

Andy scowled at Burt and took a step toward him with hands clenched at his sides.

Fortunately, Zach's mother happened to see the storm brewing and intervened. "Miss Lennox, it would make me so happy if you'd come home with us for lunch. I'd dearly love the opportunity to visit with you for a while. We could bring you back before supper."

Lorna turned to the older woman she'd introduced as Dodi Truman, her former nanny, who'd been glued to her side since the service ended.

The woman smiled and patted Lorna's hand. "Go on, child. Enjoy your day."

"But what about you and Maude and Marcus?"

"They're all welcome to come," Cora Lee hurried to assure Lorna and Dodi.

Dodi shook her head. "We'll welcome a quiet day of rest, Miss Lennox. You go on and have a grand time."

Lorna looked as though she'd refuse; then she lifted her gaze, and it tangled with Zach's. He smiled, and Lorna nodded at his mother. "Your invitation is greatly appreciated, Mrs. Coleman. If you're certain I wouldn't be imposing, it would be with sincere gratitude that I accept your kind offer."

"Splendid!"

Zach watched as his mother looped her arm around Lorna's, then introduced her to Pastor John Ryan and his wife, Maureen. The pastor's youngest child, Rogan, stood off to one side of the churchyard with Timothy Milton. The two boys appeared deep in a discussion about a pocket knife as they took turns studying it.

While his mother escorted Lorna through the throng waiting to meet her, Zach crossed the churchyard to where he'd parked their automobile. Although it belonged to his parents, he was the one who most often drove it. Then again, he was the one who liked to tinker with anything mechanical.

Noah refused to drive an automobile. Zach watched as Jenny herded Tilly and Hayes out to their buggy, helping the little ones climb in. He waved to her as Noah slid onto the seat. His brother gave him an odd look, then tipped his head toward their mother as she stood in the middle of the churchyard, surrounded by females, all eager to make Lorna's acquaintance.

Zach had told his parents the truth about what he was doing the previous evening when he'd asked to borrow the car to drive Lorna home. Of course, he'd waited to explain the mysterious scarecrow's identity until after they'd left the Milton family and headed toward the ranch.

His mother had been so giddy about him escorting Lorna home, she'd nearly bounced in her seat. This morning, she'd been equally excited at the prospect of meeting the girl. It hadn't surprised him in the least that she'd invited Lorna to eat the noon meal with them.

And if he knew his mother, which he did, quite well, she'd make sure he was the one to return Lorna to her home later this afternoon.

That was fine with him.

In fact, he was looking forward to spending more time with the intriguing woman. He'd been eager to see her at the party last night, anticipating she might come dressed as a witch or a fairy or perhaps a mythical being. He could easily see her in a Grecian gown, pretending to be Aphrodite.

Acute disappointment had settled over him when she hadn't shown up at the party. Then Zach had become aware of a scarecrow lingering around the edges of the gathering. Because she was tall, Lorna had managed to pull off her ruse of being a man in costume.

He wasn't sure when he'd figured out it was her, but at some point before Lorna had found the button in her cake, he'd begun to suspect she was the scarecrow. By the time she'd won the costume contest, he'd been sure of it.

It had shocked him speechless when she'd spoken to him in a voice that sounded like she'd chewed up gravel, telling him he'd made a mistake about her identity. He'd even believed her for a few seconds until she started to giggle.

Zach liked that she was full of fun. He'd always thought life was far too short to be taken too seriously. The idea that Lorna seemed to be of the same mind made him whistle a lively tune as he started the car.

"Looks like someone is getting their wish," his father said under his breath as he approached the automobile. "You want me to drive so you can sit in the back with Miss Lennox?"

"I think Mamie will want to keep her all to herself for a little while longer, Dad, but thanks for the offer."

"All righty, then, son. I'll leave driving home to you." His father walked around the car and opened both the back and front passenger doors. His mother climbed in the back, and Lorna scooted in beside her, leaving Zach to sit next to his dad. It wasn't exactly the seating arrangement he had in mind, but he'd have the trip back to town alone with Lorna; at least he hoped his parents wouldn't feel the need to chaperone them. It wasn't like he was sixteen and in need of their supervision when he was around a female.

His mother pointed out people and places as they drove through town and turned onto the road that headed out to the ranch. A trip that used to take the better part of an hour in the wagon if the team felt like plodding along could be made in less than fifteen minutes in the automobile, if the road was dry. If it was muddy, they were better off traveling in the wagon.

Thankfully, today provided a beautiful, sunny, unseasonably warm beginning to the month of November.

Zach glanced into the back seat and saw Lorna leaning closer to his mother as she pointed out neighboring farms and ranches.

"The Milton family is certainly large," he heard Lorna say.

His father chuckled and turned around to glance at her. "All those big boys overwhelm you?"

Lorna smiled. "They certainly did, Mr. Coleman. Which one is the oldest son?"

"Oh, that's Charles. Charles, then Rance, and Mike. They're all married to such lovely girls. Andy is still single, as you may have surmised from his enthusiastic greeting this morning. Next in line is James, but he's getting married in two weeks. Then there's Burton, or Burt, as we all call him, and Timothy, who is just twelve. Then there are the girls. Ellery arrived between Andy and James. The twins, Mariah and Mercy, are just a year and a half younger than Burt."

"And you've been friends with the Milton family for several years?" Lorna asked.

"Oh, yes," Zach heard his mother respond. "R.C. and Jace were friends before Anne and I met them. You see, Anne and I arrived in Holiday on the same train to be mail-order brides. Back then, she was Anne Charles and I was Cora Lee Schuster. She took one look at R.C. when he met us at the depot and was immediately smitten."

"What an amazing story. Is that what happened to you and Mr. Coleman?"

Cora Lee glanced at Jace and shook her head. "No. Jace's father decided to play matchmaker for Jace's brother. He sent for me, pretending to be Jude. Pops met the train and brought me out to Elk Creek Ranch, but it was evident from the start Jude had no idea about my arrival and no interest in marrying me. It wouldn't have mattered what Jude wanted anyway because I fell in love the moment I set eyes on Jace."

Zach watched as his father reached back and squeezed his mother's hand, giving her a look full of love and tenderness. "I think it was the second look when you fell in love. The first one, you accused me of robbing the very train I was driving."

"That I did." Cora Lee looked over at Lorna. "You see, Jace and his brother were identical twins, much like Mariah and Mercy Milton. Jude had robbed the train, and I'd accidentally caught a glimpse of part of his face, so when I saw Jace, I thought he was the robber. I quickly discovered it would have been impossible for him to rob the train since he was the engineer. At any rate, it all worked out like it was supposed to."

"It did. For us and the Milton family," Jace said, giving Cora Lee's hand another squeeze before he released it. "What about you, Miss Lennox? Any family beyond your father? Any beaus who'll be coming to Holiday?"

Zach rolled his eyes, annoyed with his father's less than subtle approach to finding out more about Lorna, although he was interested in knowing the answers to the questions.

"No, sir. My mother passed two years ago, not long after my father started building the house here in Holiday. Originally, he intended for it to be our summer home, but after we lost Mama, the house in Philadelphia seemed empty. And it teemed with memories of her. I think that's why Papa spends so much time traveling. Now that we are settled into the house here, I do so hope he'll be at home more often. As for beaus, there hasn't been anyone who's met both my approval and Papa's."

"Is it a joint agreement, then?" Cora Lee asked. Zach wondered when his parents had gotten so inquisitive, or downright nosy. They were nearly as bad as Pops with their thinly veiled attempts at extracting Lorna's personal information.

Lorna laughed. "My father thinks it is, but under the right circumstances, I might disagree. So far, his disapproval has conveniently served to keep the fortune-hunters at bay."

"I'm sorry, Miss Lennox. It must be hard to discern the people who like you for you and those who are interested only in furthering their financial situation," Cora Lee said in a sympathetic tone.

"Thank you. It has been a wearisome challenge, but nothing I haven't been able to manage."

"Will your father be returning soon?" Cora Lee asked.

"He is supposed to return next Saturday, but his business meetings often result in delays. I've learned to not worry overly much if he's late and to enjoy the time when he's home."

"That's wise, Miss Lennox."

Zach turned onto the lane that led to their house. He loved their home and the ranch but wondered what Lorna would think of it. It certainly didn't compare to the grandeur of the Lennox mansion.

He heard her gasp and glanced back to see her leaning forward as the house and barn came into view. The barn had received a new coat of red paint back in September, and his mother's autumn flowers bloomed all around the porch of the house. A maple tree and an oak tree that provided shade to the side of the house in the summer hadn't yet lost their leaves. The hues of gold, orange, and red looked quite striking in the midday sunlight.

"It's gorgeous!" Lorna said, excitedly. "Oh, look at the horses! And there are cows!"

From the tone of her voice, he was certain her enthusiasm was genuine. Lorna seemed truly pleased to be there.

"Welcome to Elk Creek Ranch, Miss Lennox," his father said, grinning over his shoulder as Zach stopped the car at the end of the front walk.

"Yes, Miss Lennox. Welcome to our home," Cora Lee said, accepting Zach's hand as she climbed out of the car. His father opened Lorna's door and helped her out.

Zach hurried to push open the gate to the yard, then stepped back as his mother and Lorna, followed by his father, started up the walk. Two dogs raised their heads from where they'd been asleep on the porch and began thumping their tails against the floorboards.

With her head swiveling from right to left, it appeared as though Lorna wanted to take in everything at once. Zach stepped forward and placed his hand on her elbow when, in her gawking at the ranch, she misstepped off the edge of the walk and nearly tripped. If he hadn't caught her arms and steadied her, she surely would have taken a tumble.

Lorna glanced at him with gratitude and embarrassment plainly visible on her face. "Thank you."

"My pleasure, Miss Lennox."

His parents led the way up the porch steps. Lorna lingered on the top step, staring at the barn and the bunkhouse. She jumped in surprise when the dogs bumped into her legs. Rather than give the dogs a repugnant look, she dropped to her knees, removed her gloves, and looked to Jace for permission. "May I pet them?"

"Of course," Jace said, grinning at her as he opened the front door. "You two play with the dogs for a minute. Come in whenever you're ready."

Zach watched his parents disappear inside before he knelt next to Lorna. She held out her hand, and Barnum licked her fingers.

"Oh, they're sweet, Mr. Coleman."

"Call me Zach, or Dad and I will spend all day confused about who you're talking to." He grinned and scratched behind Bailey's neck. "They are good dogs. The one slobbering all over your hand is Barnum, and this pretty girl is Bailey."

Lorna's eyebrows arched upward. "Barnum and Bailey? From the circus?"

Zach nodded. "That's right. Pops took me and my brothers to the circus when it came through Baker City years ago. I think I was probably around eleven. At the time, it was a grand adventure. Anyway, when we got the dogs a few years back, those names seemed like a perfect fit."

"They are perfect." Lorna gave Barnum a few more scratches behind his ears before she showered Bailey with affection. The moment she stopped petting Bailey, both dogs leaned against her, eager for more attention.

"I think you've made two friends for life." Zach reached over and playfully thumped Barnum on the side. The dog's tongue lolled out in pleasure; then he scooted closer to Lorna, licking her chin.

Laughing, she lifted her face out of reach. "They are so loveable. What kind of dogs are they?"

"Mutt, mostly, with just enough collie in the mix to make them useful for herding the cattle." Zach ruffled the fur of both dogs, then straightened and held out a hand to Lorna. "If you aren't careful, they'll lick the freckles right off your face."

She stopped laughing and glared at him. Too late, he realized Lorna might be sensitive about her freckles. According to Ellery Milton, most women detested them, along with sunburned noses. He supposed she was as good an authority as any on the subject, since she sported a smattering of freckles and frequently sunburned her nose while trying to keep up with her younger siblings.

"I … um … I wasn't … I didn't mean anything by that comment." He started to drop his hand, but Lorna clasped it with hers as she stood.

He offered her a cautious look. "I meant no offense, Miss Lennox. Your freckles are quite fetching."

A smile eased across her lips and brightened her eyes. "Thank you. No offense taken, although I detest having freckles." She sighed and turned so she could see out across Elk Creek Ranch. "It's so lovely here. So peaceful. It must have been a nearly perfect place to grow up."

"It was. If you're interested, I could show you around after we eat."

"I'd like that very much." She drew in a breath. Zach wondered if she could smell the pine trees mingling with the hint of woodsmoke and the aroma of frying chicken that made his stomach growl with hunger.

"Would you like to come inside?" Zach took a step toward the door, making a grand sweeping motion for her to enter.

"Thank you, kind sir." Lorna smiled at him as she walked inside the house. Her gaze slid around their comfortable family room; then she looked beyond it to the wide doorway that opened into the kitchen and dining area. He could see his father setting plates on the table, while his mother bustled between the stove and the sink.

"I'll give you a tour. It won't take long." Zach led her from the family room, which his grandfather always called the great room, to a hallway located to the left of the main section of the house. His parents slept in the largest bedroom on that side of the house. Two other bedrooms currently stood empty. On the other side of the family room, he led her down another hallway where three more bedrooms, including his, were located.

"These other rooms must have belonged to your brothers," she said as she looked at the darker, masculine curtains and furnishings in the rooms.

"That's right. Jonah and his family use them when they come to visit. Mamie keeps threatening to redo them, but Jonah talks her out of it every time."

Lorna laughed softly. "I get the distinct idea that you and your brothers know just how to get your way with your mother."

Zach tossed an innocent look at Lorna as he guided her back toward the family room. "I would take great offense at that if it weren't mostly true. On things that really matter, Mamie lays down the law and demands it be kept. The rest of the time, she probably lets us get away with more than we should."

"If your brothers are like you, I don't see any lasting harm in it."

Zach grinned at her and escorted her to the kitchen. "That chicken smells so good, Mamie. I can't wait to eat."

"May I help with anything?" Lorna asked,

nervously clasping her hands in front of her.

"It's all just about ready to set on the table," Cora Lee said, smiling at Lorna, then looking at Zach. "Why don't you wash up?"

Zach showed Lorna the washroom that had been added off the kitchen. He gathered an armload of firewood and carried it inside while she washed her hands; then he washed his before returning to the kitchen. As her eyes looked observantly around the room, he wondered what she saw, what she thought of their home. His parents had updated the kitchen two years ago, adding a bigger cookstove, more cabinets, and even a porcelain-lined refrigerator that kept their food cool year-round. He could be wrong, but he was sure his mother's favorite thing in the house was that refrigerator.

He walked over to the table and pulled out a chair, offering Lorna a warm smile. "Please, have a seat, Miss Lennox."

"Thank you," she said, gracefully poising on the chair. As she did, Zach drew in a breath, inhaling her tantalizing scent. Once again, a ridiculous word—*scrumptious*—entered his thoughts. He mentally tossed it aside and took a seat in his chair.

After his father asked a blessing on the meal, the four of them discussed the party the previous evening and upcoming events in Holiday. His parents asked Lorna about life in Philadelphia, and she asked about Holiday and their family.

As soon as the meal was over, his mother hopped up from the table and began carrying plates to the sink.

"Why don't you take Lorna out and show her around a bit, Zach? When you come back, we'll have dessert. That will give my apple cake time to finish baking."

"Yes, ma'am," Zach said, pulling out Lorna's chair. "You don't want to miss out on Mamie's apple cake."

"Was it the deliciously moist apple cake at the party last night?"

Cora Lee nodded. "I did take an apple cake. I'm glad you had a piece of it."

Jace chuckled. "You're lucky you got some. Everyone loves Cora Lee's apple cake. It usually disappears quickly at community gatherings. I didn't even get a piece."

"Then you can have two today," Cora Lee said, kissing Jace's cheek. He tugged her onto his lap and kissed her square on the mouth.

Zach rolled his eyes while escorting Lorna from the room. "You have to forgive them. Dad and Mamie sometimes forget they're old married folk instead of a young newlywed couple."

"I think it's sweet," Lorna said. A soft look settled on her face as she slid her arms into the sleeves of the coat he held for her. "My parents weren't nearly as demonstrative with their affections, but how delightful your parents are still so much in love, especially after raising three wild boys."

Zach scowled as he tugged on his coat and opened the door. "Wild boys? Who said we were wild?"

"Several of the stories your parents shared

about you and your brothers give every indication that the three of you were wild." She lifted an eyebrow, as though challenging him to argue before she stepped outside. "Perhaps a better word would be rambunctious."

"We were that." He cupped her elbow and guided her down the porch steps. "Some might even say we were a little wild."

The knowing grin she cast in his direction made something inside him feel warm and tender.

He spent the next hour showing Lorna around Elk Creek Ranch. She climbed on the fence and admired the handful of horses in the corral next to the barn, studied the chickens, and wrinkled her nose at the pigs. Inside the barn, she spent several minutes petting one of the milk cows, Bunny, and was quite taken with her big, brown eyes. He introduced Lorna to some of the ranch hands when they stepped out of the bunkhouse to greet her.

Zach tamped down the urge to clobber two of the cowboys who continued to stare at Lorna like she was the first and only woman they'd ever seen.

He steered her back toward the house, giving her a chance to wander around the yard, taking in his mother's colorful flowers. While she stopped to study a bush with burnished bronze leaves, he tossed a stick for Barnum and Bailey to chase.

The dogs woofed and took off running across the yard, tails wagging in delight as Noah and Jenny arrived with his grandparents.

"This won't be good," Zach muttered to himself, hurrying to Lorna's side. A part of him longed to grab her hand, race to the automobile, and make a hasty retreat to Holiday. But it was too late to escape, especially with Hayes and Tilly running toward them with the dogs close at their heels.

"Who have we here?" Lorna asked, hunkering down until she was on eye level with the children.

Hayes stuck his hand out and grinned at her. "I'm Hayes. I'm five. You're pretty. I like your hair."

Zach had to hand it to his nephew, the kid wasn't a bit shy, and he had an eye for beauty. With the autumn sunshine caressing Lorna's head, her hair appeared to be a glorious shade of deep red.

"How lovely to meet you, Hayes." Lorna shook his hand, then turned to Tilly.

The little one wasn't nearly as bold as her brother and hid her face against Zach's legs. He picked her up and rubbed her back as she clamped her arms around his neck. One of his favorite things in the world was hugs and kisses from Tilly. She'd wrapped her little fingers all the way around his heart the first time he'd seen her, just as Hayes had, but Tilly looked like a wood sprite with her delicate features, tiny fingers, and halo of soft golden curls.

"This is Tilly. She just turned three." Zach turned slightly to the side as Lorna stood and took a step toward him.

"Oh, she's precious, Zach. She looks like a beautiful doll." Lorna smiled at his niece in a way he found entirely becoming.

"A dolly?" Tilly asked, lifting her head from where she'd tucked it beneath Zach's chin. "I likes dolls."

"I'm sure you do, Tilly." Lorna reached out and

ran a gentle hand over Tilly's curls. "She's so pretty, Zach."

"That's because she took after her mama instead of us Coleman boys," Zach said, tickling his niece and making her squirm and giggle.

"Down, please," Tilly said, wiggling in his arms. Zach set her on her feet, and she took off running for the house with Hayes right behind her.

"They're adorable, Zach. What sweet children."

He grinned. "You might not say that if you saw Tilly during one of her tantrums, or Hayes when he's come to visit with his pockets full of treasures like frogs and bugs."

Lorna shuddered in revulsion, and Zach chuckled. He introduced her to Noah and Jenny, his grandfather, and Ava; then they all went inside, where the scent of his mother's apple cake filled the kitchen with a rich cinnamon-laden fragrance.

Much to his pleasure, Lorna teased Noah and his grandfather, played with the children, complimented Jenny on her hairstyle and raved about his mother's cake as though she were part of the family. For a brief, intensely crazy moment, Zach wished it were so. Wished she belonged to them—to him.

To distract himself from his outrageous notions, he rose and refilled cups with coffee, then helped himself to a second piece of warm apple cake. No one made it as good as Mamie could.

Although he'd been prepared for his family to ask probing, increasingly embarrassing questions of Lorna, they all seemed to be on their best behavior.

By the time they'd spent an hour sitting in the family room enjoying one another's company, he relaxed. Tilly climbed onto Lorna's lap and fell asleep.

"Let me take her. I know she gets heavy," Jenny said, starting to rise from her seat next to Noah.

"She's fine. I don't mind holding her at all," Lorna said, brushing the curls away from Tilly's face with a gentle hand.

The sight of her holding the little one so tenderly did something to Zach. Something that made him ache for things he'd never longed for, like a wife and children of his own. He was still young. He had plenty of time to think about settling down, but seeing Lorna rock his niece certainly brought ideas of marriage and babies to the forefront of his mind.

Another half an hour passed, and clouds rolled across the sky.

"You'd best see Miss Lennox home, son," Grant said as he rose and looked out the window. "My old bones are telling me a storm is on its way."

Zach would have laughed and dismissed such nonsense, but he'd learned long ago, when his grandfather said it was going to storm, it generally did.

Noah took Tilly from Lorna; then everyone made quite a display of bidding her farewell and inviting her to come again. His mother packed pieces of cake into a tin and handed it to Lorna after Zach helped her with her coat.

"I can't thank you enough for such a lovely

day. I don't know when I've enjoyed a Sunday afternoon more." Lorna hugged his mother and tweaked Hayes' little nose, then hurried outside. Zach helped her into the automobile while his father started it.

A stiff wind threatened to blow the hat from his head, so he tossed it to his father and waved to his family.

"Goodbye! Thank you, again!" Lorna called, half rising in the seat as he drove down the lane headed for the road.

She plopped back next to him and smiled. "Your family is splendid. Just splendid."

"I'm kinda fond of them myself," he said, grinning at her. "How do you usually spend your Sunday afternoons?"

"Reading or walking in the park. Father thinks Sundays should be a quiet and reflective time, so I was never allowed to visit with friends. We normally give the staff the day off, so not even Dodi is available to ease my boredom. Before my mother passed, she and I often spent the afternoon together, looking at magazines or working on embroidery projects."

"You must miss her a great deal."

Lorna nodded. "I do. My mother was such a lovely person, both inside and out. Her absence has been hard on us all, but perhaps none as much as my father."

Zach swerved to miss a rabbit that hopped into the road. Lorna squealed and grabbed onto the door to have something to hold onto as he straightened his course.

"Sorry about that."

"It caught me by surprise. I would have hated it if you'd accidentally hit the little fellow."

Zach raised an eyebrow. "Perhaps it was a mama bunny in need of a rest from her young ones."

Lorna gave him a long look. "Or perhaps it was an ornery little boy bunny that torments his mother. Perhaps, even, his name might be Peter."

"Peter Rabbit, from Beatrix Potter," Zach grinned. "Tilly is quite enamored with that book. In fact, Noah has bemoaned the dozens of times he and Jenny have read it to her, but she enjoys hearing the story before she falls asleep at night."

"It is a delightful story." Lorna glanced at him, then tipped her head to look up at the sky. "Those clouds do appear rather ominous. Is your grandfather always so good at predicting the weather?"

"Usually. He once told me it was going to snow overnight, and I didn't believe him. Four months later, after all the snow melted, I recovered the toy I'd left in the yard. It was a horse made of metal and had a string on the front so I could pull it around. It was a rusted mess when I finally found it. Uncle R.C. worked most of the rust off, but it was never quite the same."

"I suppose that was a hard-learned lesson."

Zach sighed. "In more ways than one. I learned to trust Pops when he said it was going to storm. I also learned to put my things away or face the consequences of them being lost or ruined."

"Some of the best lessons are those we learn at

the hand of experience."

"True." Zach cast a quick glimpse at Lorna as they neared Holiday. There were so many questions he wanted to ask her, so many things he wanted to say, but his tongue suddenly felt tied in knots, along with his brain.

Lorna didn't seem to notice as she asked questions about the town, and people she'd met at church. They were nearly to her house when she turned to him. "I've spent the day with you and your family and still have no idea what it is you do, Zach Coleman."

The conversations they'd had that day flickered through his thoughts. He realized they hadn't once discussed his job. Since Lorna would learn soon enough if she cared to ask after him in town, he saw no reason to be anything but forthcoming. Besides, his parents had raised him to tell the truth, even when he didn't want to. Like now. How did one explain to the girl who had finally captured his interest that he worked for her father? And not just for her father, but was so far down the line, her father had no idea who he was and never would.

"I work for the railroad, repairing and maintaining engines and other equipment as needed."

To her credit, Lorna didn't appear shocked or distressed by this news. Not in the least. "Oh, I've always wanted to climb down in the pit under the engines and see what it looks like from that view. Papa assures me it is no place for a lady."

Zach almost chuckled at her words. That was certainly not what he'd expected to hear from her.

He half thought she might curl up her cute little nose at him for being one of her father's low-ranking employees.

"Your father is correct. It's greasy, dirty, dark, and dank down in the pit." He made a show of studying her. "I think you'd find it much more enjoyable climbing into a smokestack to clean it."

Lorna laughed. "I know when I'm being teased, sir. You'd better watch out. I might just show up ready to climb in the pit or into the smokestack one day."

If she did arrive and make the request, Zach knew there wasn't much he could do to dissuade her. Technically, she owned the railroad and was effectively his boss by association with her father.

Rather than dwell on the thought, on the idea that Lorna belonged in a mansion in gowns that cost more than he earned in a year, he kicked them aside. Instead, he gloried in the moment, pleased she'd spent the day with him and his family.

He drove up and parked at the end of the walk to her impressive house.

"I'd invite you in, but it's probably best if you head home before the storm hits. I can feel a chill in the air that wasn't there earlier," she said, rubbing her hands on her arms as Zach hurried around the vehicle and opened the door for her.

"Thank you for spending the day with us. It was nice to have you come out to Elk Creek Ranch." Zach held her hand as he helped her out and walked her to the gate in the high wrought-iron fence surrounding the yard.

"It was a magnificent day, Zach. One I'll long

remember. Please thank your family for their hospitality." She started up the walk, then rushed back and retrieved the tin of cake she'd left on the seat. "I can't forget the cake. Maude will be thrilled with it and will hound your mother for the recipe."

Zach smiled. "All she has to do is ask. Mamie loves to share her recipes. In fact, if Maude or Dodi ever want to come out to the ranch for a visit, Mamie would welcome their company."

"I'll let them know." Lorna took two steps away from the vehicle, then grinned at Zach. "Don't let Peter or Cottontail slow you down on the way home."

"No, ma'am," he said, reaching to tip his hat to her, then remembering he'd left it at home. He so badly wanted to walk her to the door, to kiss her cheek, but she'd already raced down the walk and stood waving to him from the top of the steps.

He returned her wave, then started the car. All the way home, his thoughts were on a pair of icy green eyes and a head crowned with autumn's finest fiery hues.

Chapter Five

"A proper young woman, unwed though she might be, must never go out alone. A chaperone should always accompany her, even if the journey is just down the street to visit a friend. Otherwise, her reputation may be left in irreparable tatters."

Miss Mulberry's Advice for Today's Young Woman

"Oh, this one would look lovely on you," Lorna said, holding up a copy of the latest fashion magazine and handing it to Ellery Milton as they sat in the Milton parlor by the fire.

Outside, a strong breeze blew leaves in swirls of crisp colors, sending them skittering across the yard and over the fence. Lorna felt as though she'd walked through a gale on the way to the Milton house from Lennox Manor. Her skirts had wrapped around her legs until they'd nearly tripped her, while she'd had to lean into the wind with one hand plastered on top of her head to keep her hat from sailing away.

Regardless of the nippy gusts blowing beyond

the windows of the Milton family's cozy home, Lorna was glad she'd braved the weather to visit Ellery. The oldest Milton daughter was someone she considered a friend.

When Lorna had received a telegram from her father right after lunch, letting her know he was still delayed on business but hoped to be home the next week, she'd felt like throwing something or stamping her feet. She'd been in Holiday for three weeks, but her father had yet to join her. He'd sent his apologies in a letter, explaining he had business dealings in the east that were taking far longer than he anticipated.

Lorna knew he was busy, but he purposely kept himself that way so memories of her mother didn't have a chance to eat away at him, although she knew his grief plagued him.

Still, it left Lorna alone far more than she liked. With Dodi to accompany her, she'd wandered through all the shops in town several times. She'd improved her embroidery skills as she had worked on Christmas gifts. She'd read several books her father had previously recommended, even though she found them dry and uninteresting. She'd even asked Maude to let her help make cookies like she used to when she was a young girl back in Philadelphia.

But today, when she received the news her father was delayed again, Lorna had decided enough was enough. She was bored and in need of company her own age. Without stopping to consider proper etiquette on the matter, Lorna had packed a basket with the magazines she'd recently received in the mail, a tin of Maude's freshly baked oatmeal cookies, and a packet of fabric swatches she'd brought along from her former dressmaker and headed to the Milton house.

The farmhouse was large and inviting and offered such a glorious feeling of family from the old dog lounging on the porch steps to a wind-battered wreath of acorns and pine cones hanging on the door.

Anne and Ellery had welcomed her with warm smiles, making her feel right at home, even though she knew it was rude to show up unexpectedly. After making tea and setting the cookies Lorna had brought on a tray, Anne left the two girls in the parlor to visit. Lorna could hear sounds from the kitchen and wondered if Anne was already busy with dinner preparations.

Lorna pointed to the gown in question. "It would be perfect for you, Ellery."

"It is a beautiful gown, but a fine gown like that would be wasted on me." Ellery handed the magazine back to Lorna.

"I disagree. You always appear quite stylish and lovely. I wish my hair looked more like yours." For emphasis, Lorna blew one of the curls that had worked free of her hairpins away from the corner of her eye.

"You're so vibrant and splendid, Lorna. Why on earth would you want straight blonde hair like mine? I look like I've been left out too long in the sun and all the color has faded away." Ellery picked up the teapot on the low table in front of them and refilled their cups with the best tea Lorna had ever tasted.

Anne had come from England to New York before she ended up traveling across the country as a mail-order bride. Lorna had looked on with interest when Anne had set a tea tray out for her and Ellery to enjoy.

"Mum makes the best tea," Ellery had proclaimed.

Now that she'd tasted it, Lorna quite agreed. She'd never savored any tea that was better and wondered if Anne would share her recipe with Maude.

Lorna picked up her cup, then nudged her friend with her elbow. "You do not look like you've been left out in the sun. Quite the opposite. Your hair makes me think of that fairy tale with Rapunzel. It's gorgeous. I'm not the only one who thinks so. I noticed Tom Stewart couldn't take his eyes off you at James and Clara's wedding. He spent more time at church studying you than listening to Pastor Ryan."

Ellery stopped thumbing through the magazine on her lap and shook her head. "Don't tease about Tom. He has no idea I even exist."

Lorna shook her head. "Believe me, he knows. He most definitely knows. How long have you been sweet on him?"

"Since I was eight and his family moved to Holiday." Ellery sighed and slumped back against the cushions of the couch. "It's hopeless, though. If he does recall my existence, it's only because I'm a sister to the Milton boys."

"I highly doubt that is the reason you come to

mind. Did I hear Mariah mention something about Tom being best friends with your brother Mike?"

"Yes. They were always close chums in school. Even though Mike has married and started his own electrical business, he and Tom still find ways to spend time together. Gwen said she thinks Mike uses the excuse of going fishing with Tom to get out of fixing things around their house."

Lorna grinned. "Possibly. Tell me more about Tom. What does he like? What's his favorite color? What does he enjoy eating? Where does he work?"

"Tom's favorite color is yellow. He will eat just about anything, although he's not fond of liver. He especially enjoys it when we have cottage pie. Mum got the recipe from a friend in England. She says it reminds her of happy childhood days."

"Cottage pie? What is that?"

"It has beef and vegetables and is topped with mashed potatoes. It's a delicious treat on a cold winter night."

"It does sound filling and hearty." Lorna picked up another magazine from her basket and opened it. "Where does Tom work?"

"With Zach at the engine house."

Lorna tried not to perk up at the mention of Zach. Admittedly, at least to herself, any mention of the handsome man made her pulse flutter. She saw him each Sunday at church. Of course, he'd been at the wedding of James and Clara Milton last Saturday. And a week ago, she'd convinced Maude and Dodi to go with her out to Elk Creek Ranch. They'd sent word with Zach to see if it was acceptable for a visit, and had been greeted by a happy Cora Lee when they arrived. The older women had a marvelous time talking and trading recipes and household tips while Lorna had let her gaze wander around the house, imagining what Zach had been like as a boy. Then he'd shown up and escorted them home. Lorna had been thrilled to sit beside him in the automobile all the way back to town.

Zach had also stopped by Tuesday evening after work to deliver a telegram that had come for her. He'd happened to overhear one of the delivery boys talking about taking it to her, so he'd volunteered to do it. She'd insisted he come inside to warm up before he headed home on his Henderson motorcycle. How he could ride that thing when the temperatures were so brisk was beyond her ability to understand. Afraid he'd be completely frozen before he made it to Elk Creek Ranch, she'd asked him to stay long enough to drink a cup of hot chocolate. They'd sat by the fire and talked; then Maude had insisted he stay for supper. Hours flew by, and rather than ride home in the dark and cold, he'd telephoned his parents and let them know he would stay in town at the Milton place.

Lorna would have gladly given him a room at Lennox Manor, but Dodi would have been fit to be tied if she'd done that.

Nevertheless, she enjoyed every moment spent in Zach's company. He was witty, intelligent, amusing, thoughtful, and kind. He loved his family with a deep devotion, held a great passion for his work and trains, and made her days brighter just by tossing one of his crooked smiles her way.

"I see," Lorna finally said when she realized she must have been daydreaming as Ellery nudged her arm, drawing her back to their conversation.

"Sure, you do," Ellery said in a teasing voice. "You're as smitten with Zach as I am with Tom."

"What a thing to say!" Lorna rapidly flipped through the magazine, then handed it to Ellery. Desperate to change the subject, she pulled the fabric swatches from her basket. She selected a dusty rose swatch of hand-dyed silk velvet embossed with a floral pattern and held it up to Ellery's cheek. "This would be divine on you."

"Oh, Lorna! It's gorgeous!" Ellery took the sample from her and rubbed her fingers over the soft fabric. "It looks terribly expensive."

Lorna shrugged. She had no concerns about the cost of the material. And for all the kindness Ellery and the Milton family had extended to her, she wanted to give something back. Like a dress fit for a princess.

"Is there a dressmaker here in town?" Lorna asked in a casual tone as she browsed through the other samples she'd brought along.

"There is one, although Mum says there's a fantastic dressmaker in Baker City. She's had a shop there for years."

Lorna looked from the samples to Ellery. "That's wonderful to hear. Do you and your family ever go to Baker City to shop?"

"Once in a great while. Mum said she and Aunt Mamie went with Uncle Jace's Aunt Mae the first Christmas they were here. It sounded like they had an extraordinary day, and they both ended up with new dresses for Christmas from Dad and Uncle Jace. Aunt Mamie wore hers as her wedding gown."

"That's such a romantic story. Perhaps your mother and Mrs. Coleman would be interested in taking a trip to Baker City before Christmas." The luxurious train car she had ridden in to Holiday was parked at the engine yard, waiting for her father's return. In fact, her father had several similar cars. He wouldn't care if she took her friends to Baker City in it for the day.

She loved the idea of giving them an adventure. After working out the details, she'd extend an invitation. Maybe even Jenny Coleman would like to come along if she could find someone to watch Hayes and Tilly for her.

"This is a spectacular color for you, Lorna." Ellery held up a swatch of emerald green taffeta that enhanced the color of Lorna's eyes and made her cheeks rosy. "If you order a new gown, it should be that shade of green."

Lorna grinned. "As a matter of fact, my former seamstress is finishing up one in that color. I just hope it arrives in time for Christmas."

"You'll be the most beautiful girl in town in it, I'm sure." Ellery squeezed her hands and smiled. "Not that you aren't already."

Lorna blushed at Ellery's comment. "I do believe you exaggerate, my sweet friend. You are far, far prettier than I could ever hope to be, and I think Jenny Coleman is also quite lovely. Then there are your sisters. The boys their age had better watch out."

Ellery laughed. "Mum frets so about Mariah and Mercy—those two conceited little things. They spend far too much time primping and fussing with their appearances. I hope it's merely a phase they'll grow out of as they mature."

"I'm sure they will."

The two young women sipped tea, nibbled cookies, and continued talking like old friends for the next hour; until Lorna glanced at the clock and realized it was past time for her to return home.

"Thank you so much for allowing me to impose on your hospitality, Ellery. I so appreciate your time and friendship." Lorna rose to her feet and wondered at the most gracious way to bid adieu to Mrs. Milton. "May I give your mother my regards?"

"Sure. Go on to the kitchen. Mum is likely in there. I'll fetch your coat and hat."

Lorna stepped out of the parlor into the hallway and followed the scent of roasting meat to a large, airy kitchen. Anne Milton sat at the table peeling potatoes, humming a lively tune, while Peg Jenkins, a widow the Milton family hired to help around the house, rolled out pie crust.

"Mrs. Milton, I just wanted to extend my gratitude to you for the lovely tea. It was delicious." Lorna smiled at Anne and then Peg.

"I'm so glad you enjoyed it." Anne wiped her hands on a dish towel, then rose from the table and walked over to where Lorna lingered in the doorway. "Thank you for coming to visit."

"It was rather rude of me to just pop in. I'll send a calling card before I come again."

Anne slipped an arm around her waist and gave

her a hug. "That is not necessary. I'm so glad you thought to drop by, my dear. Ellery so enjoys your company, so please know you are welcome anytime."

"Thank you, ma'am. I greatly appreciate the kindness and the invitation. Your tea truly was the best I've ever had."

Anne smiled as they reached the doorway where Ellery waited with Lorna's coat and hat. "There is nothing quite as satisfying as a proper cup of tea on a wintery afternoon." Anne glanced outside, then back at Lorna. "Would you like me to telephone Mr. Barnes and have him come get you?"

"No, but thank you. It's not that far and an invigorating walk will do me good." Lorna tugged on her coat, pinned on her hat, and pulled gloves from her coat pocket, sliding them on her hands. "Thank you again for a most pleasant afternoon."

"It was our pleasure, Lorna. Come again soon!" Ellery gave her a quick hug, then pulled open the door. Frigid air blew around her as Lorna hastened outside and down the porch steps. She turned and waved at Ellery, then rushed down the walk and out the gate, and headed toward home. She was halfway there before she realized she'd left behind her magazines and fabric swatches. Not that it mattered. She was sure Ellery would return them to her soon.

Lorna held onto her hat to keep it from sailing into a sky the color of pewter as she made her way back to Lennox Manor. She could picture Mercy and Mariah poring over the magazines, holding up the swatches of fabric, dreaming about glorious gowns and handsome boys coming to call.

Oh, to be sixteen again, when life seemed much simpler.

Not that Lorna's life was complicated now, but she so often felt unsettled these days, as though she had come unmoored and bobbed about in an ocean of uncertainty with no particular direction in mind.

Years ago, she'd wanted to become a teacher, an idea her father quickly dismissed. She'd considered other ways she could volunteer, to be a help to others, but her father constantly reminded her there were things people of their station simply did not do.

Lorna did what little she could, but she longed to make a difference to others. She wondered if there was something in Holiday she could do that would be a help to the community. Perhaps Zach would have some ideas.

Mindful her thoughts had once again settled on the handsome man who was in her father's employ, she tried to shift her attention to the approaching Thanksgiving holiday. Her father hoped to join her by then. If he hadn't returned, though, Lorna, along with Dodi, Maude and Marcus, had been invited to the Coleman home for Thanksgiving dinner. Wrong as it might be, there was a part of Lorna that hoped her father wouldn't arrive on time just so they could spend the day with the Coleman family.

She knew Cora Lee and Jace wouldn't care if her father accompanied them, but she hated to think about how her father might treat them. George Lennox was a good father, for the most part, and he had been a devoted and loving husband, but he'd grown up seeing people not as people but as part of social classes.

Lorna detested it when he looked down his nose at someone merely because they labored with their hands for a living. As long as they put in a day of honest work, what did it matter how much they earned or where they lived? Why should those trivial things dictate whom she could be friends with and whom she was expected to ignore?

If her father had even an inkling of how much she liked and admired Zach Coleman, she feared he would be fired and sent packing without a moment's hesitation.

Which was why she really should stay away from Zach, no matter how much she wanted to spend more and more time with him.

"Miss Lennox. Miss Lennox!" One of the messenger boys caught her attention as she waited to cross the street at an intersection.

"Hello, Willie. How does this day find you?" she asked when he dodged between two wagons and rushed across Milton Road to her.

"Fair enough, I s'pose." Willie handed her a telegram, then rubbed a grubby finger beneath his nose.

Lorna wasn't sure how old the lad was, but she doubted he was more than nine or ten. He should be in school, learning and playing and enjoying his childhood instead of working to help support his family. Lorna had learned he had six brothers and sisters, a father who drank more than he was sober, and a mother who'd disappeared a few months after the last baby had arrived. Lorna longed to take Willie home and give him a decent meal and a bath, and a set of warm clothes. The thin jacket he wore surely wasn't enough to keep out the chill. What would the poor boy do when it began to snow?

Before Willie could run off, Lorna took a dime from her pocket, pressed it into his hand and smiled at him. "Thank you for bringing this to me, Willie. Have a good evening."

He smiled at her and tipped his worn cap. "I will, Miss Lennox. Thank you!"

"You're welcome, Willie!" she called after the child as he raced to the corner and disappeared down Main Street.

Lorna considered waiting to open the telegram until she returned home, but curiosity got the best of her. Despite her early musing that it might be nice to celebrate Thanksgiving at the Elk Creek Ranch without her father, she hoped the missive was letting her know he was on his way home.

She opened it, read the few lines, squealed with excitement, and took off at a most unladylike trot toward the depot. The train whistle blew as the Holiday Express rolled into the station, right on time.

Her father had expressed his regrets for his lengthy delay in returning home. To make it up to her, he said she would find a gift on the afternoon train. Lorna loved surprises and couldn't wait to see what her father had sent. Maybe it was a bouquet of hothouse flowers. She, Dodi, and Maude would all enjoy them. Or perhaps he'd sent a crate of oranges. It might even be a box of the European chocolates she loved so much. With the war raging overseas, she rather doubted there'd be much candy exported for a while.

No matter what he sent, she was sure she'd enjoy it. Hopefully, it would be something she could share with others.

Lorna stopped outside the depot building and caught her breath before tucking loose curls up beneath her hat, tugged down her coat to straighten it, and stepped inside. She waited in line and finally, it was her turn at the window.

"May I help you, miss?" asked the gentleman seated there, barely giving her more than a dismissive glance.

"Yes. My father sent something on the train for me to pick up, but I don't know what he sent, and I don't have a claim ticket." Lorna took in his thin face and thinning hair, and the weary set to his shoulders. She assumed his was most likely a stressful position.

The man sighed and looked up at her. "Name of the sender?"

"Lennox. George Lennox." Lorna didn't feel the need to let the man know her father owned the train and the building where they stood, not to mention the fact that her father was his employer.

"Lennox?" The man's eyebrows shot up to his receding hairline. "*The* George Lennox? The one who owns this building?"

Lorna smiled. "That's correct. I'm his daughter, Lorna Lennox."

The man's prominent Adam's apple bobbed as he swallowed hard. "I'll find the paperwork right away, Miss Lennox."

"Thank you," she said, primly folding her

hands together on the counter as she waited.

The poor man looked near panic as he riffled through the papers, then went through them a second time before he pulled one from the stack. "Here it is. I'll have someone bring that out of the car for you. Would you like it delivered to your home?"

"That won't be necessary, sir. Shall I wait here or outside for it?"

"It might be best for you to wait inside out of that chilly breeze, Miss Lennox. As soon as it is unloaded, I'll let you know."

"Thank you." Lorna looked around, spying an empty bench along the wall. She strode over to it and took a seat. Anticipation bubbled in her until she could hardly sit still. Momentarily, she thought about walking over to the engine house and seeing if Zach was there, but she wouldn't. It would be wrong to disturb him during his work hours. Besides, she'd just lectured herself about leaving that handsome man alone, not spending more time with him.

Determined not to act like a child on Christmas morning, overly eager for a gift, she placed her hands on her lap, straightened her spine, and waited.

Chapter Six

"Henry! I need help. Can you spare a couple of the boys for a few minutes?" Ralph Coons hollered as he raced inside the engine house.

Henry straightened from where he labored over a brake cylinder. "What's the problem?"

"I got a delivery of an automobile for Mr. Lennox's daughter and need some help getting it off the train. She's here to retrieve it."

"All righty." Henry pointed the wrench in his hand toward where Zach was working in the pit beneath one of the engines not being used that day. "Take Zach and Corliss."

At the mention of Lorna, Zach had started to climb out of the pit, ready to volunteer if Henry didn't suggest he go along. Corliss, ever anxious for adventure, appeared at his side when he stepped off the ladder and wiped his hands on a rag. Zach grinned at him and shrugged out of his filthy coveralls. Corliss followed his example as Ralph hurried toward them.

"Can you two please unload a vehicle and get it running?"

"Sure, Ralph. Just give us a minute to wash up. I don't want to get any grease on the lady's automobile."

"Fine, fine, but hurry!" Ralph ran his hand over his nearly bald head.

Zach knew Ralph had yet to reach thirty and wondered if his nervous tendencies or his job as assistant stationmaster had contributed to the loss of his hair and the deep furrows etched across his brow. If his position was the reason, Zach was glad he rarely had to interact with the public and their odd, sometimes ridiculous demands.

He and Corliss washed their hands, then followed Ralph's agitated gait to one of the freight cars. When they pushed open the door on the side, it revealed something large covered by a tarp.

"I'll get some planks," Corliss offered, jogging off to where thick wooden boards were kept for unloading autos and equipment.

Zach hopped into the freight car and began loosening the straps holding on the tarp. He eyed the equipment in the back of the car and knew it would head up to the mine without being unloaded.

Carefully, he pulled off the tarp and stared wide-eyed at the cream-colored four-door automobile accented with shiny brass trim. The bottom of the car was painted shiny black, giving it quite a distinctive appearance.

"Wow!" Corliss said as he returned with two heavy planks. "What is it?"

"One of the new Dodge vehicles. This is a Model 30 touring car." Zach glanced inside at the leather seats and the leather-wrapped steering wheel, then went about starting the car. "It's a beaut."

"Well, from what I've seen, so is Miss Lennox." Corliss offered him a sly look as he slid the planks into the freight car and braced them against the platform.

Zach scowled at him, refusing to rise to the boy's bait. No one needed to know how much attention he'd paid to Lorna. He'd memorized her smile, the tilt of her chin, the laughter that danced in her eyes, the way her step almost bounced when she was excited. He'd studied the way the light set her auburn curls aflame and the perfectly peachy hue of her lips that made him want to kiss them over and over again.

"Ready?" Corliss asked as he stepped back and raised his hands to guide Zach as he drove the car onto the planks. If a plank slipped or he drove too close to an edge, they'd wreck the car, and that would never do.

Nervous but confident since he'd driven many autos and pieces of equipment off the freight cars, he slowly moved forward, feeling the bump as the tires climbed onto the wooden planks.

"Keep it straight," Corliss said, moving backward as Zach started down the planks. "A little to the left."

Zach turned the wheel slightly, then adjusted when Corliss motioned to the right. With another bump, the automobile was on the platform. He drove it down the sloped area that led to level ground and the street, then stopped.

Ralph and Corliss both came over and gave the

automobile a long glance.

"What is that thing?" Ralph asked, leaning to look inside the luxurious interior.

"One of the brand-new Dodge automobiles. Production started a few weeks ago. I wonder how Mr. Lennox came to be in possession of this one." Zach figured there was probably nothing the man couldn't acquire if he wanted it.

"Dunno, but I'll let Miss Lennox know it's ready." Ralph took two steps toward the depot. "It is ready, isn't it?"

"Should be. I'll give it a quick look to make sure everything appears in good shape." Zach glanced at the engine, checked the fuel, studied the tires, and decided it was ready for Lorna to drive. He couldn't recall if she'd mentioned knowing how to drive and wondered if she'd ever driven a vehicle. He wouldn't mind giving her a few lessons if she needed them.

He heard footsteps followed by a gasp and turned as Lorna pressed her hands to her cheeks, gaping at the car.

"Oh, my stars!" she said, continuing to stare in disbelief.

"Looks like you are the proud owner of one of the new Dodge automobiles."

"I can't believe it." She moved beside him and ran a gloved hand over the fender. "It's magnificent!"

"It is." Zach somehow managed not to blurt out his opinion that the car didn't begin to compare to her. Especially not when the wind had loosened several curls from her hairpins and they danced around a sweet face that shone with eager anticipation. Lorna fairly oozed energy, as though it bubbled inside her and couldn't help but spill out. Her gorgeous eyes snapped with excitement, and it required a great deal of restraint on his part not to lean over and kiss her upturned, smiling lips.

"I wonder how Papa acquired it. The Dodge brothers just started releasing these a few weeks ago." Lorna walked around the car, then took a peek at the engine. "It's an inline four-cylinder L-head engine. Did you know it produces thirty-five brake horsepower?"

Zach gaped at Lorna, left speechless that she knew so much about any vehicle, let alone one so new.

She glanced at him and pointed to the engine. "I read in the newspaper it has a three-speed sliding gear transmission, which is revolutionary. And it's made from a steel body, something most other automobile producers don't do. Wooden frames are the standard."

"That's right," he said, finally recovering his voice. "It also has a twelve-volt charging system instead of the industry standard of six. It really is quite an innovative wonder, Miss Lennox."

Her smile widened as she moved around to the driver's side door. "And it's all mine. I can't believe Papa sent this as a surprise, but I'm so glad he did. Want to take a ride with me?"

Zach glanced back at the engine house. It was almost time to call it a day, and Henry wouldn't care if he left a little early. "I'd like that. Can you give me a few minutes to let my boss know I'm leaving?"

"I didn't mean to interrupt your work, Zach. Of course, you're busy." She opened the door, but his hand on her arm kept her from sliding into the car.

"Henry won't mind if I leave a few minutes before quitting time. Besides, I wouldn't want you to take the car out and have it leave you stranded somewhere. Sometimes they get jostled a bit in transport and need a little fine-tuning."

"I hadn't thought of that. If you're sure it's no imposition to you or to Mr. Biggins, I would very much appreciate your presence when I take it out for an inaugural drive."

Zach grinned and backed toward the engine house. "It will just take a minute. Don't rush off."

He turned and jogged back to the engine house. Henry was wiping grease off tools and preparing to hang them back in their proper place when Zach stepped inside.

"You get Miss Lennox on her way?" Henry asked as he hung a wrench on a hook.

"Not yet. I thought it might be a good idea to accompany her in case there are any problems with the auto."

Henry gave Zach a thoughtful look. Although his eyes danced with humor, he kept his expression neutral. "I reckon that would be a good idea. You go on, son. I'll see you tomorrow."

"Thank you, Henry. Have a nice evening."

"Will do, my boy." Henry began to whistle a lively off-key tune.

Zach grabbed his coat and lunch pail, pushed his motorcycle outside, and left the pail hanging from the handlebars after he leaned the motorcycle against the side of the depot. He didn't think anyone would bother it in the time it took him to see Lorna home. Besides, the stationmaster could see the motorcycle from his office and would keep an eye on it.

He rushed back to where Lorna waited. She'd already climbed inside the car and slowly ran her hand over the smooth leather seat. When she spied him, her whole face brightened, as though she was pleased beyond anything to spend time with him.

Zach gave her a studying look. "Do you know how to drive?"

"I certainly do." She tipped her head toward the passenger seat beside her, and he got in after he helped her start the car. Lorna carefully looked both ways before pulling out onto the street. Rather than turn onto Park Street that would take them into the heart of town, she continued heading north toward the newly opened hospital. She turned a few blocks past it and drove east until they came to the last street at the edge of Holiday's city limits, then ventured south.

"It rides as smooth as a raindrop sliding down a sheet of polished glass," Zach commented as they chugged along, enjoying the opportunity to ride in the new vehicle. He waved at Pastor Ryan as the man walked on the opposite side of the road, most likely heading home after visiting one of the church members.

"Would you like to drive it?" Lorna asked, giving him an inviting smile.

Zach started to refuse, to tell her it was her car

to drive, but he really wanted to give it a whirl. "Are you sure you want to share?"

Lorna laughed. "Absolutely. I'll find a good spot to pull over, then you can drive me home."

Rather than stop right away, Lorna turned and headed west until they reached the far edge of town a few blocks from the depot. She parked in an empty lot near the tracks. It didn't take long for them to switch places, and Zach was soon driving the automobile down the street. The car was even more pleasurable to drive than he'd expected. He was thankful for Lorna's generosity that allowed him to experience it.

As they rolled down a quiet street with a few run-down houses, he pointed to a small abode, barely more than a shack. "Remember the basket you won the night of the Halloween party?"

Lorna nodded.

"I left it there. The family is struggling. The mother ran off, and their father spends more time drinking than anything. Those poor kids would starve to death if they weren't an ambitious lot. The oldest girl works at the hotel in the kitchen, and the older boy delivers messages around town."

"Willie?" Lorna asked, peering out the window at the ramshackle house. "Young Willie lives there?"

"That's right. That basket full of treats was something special for them. It was nice of you to share."

"I'd like to do more for those less fortunate in town. Is there an organization that helps them?"

"Talk to Mamie or Aunt Anne. The Women's

League tries to gather donations of food and clothing at Christmastime, but they'd welcome any and all assistance."

"I'll do that," Lorna said, looking determined as he turned down Milton Road. They waved to Burt and James as the two of them stood outside the feed store. Zach laughed at the shocked looks on their faces as they realized he was the one driving the brand-new automobile.

"That will give them all something to chew on over dinner besides Aunt Anne's roast beef."

Lorna giggled. "I'll have to visit Ellery again soon and take her for a ride."

Zach looked at her as he paused on Main Street, waiting for a buggy and two wagons to pass. "Ellery would love that. It's nice the two of you have become friends."

"I am grateful for her friendship and her companionship. She and Mrs. Milton were most gracious when I dropped by unannounced today. I just needed to get out of the house, and my feet carried me there."

Zach smiled. "I'm sure they were happy you stopped in. Ellery could use a friend her age."

"And so could I." Lorna gave him a studying glance as he continued down the road. "I've noticed there are several young ladies around my age. Is Ellery not friends with them?"

"Ellery's a little shy and doesn't make friends as easily as Mariah and Mercy. Those two girls could talk to anyone, anytime, about anything."

Lorna laughed. "I did make note of that tendency, and of Ellery's shyness. I assumed she might be when we first met, but we've gotten along quite well and had a lovely visit this afternoon over tea."

"I'm not much of a tea drinker, but even I enjoy a cup of Aunt Anne's tea. No one makes it quite like she does." Zach turned down the lane to her house. "Any word on when your father will return?"

Lorna shrugged. "I'm not certain. He hopes to be back in time for Thanksgiving."

"If he is, you know you all are still welcome to join us at Elk Creek Ranch."

"I know, and I appreciate the invitation. Might I let you know for certain next week of our plans?"

"Of course. If you decide that very morning to join us, please do. Mamie always makes plenty of food, and we'd love to have you." Zach stopped the car at the end of the front walk. "Thank you for letting me drive your Dodge. It's a mechanical wonder."

Lorna smiled as they both got out of the car. "Would you like a ride back to the depot? I could have Marcus drive us. I'm sure he'd be thrilled at the opportunity to take it for a drive."

"I'll walk, but I do appreciate the offer. Enjoy your automobile, Miss Lennox." Zach tipped his head to her, since he'd forgotten to tug on his cap, and started to walk away. Before he made it more than half a dozen steps, he stopped and looked back, finding her watching him. He returned to stand next to her. "I was wondering, if you don't already have plans, would you consider accompanying me to a performance at the Opera House? There's a showing of *Snow White and the Seven Dwarfs* coming up week after next."

"I would be honored to attend with you, Zach. Thank you for the invitation." Lorna looked like she was about ready to bounce with excitement and the fact that she was made him elated. Suddenly, she clasped her hands together beneath her chin and gave him a look full of mischief. "You work with Tom Stewart, don't you?"

"That's right."

"And are you aware Ellery is quite smitten with him?"

Zach nodded. "I may have heard something along those lines from Andy. Why?"

"Well, I was just thinking, if you wouldn't object, perhaps we could encourage Tom and Ellery to join us that evening."

Zach grinned, amused to find Lorna fancied herself a matchmaker. The pleading look on her face was enough to get him to agree to her schemes, but he did like the idea of giving love a nudge when it came to Ellery and his friend Tom.

"That's a grand idea, Lorna. I'll mention it to Tom tomorrow."

"Wonderful. Thank you, Zach, for being … you."

"Who else would I be?" he teased. Before he did something crazy, like pull her into his arms and give her a kiss, he backed away from her. He'd been wanting to kiss her from the moment he'd seen her that afternoon, looking windblown and wonderful. "You're welcome, Lorna. I'll see you later."

He ran through town to the depot and retrieved his motorcycle. Zach barely even noticed the cold air slapping against his cheeks as he made the chilly ride home. Despite the voice in his head cautioning him to leave Lorna alone, his heart rejoiced at the knowledge he'd soon spend more time with her.

Chapter Seven

*"Should a young man become besotted with
you, a young lady should never coyly toy with his
affections, nor encourage untoward behavior. Make
it clear he must act the part of a gentleman,
otherwise, you shall never gain his respect or retain
your own."*

Miss Mulberry's Advice for Today's Young Woman

"That's splendid! Absolutely splendid!" Lorna
smiled excitedly into the mirror at her vanity table.
For the last hour, Dodi had styled first Lorna's hair,
and then Ellery's. "Tom Stewart will drop his teeth
when he sees you."

Ellery laughed as she reached up and touched
one perfectly fashioned curl as it rested above her
left ear. "If he drops his teeth, he won't be nearly as
handsome."

"Or as fun to kiss," Dodi teased as she moved
back so the two of them could study their
reflections in the mirror.

Ellery's cheeks turned bright pink as she turned toward Dodi. "I have never kissed that man. Not once!"

"But you want to." Lorna tugged on Ellery's hands, pulling her to her feet.

"No more than you want to kiss Zach."

Lorna shrugged but didn't offer a denial. Truthfully, she'd like nothing better than for Zach to take her in his arms and kiss her until she was senseless. She'd dreamed about him doing that exact thing so many times, she'd awakened with the imagined taste of his kiss on her lips several mornings.

Not that she minded starting the day on such a marvelous note, but she was beginning to think he'd never get around to kissing her.

Then again, he couldn't be blamed since they'd had few opportunities to be alone. Since her father still hadn't returned by the time Thanksgiving arrived, she and Dodi, along with Maude and Marcus, had gone out to Elk Creek Ranch for dinner. Cora Lee and Jace had warmly welcomed them. Lorna had a grand time playing with Noah and Jenny's children. The little ones had been particularly excited by the crayons and sheaf of paper she'd brought for them to enjoy. Zach had suggested they go for a stroll after the meal, but Hayes had begged to tag along, and she didn't have the heart to tell the adorable little boy no.

Zach had invited her to come out to the ranch Sunday after church, but she'd already promised to spend the afternoon with Ellery at the Milton's home. She, Ellery, and the twins had spent half the afternoon being teased mercilessly by Andy and Burt. Anne had finally chased the two boys out of the parlor with threats of making them learn to sew if they lingered any longer.

Lorna had encountered Zach at the mercantile a few evenings ago when she'd offered to pick up the nutmeg Maude needed for a cake she was in the midst of baking. Zach had walked her home, leading the horse he was riding since the snow was too deep for excursions on his motorcycle.

In fact, Lorna had begun to despair the snow would never stop. It had snowed every day since Thanksgiving. Twice, it snowed so hard no one dared venture out, although she had heard the whistle of the train as it had arrived and departed the station. She had no idea how the workers kept the track cleared, but she assumed they must since the trains had been on time every day.

Marcus had spent the better part of yesterday shoveling pathways through the snow that was already piled as high as Lorna's knees. She'd caught a glimpse of Zach and three of the Milton brothers shoveling snow early one morning as she glanced out her window after rubbing away the frost clinging to the panes.

Excited for an evening spent in Zach's company, she was glad Tom had mustered the courage to invite Ellery to the performance this evening. Lorna had never seen this particular play, but she'd often attended events at the opera house in Philadelphia.

"You both look lovely," Dodi said, beaming at them like a doting grandmother. "Those boys will be beside themselves."

"I hope so," Lorna said, adjusting the bow on the back of Ellery's gown. The ends of it flowed down to the hem.

"This is like something from a dream," Ellery said, hesitantly brushing her hand along the skirt of the pink velvet gown trimmed with matching satin ribbons and embroidery.

Lorna had ordered the dress two years ago but hadn't liked the way it looked on her once it was finished, so she'd tucked it away. Now, she was glad she'd kept it instead of leaving it behind when she'd packed her belongings a few months ago. The dress looked like it was made for Ellery. The soft fabric glided over her curves, and the light hue brought out the pink in Ellery's cheeks and a rosy glow to her skin.

Or perhaps it was the thought of spending the evening with Tom that made her appear so lovely.

"Thank you for letting me borrow a gown, Lorna. I've never seen, let alone touched, anything so fine."

Lorna hugged her friend's narrow shoulders. "My pleasure, Ellery. But you aren't borrowing the gown. It's yours to keep."

Ellery's eyes widened, and she shook her head. "I can't keep this, Lorna. I'm nervous enough about spilling something on it as it is."

"Ask Dodi. I never wear it, and someone should who enjoys it. Besides, it suits your coloring far better than mine."

"Thank you!" Ellery gave her a tight hug, then spun around to look in the mirror again before she picked up Lorna's hand and held it out to the side. "You look so beautiful. That deep color of green makes your eyes stand out."

"Two lovely, sweet girls," Dodi said, putting her arms around their waists and walking toward the door with them. "But if you don't hurry along, Mr. Coleman and Mr. Stewart will be anxiously waiting for you."

"We're nearly ready," Lorna said, pecking Dodi's cheek, then glancing over at Ellery. "We just need to slip on our boots and cloaks."

"And don't forget your gloves. It's so cold out this evening." Dodi gave them one more motherly look before she disappeared down the hallway.

Lorna had already taken two of her heaviest fur-lined winter cloaks from her closet and tossed them on the bed. Ellery had protested about borrowing one, but Lorna insisted she must wear the cloak in a deep shade of pink that complimented the dress.

After pinning silk flowers in their hair, Lorna gave their reflections in the mirror one more appraising glance. Ellery looked as lovely as she'd ever seen her. Lorna straightened a seam on her skirt, pleased the last of the new gowns she'd ordered before they'd headed West had finally arrived. This one, in a forest green hue made of silk velvet, felt as rich and incredible as it looked. She loved the way the fabric almost shimmered in the light. And Ellery was correct: it did make her eyes sparkle. Lorna adjusted the silk burgundy flower pinned amidst the riot of her auburn curls, then turned to sit on the bench at the foot of the bed.

"Let's pull on our boots. We can slip on our cloaks downstairs," Lorna said, tugging on winter boots that would keep her feet warm. She hated to wear them beneath such an elegant gown, but no one would see her footwear, and she positively couldn't bear the thought of anything, not even frozen toes, causing her discomfort this evening. The only distraction she longed for was one provided by handsome Zach Coleman.

Ellery pulled on her equally sensible boots and tied the ribbons that held them closed at the top.

Together, she and Lorna gathered their little opera bags that would hang from their wrists. The bags were just big enough to carry a handkerchief, money, and a package of gum, which was exactly what Lorna's bag contained.

She'd just reached out to pick up her cloak when Dodi appeared in the doorway.

"The young gentlemen have arrived. They both look quite dashing." Dodi grinned before she hustled down the hallway toward the back stairs. Lorna assumed she'd go to the kitchen and let Maude know Zach and Tom had arrived. She had no doubt the two women, and probably Marcus, would watch unobtrusively as she and Ellery descended the stairs and left with their escorts.

"Come on," Lorna said, snatching up both cloaks and handing the pink one to Ellery. Lorna draped her cloak over her left arm and hurried out of her room. "Let's make a grand entrance," she whispered, pointing for Ellery to go one way down the hall while Lorna went the other to meet at the head of the stairs where it curved both to the right and the left.

Ellery remained hidden in the shadows until Lorna appeared in the right curve of the grand staircase.

Together, they slowly descended the marble steps to the entry foyer. Lorna felt the cool wood of the banister beneath her palm as she slid her hand along it and took one graceful step at a time. Head held high, she kept her spine perfectly aligned as she made her way to the bottom of the stairs.

Much to her gratification, the moment she and Ellery started down the stairs, Zach and Tom, who'd been speaking quietly in the foyer, noticed the movement and turned to watch them. Tom's jaw dropped open, but, unlike her joking prediction, his teeth did not clatter to the floor like broken piano keys.

Zach gave her that lopsided grin she adored, nearly stealing her breath away. He looked outrageously handsome in a fine wool suit with a crisp white shirt and a dark blue tie knotted at his throat. His hair, which was frequently mussed, had been carefully combed. Even the boots on his feet had been polished to a high shine.

"Good evening," Zach said, holding out a hand to Lorna and dipping his head with a rascally wink.

She smiled and took his hand, dipping her knees slightly in an abbreviated curtsy.

Ellery settled her hand on Tom's when he reached out to her and offered him a look so full of love, Lorna wondered if Tom was blind or had rocks rattling around in his head. She had no idea how he hadn't already arrived at the conclusion the woman was mad about him.

Zach waggled his eyebrows at Lorna and tipped his head toward Tom. The man still hadn't recovered from his shock of seeing Ellery in her finery, causing Lorna to tamp down her mirth.

"Shall we be on our way?" Lorna asked, handing Zach her cloak, then turning so he could slip it over her shoulders. Ellery mimicked her actions, and Tom rested his hands on Ellery's arms for a moment after the cloak engulfed her in its warmth. Lorna noticed her friend made no move to pull away from him.

"We shall," Zach said, motioning to the door.

Marcus practically ran from the shadows of the music room where Lorna was sure he'd been hiding with Maude and Dodi to pull open the door.

He handed Tom and Zach their coats and hats, then waved as the four of them made their way down the steps and out to a large sleigh that could accommodate at least six people. Burt Milton sat on the front seat, holding the reins in his hands. The boy grinned and tipped his hat to them as Zach and Tom helped her and Ellery into the sleigh and settled onto the plush seats.

Zach pulled a blanket over her lap, then nodded to Burt, who glanced back at them over his shoulder.

"I'm impressed you even hired a driver," Lorna whispered to Zach.

He chuckled. "Oh, I'm not paying him, not in cash. Burt needs a hand with a project he's working on, and I promised to help him with it this Saturday. Even if I hadn't, Aunt Anne would have made him do it for Ellery."

"Well, it's nice he was willing to brave the cold and drive the sleigh tonight." Lorna glanced up, pleased to see the moon shone brightly overhead and the snow had finally stopped falling. The world around them appeared almost magical with moonbeams adding a soft, silver glow to a landscape draped in white.

"What an incredible evening," Ellery said, pointing to the snow-shrouded trees that looked like they'd been dipped in a bowl of white frosting and dusted with sugar as snow clung to each branch.

"Incredible," Tom muttered, as though he couldn't quite find his tongue or gather his wits. His gaze hadn't left Ellery since he'd glanced up and noticed her on the stairs.

Pleased Tom seemed to finally be falling under Ellery's spell, Lorna cast a glimpse at Zach. The moonlight mingling with shadows made his face look like it was carved from the same marble as the stairs at Lennox Manor. She could envision a likeness of him gracing a Grecian garden. Zach was not only good-looking, but he was also good-hearted. Each time she saw him, spent time with him, she fell more in love with him.

Although she knew Zach considered her to be a friend, she wasn't certain he felt the same intense attraction to her that she experienced for him. Perhaps he never would. The possibility of Zach one day falling in love and marrying another made her heart clench with pain.

Lorna refused to allow anything to dim her joy this evening, so she shoved such thoughts from her mind and studied Main Street as they headed toward the Opera House. Even though Christmas was three weeks away, many businesses had already hung decorations and strung ropes of garlands outside their shops. Even the post office had a wreath with a big red bow hanging on the door.

It seemed the town of Holiday loved the Christmas season as much as Lorna did. She and Dodi had been discussing decorating Lennox Manor, but Lorna had wanted to wait until her father came home. Unfortunately, he still wasn't certain when that would be. Lorna had decided just that morning if he wasn't home by Sunday evening, they would begin decking the halls on Monday. She planned to invite Ellery, her sisters, and sisters-in-law to join in what Lorna viewed as a fun activity.

The idea of having the house decorated for her father upon his return made Lorna even more determined to get started. Maybe she'd begin unpacking boxes of decorations tomorrow. Despite his busy schedule throughout the year, her father always took a few weeks off at Christmas. Lorna owned fond memories of her parents setting out decorations together and trimming the tree in the main parlor on Christmas Eve.

This year would be far different for them, being in Holiday, but she couldn't help but feel it would be a memorable Christmas.

Before she could give decorations and Christmas surprises more consideration, Burt stopped the sleigh outside the Holiday Opera House. Lorna had learned from Anne Milton the building had been constructed just two years ago but hadn't been used nearly as much as they'd hoped. It was a challenge to get quality entertainers to travel all the way to Holiday.

Tonight, though, every seat in the place had been sold, or so she'd heard from Marcus who'd gotten the information from the assistant manager when he'd gone to pick up the tickets Lorna had purchased for the household staff.

Couples and several families made their way inside the imposing brick building. Lights seemed to glow from every window as Zach and Tom both hopped out of the sleigh. Lorna waited as Tom helped Ellery onto the boardwalk before she tossed off the blanket on her lap and took the hand Zach held out to her. She wished she didn't have to wear gloves. The contact of his warm palm against hers would have been welcome.

As it was, she lightly squeezed his fingers and offered him a warm smile as she stepped onto the boardwalk.

Zach flipped a silver dollar to Burt, who caught it in mid-air. "Have fun!" Burt called before he snapped the lines and headed down the street, making way for a wagon full of people to stop in front of the door.

"Ready to go in?" Zach asked, leaning close to Lorna to be heard above the noise of the attendees.

The warmth of his breath blew across her ear, making a delicious shiver pass over her.

"You must be freezing," Zach said, mistaking her shiver for a reaction to the bitterly cold temperatures instead of his presence. "Let's get you ladies inside."

He cupped her elbow and guided her through the crowd to the entrance. Two men, dressed in tailed coats and top hats, yanked open the doors, and Zach walked beside her into the resplendent foyer.

Decorated in rich burgundy tones, the Opera House and everything in it, from the flocked wallpaper to the six-foot-tall bouquet on a round table with a stack of printed programs, hinted at opulence.

"It's wonderful," Lorna said, barely standing still as Zach helped her remove her cloak. He waited as Tom helped Ellery with her cloak, then took their outerwear to a desk, where two harried-looking women tried to keep track of all the clothing and hats tossed at them.

Lorna turned in a slow circle while Zach waited in line to leave their coats. A chandelier that hung from the second story glittered in light glowing from the electric wall sconces, drawing her gaze to it. Stairs, covered with a thick ruby-hued embossed carpet, wound along the wall to her left, while a refreshment table was set up to the right.

"It's wonderful," Lorna repeated, smiling at Ellery and wrapping her hand around her friend's arm. Together, they went over to admire a huge fir tree decorated with satin bows, hand-blown glass balls, paper cornucopias full of candy, figurines of St. Nicholas, lush roses made of paper, and what seemed like thousands of strands of tinsel as it refracted the lights and made the tree sparkle with radiance.

"Now that's a tree," Zach mused as he rejoined

them. "I heard they cut that up above the mill and it took four men to haul it in here and get it set up."

"I've been to numerous opera houses, but this one could compete with the very best," Lorna said, smiling at her friends.

A frown appeared on Zach's face but disappeared so quickly, she thought for a moment that she'd perhaps imagined it.

"May we head to our seats?" Ellery asked. "I know we have plenty of time, but I'm so excited to see where we'll be sitting."

"Absolutely," Lorna said, looking at Zach as he nodded his head in agreement.

"Does anyone want refreshments now?" Zach tipped his head toward the table where punch and cookies were available.

"I'm fine, but thank you." Lorna smiled at Zach, then looked to Ellery. "Do you want anything?"

"Goodness, no. I'm still stuffed from Maude's delicious dinner. Lorna invited me to eat with them. Maude made a casserole with cheese and ham—it was so good—and there were little cups of fruit, pickles, creamed peas, and warm slices of oat bread." Ellery looked embarrassed that she'd gone on and on about the meal. "It was all delicious."

"I'm just glad you could join me, Ellery." Lorna patted her friend's hand. They both turned to Tom and grinned when they heard his stomach rumble.

His face turned red as he shrugged in embarrassment. "I didn't have time to eat."

"Then, by all means, you should at least

partake of a few cookies," Lorna said, giving Ellery a nudge toward Tom.

Ellery led the way toward the refreshment table, while Zach shifted closer to Lorna. "Thank you for being so kind to her. She's like a sister to me, and I have never seen her this happy. Her face is glowing with joy."

Lorna took a step that placed her so close to Zach, she could have counted his incredibly long eyelashes when she looked up into his face. "She's a sweet, caring person, and a dear friend. Ellery has been a blessing to me in so many ways."

"I'm glad to hear that, but she'd say the same about you." Zach offered her a tender smile. "If I'm not mistaken, she's wearing your gown and cloak. I assume you also had a hand in the new style of her hair?"

Lorna nodded, pleased when Tom handed Ellery a cup of punch and a napkin with a cookie before he helped himself. "Doesn't she look exquisite? Her coloring is much better suited to that gown than mine. I'm just thrilled she agreed to come this evening. Tom also seems delighted she's here."

Zach smirked. "That he is. I thought he was going to swallow his tongue when you two started down the stairs." He looked at her, his gaze tangling with hers, pulling Lorna into a place where no one else existed beyond the two of them. Time seemed to stand still as Zach raised his hand and trailed one work-roughened finger over the slight dimple in her chin. "Tom wasn't the only one knocked right out of his boots. You are about the prettiest thing I've ever seen, Lorna Lennox. I'm not a man given to flowery speeches, but you make me wish I were a poet. If I were, I'd put pen to paper to describe your eyes that always make me think of frost edging a forest glade, one with depths beyond the ability to imagine. Then there's your gorgeous hair. In the sunlight, it's as though the silky tresses have been touched with a heavenly flame. And I'd be remiss not to mention those sweet lips. They are far too tempting for mere mortal men to resist."

A flush started at the top of her head and slid all the way to her toes. She could feel heat blazing in her cheeks, but cherished each word Zach had spoken. "And you say you aren't a poet, Mr. Coleman. Shame on you." She tossed him a coy smile and pretended to be unaffected by his descriptions. Inside, her stomach felt weightless and her limbs entirely languid. No one had ever dared to utter such things to her, and Lorna quite liked it, at least when Zach uttered such words of praise. Had anyone else spoken in such a forward manner, she would have immediately set them in their place for their impudence.

"I'm telling you the truth, Lorna," Zach said, taking her hand in his and bringing it to his lips, kissing the back of her gloved fingers. "You have left me beguiled and quite often befuddled. I've never felt so …"

"These cookies are divine," Ellery said as she and Tom returned. "Try one." She held out a napkin with cookies on it.

Lorna wanted to stamp her foot in frustration. Finally, she'd been making headway with Zach, only to be interrupted when she was certain he was on the verge of telling her something important. However, tonight was about giving Ellery an experience to remember. From the way Tom couldn't take his eyes off her, she hoped it would be the beginning of something wonderful between the two of them.

She and Zach each took a cookie from those Ellery offered.

"Delicious," Lorna said, wondering if Zach's mother had made them. She'd noticed some of the women in the community helping with the refreshments. The cookies tasted just like a batch Cora Lee had served one afternoon at a Women's League meeting. She looked at Zach. "Are your parents here?"

"Yep," Zach said, looking at her with a hint of displeasure. She wondered if it stemmed from Ellery and Tom intruding on what had been an intimate moment, or if something else bothered him. "Mamie and Dad came, but Pops and Grams decided it was too cold to venture out this evening. My folks are spending the night at the hotel as a special treat. I hated the thought of them heading home in the dark and cold after the show."

"That's delightful," Lorna said. "I hope they have a marvelous time. Do you think our seats are close to theirs?"

"Only one way to find out." Zach took four tickets from the pocket of his suit coat and motioned for Lorna and Ellery to precede him and Tom.

It didn't take long to find their seats. Lorna

took a seat between Ellery and Zach, then hopped up and gave Cora Lee a hug when she and Jace appeared in their aisle.

"You look so lovely, Mrs. Coleman!" Lorna moved back so Ellery could greet them.

"Thank you, Lorna. Both of you girls look like a picture from a magazine. Your gowns are so lovely." Cora Lee smiled at them, then pressed her hand against Zach's chest. "And you don't look too bad, son. I forgot how well you clean up when you aren't covered in grease from work."

Tom snickered at her comment, earning a glare from Zach. Lorna did her best not to giggle at the woman's teasing, but Ellery laughed.

"Are you sitting with Mum and Dad?" Ellery asked, looking around for her parents.

"Yes, we are. We have seats right over there." Cora Lee pointed across the aisle. "Your folks haven't yet arrived."

"Burt will probably drop them off soon," Zach said, glancing toward the doorway. "There are Rance and Kansas. I think Charlie and Alice were coming, too."

"Yes, they're coming," Ellery said, waving at her brother. "It looks like they have seats right behind you, Aunt Mamie."

"I suppose we'd better get settled into our seats." Cora Lee smiled at them, then wrapped her arm around Jace's, and they made their way back over to their seats.

Lorna had offered to purchase the tickets, but Zach had insisted he'd pay for them. In fact, he'd acted insulted she'd even suggest buying them. She knew they weren't overly costly, but she wondered if he could afford four of them. Perhaps Tom had paid for his and Ellery's tickets. Still, they had grand seats, right on the aisle, only four rows back from the stage. Lorna had no idea if the cost of the tickets varied by the seat location, or if they were all one price and the first to purchase got to choose the best seats.

Regardless, she looked forward to the evening ahead. Even if the play was horrible, she was content just to sit next to Zach for the next hour and a half.

When R.C. and Anne Milton arrived, Zach waved to them, as did Ellery. They'd barely taken their seats when the lights dimmed and the play began.

Lorna found herself swept into the fairy tale originally penned by the Brothers Grimm. Two years ago, it had been made into a play on Broadway where the dwarfs in the story were given names. One of her friends had attended a showing of the play and thought it silly, but Lorna wished she'd been able to see it, if, for no other reason, to compare it to this charming presentation of the tale.

When seven children, dressed in clothes made of colorful patches, wearing long wigs and fake beards, marched across the stage as the seven dwarfs, Lorna had to hold her hands tightly clasped on her lap to keep from clapping at the adorable sight they made.

As the story progressed and Snow White took a bite of an apple poisoned by the evil queen, Lorna sat forward on her seat, completely absorbed in the tale as she twisted her handkerchief in her hands.

"Don't despair. She doesn't die, you know," Zach whispered in her ear.

Lorna turned her head from the stage to Zach, finding his lips alarmingly close and his eyes full of mirth. "I know, but it's quite good, isn't it?"

He nodded indulgently, and Lorna relaxed, settling back in the comfortable theater seat.

Amazed by her handsome companion as well as the elaborate sets and costumes involved in the play, she was among the first to hop to her feet and enthusiastically applaud at the end of the performance.

"Oh, wasn't it marvelous?" she asked, turning to Zach with a bright smile. He nodded his head, looking like he wanted to say more, but Ellery grabbed Lorna's arm and pulled her attention away from him.

After making their way back to the foyer where more punch and cookies were served, Lorna found herself among those invited to the Milton home.

"Mum and I made two cakes this morning," Ellery said as Tom settled the cloak around her. "I hope you'll join us."

Tom nodded. "I'd like that very much, Miss Milton."

While Ellery and Tom headed outside, Lorna lingered with Zach. "Are you going to join them?"

"I rather hoped you'd want to come, unless you are in a rush to hurry home."

"Not at all," Lorna said, happy to spend more time with Zach and his parents, as well as the Milton family.

When they walked outside, Burt waited with a large wagon and a hulking team hitched to it. "It's getting too cold to make multiple trips in the sleigh. Everyone can pile in," the boy said, glaring at Rance when he started to complain. "If you prefer, you can walk."

Zach and Tom stood at the back of the wagon, helping everyone in before they swung up and took seats at the back on the bales of straw Burt had tossed in and covered with old blankets.

"This is fun," Lorna whispered to Zach. "Would anyone mind if we sing?"

"Sing?" he asked, giving her a strange look. "What do you want to sing?"

"Christmas carols, of course," Lorna said, then began singing *Deck the Halls*. She elbowed Ellery to join her, and soon everyone was belting out the familiar carol.

They sang all the way to the Milton home where Mariah and Mercy had hot chocolate ready to serve.

"We want to hear everything. Absolutely everything," Mercy said as she took Ellery's cloak, admiring the covering.

Mariah squealed, took Ellery's hands, and twirled her in a circle. "Your dress! Oh, it's fantastic!"

Ellery blushed, but Lorna could tell she was pleased by her younger sisters' appraisal of the gown and her appearance.

After indulging in hot chocolate and slices of cake, Lorna knew it was time for her to return to Lennox Manor. She wished she could bottle up the feeling of home and family she felt with these dear, kind people and keep it for a day when she was lonely. Even if she couldn't preserve the feeling, she would have the sweet memory to cherish.

"Want me to drive the sleigh?" Burt asked as Zach helped Lorna with her cloak.

"If you don't mind my driving it, I can take it and put it away."

"That's fine with me," Burt said, returning to the spot on the floor near the fireplace where he'd settled and stretched out his feet toward the warmth of the flames.

Zach escorted Lorna outside and over to the three-sided shelter where Burt had left the sleigh. Not only did it keep the horse protected from the elements, but it also kept the snow from covering the seats.

"Mind riding up here with me?" Zach asked as he pointed to the driver's seat.

"Not a bit." Lorna felt the air whoosh out of her when Zach settled his hands at her waist and swung her into the sleigh, then climbed up beside her. He reached back and lifted one of the heavy throws from the seat and draped it over her legs.

"Don't want you to freeze."

"Certainly not," she said, scooting closer to him.

He pretended not to notice as she edged closer to him. Beneath the cover of the blanket she had spread out so it extended over his lap, their legs bumped against each other. Lorna felt quite scandalized by the innocent touch, yet oddly invigorated too.

Something about Zach Coleman made her want to cast all caution aside and leap headlong into the possibilities love offered. Only she wouldn't. Not when she still had no idea of his feelings for her. Not when she felt so uncertain of her own.

"Did you have a nice time?" Zach asked as the horse plodded along the quiet street.

"The best," Lorna said, turning to look at Zach. As she studied his strong jaw and a mouth made for tempting kisses, light snow began to fall.

She tipped her head back and let the flakes dance across her cheeks. Because Zach made her feel so free, so unfettered, she stuck out her tongue and caught a few, causing him to laugh.

"You are something else, Lorna Lennox," he said, slipping an arm around her and tucking her against his side.

"I hope that something is good."

"Oh, it is, my lady with the frosty forest green eyes."

The way he said "my lady" made such warmth spiral through her, Lorna fought the urge to toss aside the blanket covering them. Instead, she snuggled a little closer to Zach.

He didn't seem to mind as he bent down and pressed a kiss to her temple. "You were the prettiest girl at the performance tonight."

"That's kind of you to say, even if it isn't true. I know for a fact there were dozens of women and girls far prettier."

Zach scowled. "Not to me. In my eyes, there is none more beautiful than you."

"Zach, that's so sweet." Lorna sighed and

relaxed against him. "I had such a lovely time. This was one of the best nights of my life, and I thank you for making it possible."

"All I did was invite you to go with me. You're the one who made it a grand experience for me. Thank you, again, for making it special for Ellery too. She is practically floating."

"I just hope things work out for her and Tom. He seems like a nice man."

Zach nodded. "He is a good fella—hardworking and kind. He'll be a good husband to Ellery, if she's of a mind to marry him."

"You think after one outing there are wedding bells ringing?"

He shrugged. "They've known each other for years. Tom's been infatuated with Ellery so long, he probably can't remember what life was like before he loved her. It's about time the two of them admitted their feelings and fell in love. You can take credit for having a hand in it all."

Lorna grinned. "I didn't do much other than suggesting going to the play together."

"And treating Ellery like a princess today. Honestly, with all the kids in their family, Ellery is the subdued one who sometimes gets overlooked, especially when Mariah and Mercy are around. Those two don't know the meaning of shy or quiet."

A laugh rolled out of Lorna. "They don't, but they are such nice girls, and I think they mean well."

"They do. Poor Uncle R.C. and Aunt Anne will have their hands full when those girls begin courting."

"I agree, but it will be amusing to observe."

Zach chuckled and pulled the sleigh to a stop at the end of the walk at Lennox Manor.

"Would you like to come in and warm up for a while?"

"I would love that, but it's getting late. I don't want to wear out my welcome with you on our first outing." Zach hopped out of the sleigh, then held his hands up toward her.

Lorna settled her hands on Zach's strong shoulders and rested them there as he swung her out and to the ground. For a moment, she felt dizzy and lightheaded, overwhelmed with sensations and feelings so foreign to her. She rested her head against his chest as she caught her breath, and felt his hands stroking up and down her back.

Despite the freezing cold nipping at her nose and chilling her toes, she didn't want to move. Not ever. She could have died right there in the comforting, welcoming circle of Zach's arms.

Slowly, she raised her head and found him studying her.

"You are so beautiful," he whispered, then lowered his head to hers.

His lips felt warm as they brushed over her mouth. Warm and soft and more splendid than she'd dared dream. Lorna sighed and slid her hands up his arms, encircling the back of his neck as he pulled her closer. The kiss subtly changed from a gentle caress to something far more passionate and demanding.

How long they might have stayed there, she would never know. One moment she was lost to everything but how right it felt to be loved by Zach. The next, she heard her father's voice bellowing at her from the front step.

"Lorna Adaline Lennox! What do you think you are doing?"

Startled, Lorna jumped away from Zach, bumping into the sleigh and losing her footing on the slippery ground. Zach caught her before she fell; then her father was there, yanking her away from him.

"Explain yourself, young man!" George Lennox demanded in a voice Lorna was sure could be heard all the way to Baker City. "Who in the blue blazes are you? How dare you take such liberties with my daughter!"

"But, Papa, he was …" Lorna's explanation died on her lips when she noticed someone step behind her father. Someone she'd hoped to never again see.

"Papa," she croaked. "What is *he* doing here?"

Her father's only response was a dark glower.

A groan escaped before Lorna could tamp it down. When she'd left Philadelphia, she'd hoped Gordon Pemberly would forget his intentions to make her his bride. She'd rather marry a one-eyed buffalo than be stuck with the citified dunce for a lifetime.

Zach looked from Lorna to her father and to Gordon, then back at her again. A face that had just moments before exuded such depths of affection for her now held a disappointment. Eyes that had glimmered with yearning appeared cold and hurt.

"Zach Coleman, meet Gordon Pemberly, he's

… um … he's …"

"I'm her fiancé. I've traveled to this barbaric town to marry Lorna, and I'll thank a plebeian such as yourself to keep your filthy hands off her."

Chapter Eight

The milksop glaring at Zach made him battle the urge to punch the dandy right in his hawkish nose.

"I am not going to marry you, Gordon," Lorna protested, removing her arm from her father's grasp and stepping back, closer to Zach.

"Yes, you are. Simple as that," the sissified interloper stated.

"I won't! I won't do it." She grabbed Zach's hand, offering him a pleading, apologetic look. "I'm sorry, Zach. Truly. Thank you again for such a lovely evening."

He nodded, unable to speak when the dreams he'd been building up for the future suddenly crashed around him. How could he have been so stupid? To think, even for a moment, her father would approve of him as a suitor? He'd known better. Known it was ridiculous to assume love mattered more than position or prestige.

With Gordon Pemberly there, insisting Lorna was engaged to marry him, Zach wasn't sure he could trust anything Lorna had to say. She should have been forthcoming about her fiancé in Philadelphia, rather than let him think she was interested in him. It seemed he was an amusing diversion and nothing more.

"I'll deal with you later," Mr. Lennox warned, glowering at Zach. The look he directed at him made it perfectly clear he thought Zach had to be the most insignificant being in existence. "Go on. Get out of here, and don't you dare come back."

Dismissed by the high and mighty George Lennox, Zach felt helpless as he watched Lorna's father grip her arm and march her down the walk and up the front steps. Pemberly scurried behind them, making Zach think of a marionette he'd once seen in a traveling show that had stopped in town a few years ago.

Just before Mr. Lennox pushed her inside the house, Lorna glanced over her shoulder. He wasn't certain, but it looked as though she mouthed, "I'm sorry."

Sorry for what? Lying to him about her intentions to wed some scrawny lunkhead? Sorry for leading him on? Sorry for breaking his heart?

At the moment, he wouldn't have been surprised to look down and see the ragged pieces of it lying red and lifeless against the pristine snow.

How could Lorna kiss him so passionately, so wondrously, if she was engaged to another?

Filled with questions for which there didn't appear to be any immediate answers, Zach returned the sleigh to the livery, then went to the Milton home, where he'd arranged to stay the night. Annoyed, irritated, and hurt, he refused to say anything to Andy or Burt when they kept trying to pry details out of him. Unable to speak without shouting, he refused to behave in a rude manner in Aunt Anne's home.

Finally, Zach retreated to the guest room that had once been Charlie's room, climbed beneath the covers, and spent the night unable to sleep. Every time he closed his eyes, he could see Lorna as she'd appeared in her beautiful dress, and the way she'd looked so full of yearning right before he'd kissed her. The sweet taste of her lingered on his lips, while he relived the feel of her body pressed against his as they'd embraced.

Exhausted from tossing and turning, but still unable to sleep, Zach rose and dressed, made his way to the kitchen, and left a note thanking the family for their hospitality. He headed to the engine house and got started two hours early on his day's work.

Too angry to eat, he skipped breakfast and tried to distract his thoughts with hard labor. By the time Henry arrived, Zach was even more livid than he'd been the previous evening. How dare Lorna string him along, flirt with him, make him think she cared when she was engaged!

For all Zach knew, Mr. Lennox might show up and fire him at any moment. The notion of being tossed from a job he not only loved but also excelled at, only added to his rage.

Indignant and livid, he could hardly keep from bellowing at her when Lorna arrived mid-morning, carrying a basket. The enticing fragrances of something sweet and spicy emanated from it, filling the air when she lifted the cloth covering.

"I brought a peace offering. Maude just took this out of the oven. I thought you might enjoy …"

"You thought wrong." Zach glared at her, his jaw hard, unyielding.

Tears welled in Lorna's eyes as she dropped the cloth back over the basket and set it on the workbench where Zach had been cleaning a grease-coated part. If Lorna wasn't careful, she'd end up with grease and grime all over her fancy clothes.

He eyed her from the top of her head to her toes, taking in the hat perched just so on her abundant curls with a dark green plume curling in a way it seemed to point directly at her fascinating eyes. She wore a matching green coat with a green and cream striped dress. If he hadn't been so mad at her, he might have acknowledged how utterly fetching she appeared.

Most likely, she'd gone to the extra effort with her appearance for Pemberly's benefit, not his.

"Are you going to glower at me forever, or do you think we could discuss what transpired last night?"

"What transpired, as you put it, is none of my business. You're free to marry whomever you please." Zach turned slightly so she was out of his line of vision. He couldn't bear to see the hurt in her eyes. "Besides, your father made it quite clear I'm not welcome."

"Don't pay Papa any mind. He was just being protective and dramatic. As for Gordon, I will not marry that man. Not ever. Even if he were the last of male species on the entire planet, I'd die a spinster."

Zach shrugged, feigning a disinterest he was far from feeling. "I do think you could do better than that nasally nincompoop, but who am I to say? We plebeians aren't known for our great intelligence."

Lorna blew out an exasperated sigh and stamped her foot. When Zach glanced back at her, she looked for all the world like she wanted to slap him. Since he was the innocent party, he took exception to her reaction.

"Go marry your buffoon, Miss Lennox, and have a lovely life looking down your nose at the rest of us."

"You are an idiot, Zachariah Coleman! A royal idiot! If I were a man, I'd knock some sense into you."

He turned to smirk at Lorna, knowing it would further infuriate her. Slowly he wiped his hands on a rag, as though he had all the time in the world and nothing better to do. "I'm not the one secretly engaged while pretending to be otherwise."

"I am not engaged!" she shouted, stamping both feet. "Furthermore, you infuriating man, I will decide whom I'm going to wed and when; no one else. Get that through your thick skull and cease in your sulking behavior."

Affronted, Zach dropped the rag and took a step toward her. "I think you should leave now, Miss Lennox, before I forget you are a lady, or that I should try to be a gentleman." Even as furious as he was with her, Zach ached to hold her, to kiss her again. His hands trembled with the need to touch her, so he shoved them in his pockets, plastered a dark, menacing look on his face, and straightened to his full height.

"I'm sorry for what my father and Gordon said, but they do not speak for me. Regardless, I can see you aren't of a mind to be reasonable." Lorna placed her hands on her hips and pinned him with a knowing glare. "When you're ready to talk, you know where to find me. Good day, Mr. Coleman!"

Lorna spun around and stormed out of the building, slamming the door with such force, every window rattled, and a handful of tools fell off the workbenches.

In the wake of her wrath, Zach remained unmoving, breathing in the tantalizing scent of her fragrance that wafted around him.

"Whooee! That girl has enough sass and spunk for ten females." Henry moved beside Zach and thumped him on the back. "She's a handful and then some. What are you gonna do with her?"

"Nothing." Zach turned back to his work. "Not a thing."

"Then I reckon you won't mind if we eat this cake," Corliss said, picking up a piece of cranberry cake, and taking a big bite.

"Help yourself."

The aroma of the cake spiced with ginger made his stomach growl, but Zach refused to eat even a crumb of Lorna's so-called peace offering. Not when he was still so angry with her.

Hours later, he was still trying to expel his ire through hard work. Nothing seemed to lessen the tight bands that squeezed at his chest, making him wish he'd never set foot in the park that day back in

October. Never run to Lorna's rescue. Never lost his heart to her.

He'd just climbed out of the pit beneath the engine that his father had named Hope when he saw George Lennox enter the building. His employer made a beeline for Henry, said a few words; then, after casting a glance his way, the two of them walked outside.

Zach half expected to be told to pack his things when Henry returned, but the man acted as though nothing unusual had happened.

As they left for the day, both walking toward the street that ran behind the engine house, Henry patted him on the back. "I hear you're helping young Burt Milton with a project tomorrow."

"I am. He's got a crazy plan to build himself a snow car."

"A snow car? What in tarnation is that?" Henry asked as they stopped on the corner.

"He thinks he can build an automobile that can be driven even in deep snow." Zach shrugged. "I told him I'd help."

Henry chuckled. "Well, I'll wish you luck."

"Thanks, Henry." Zach lingered a moment, hoping Henry might hint at what he and Mr. Lennox had discussed earlier, but the man remained oddly quiet. "Tell Betty I said hello."

"Will do, son. Bye."

Zach watched Henry walk off before he headed toward the Milton home, where he planned to spend the night so he could be ready to help Burt first thing in the morning.

He'd not made it more than a block when a

sleigh pulled in front of him and George Lennox stepped out, lambasting him for consorting with Lorna. Without giving him a chance to respond, the man climbed back into the sleigh and departed.

Zach was so angry, he was surprised he didn't melt all the snow in a mile radius. He did his best to bank his temper before he continued toward the Milton place. With the accusing, unkind words of George Lennox echoing in his thoughts, he had a hard time falling asleep and again woke early.

After a filling breakfast, he, Burt, and Andy spent thirty minutes shoveling snow before they headed to the blacksmith shop.

"Here's what I want to do," Burt said, rolling out his plans on the workbench. Andy volunteered to round up the wooden components, while Burt and Zach worked on the parts they'd need to build.

The more Zach thought about Lorna, her father, and that dimwit Pemberly, the more irritated he grew.

"I've come to marry Lorna," he muttered in a tone mimicking Pemberly's as he picked up a heavy hammer and tried to beat out his frustrations on a piece of metal at R.C.'s blacksmith shop.

"You say something?" Burt asked as he worked to shape a piece of red-hot metal on the anvil.

"No." Zach expelled a deep sigh that didn't prove satisfying. Nothing had been satisfying since Lorna's father had returned home. The way Zach's heart weighed heavy in his chest, he wasn't sure anything would feel satisfying again, except maybe plowing his fist into Pemberly's homely face.

He still didn't feel like talking about Lorna.

Instead, he questioned Burt and Andy, asking if they thought Ellery had enjoyed her evening with Tom.

"She hasn't stopped going on and on about it," Andy complained with a teasing smile. Everyone in the Milton family was pleased to see their shy Ellery so happy.

Unfortunately, Tom had been nearly as giddy as Ellery at work yesterday, blathering constantly about the play, Ellery, and how much he hoped the four of them could plan another outing together.

Maybe Tom wouldn't mind having pathetic Pemberly tag along since Zach highly doubted the likelihood of his spending time with Lorna again. The realization that he'd surely lost her friendship caused his chest to ache as he worked.

"What are you gonna do with this thing if it works?" Andy asked Burt as he worked to fashion two broken bar stools he'd found behind the Golden Iron Saloon into seats for the automobile.

"The first thing I'm going to do is drive straight over to Molly Turner's house and offer her a ride." Burt waggled his eyebrows with an exaggerated mischievous expression. "I'll let you know my other plans after that."

In spite of his foul mood, Zach chuckled. "You mean to tell me we're going through all this work to impress a girl?"

"What else do you think would make me spend my weekend out here slaving over a hot forge?" Burt asked with a cheeky grin.

Andy looked at Zach, and they both started to laugh.

Chapter Nine

"When a young woman is out with her friends, it behooves her to act with the utmost dignity and decorum, setting a good example for others."

Miss Mulberry's Advice for Today's Young Woman

"We're here! We're here!" Lorna exclaimed, clapping her hands as she, Ellery, and Jenny Coleman all looked out the windows of the train car on one side, while Anne, Mariah, and Mercy peered out on the other.

Excited to have a day to spend with her friends, Lorna looked forward to exploring the shops in Baker City. Her father had graciously offered the use of his private car, as Lorna knew he would, and he'd pressed a wad of money into her hand as she'd left that morning, telling her to have a grand time.

She intended to. The past two weeks had worn on her nerves until she was nearly ready to explode.

After Papa had been so rude to Zach the night of the play, a night that, up to that point, had been one of the best of her life, Lorna had to force herself to be civil to her father. She knew he was only trying to protect her, but it didn't help matters any that he'd arrived in Holiday with the detestable Gordon Pemberly in tow. As soon as they'd had a moment alone, Lorna had made her feelings on the matter quite clear.

"I know you have no intention of marrying him, sweetheart, but he insisted on coming to see you. He said you needed one last opportunity to change your mind," her father had said by way of explanation.

While Gordon had snored like a hibernating bear in one of their many guest rooms, her father had spent a full hour the following morning interrogating her about Zach. Lorna had told her father the truth. That she admired Zach. That he was a good person and came from a fine family. That she didn't care what he thought because she loved Zach.

Her father had stormed out of the house in a fit of fury. Desperate to make amends with Zach, she'd asked Maude to bake one of her delicious cranberry cakes. Lorna took it to the engine house, hoping Zach would accept her apologies and they could pretend everything was fine.

Only Zach hadn't been ready to listen to what she had to say, and her own temper had gotten the best of her.

Now, nearly two weeks had gone by, and the only time she'd seen him was at church, where he'd snuck out the back door so he wouldn't have to face her.

According to Ellery, Zach was gloomy and miserable, but Lorna didn't know what to do about it. If he let a silly thing like her father's wrath get between them, there was no hope for their future. None whatsoever. The man that married her was going to have to learn to handle George Lennox or be plowed under by her father's overbearing ways.

Lorna had tried to distract herself from her broken heart and wounded feelings. She'd invited Ellery and the twins over to help her, Dodi, and Maude decorate for Christmas. Her father had seemed pleased to see their efforts and was even quite charming to the Milton girls.

However, Gordon was rude, condescending, and annoying. Lorna had threatened to blindfold him, lead him out of town, and leave him to his own defenses. He'd merely laughed at her, as though she joked, but she was entirely serious—at least mostly serious.

With her father's blessing, she'd arranged for this excursion to Baker City today. Although she'd invited Cora Lee Coleman to join them, the woman had politely declined. Lorna thought it was out of loyalty to Zach and respected Cora Lee's decision. Nonetheless, Jenny had squealed and given her a hug when Lorna extended an invitation to her.

Lorna had wanted to talk about Zach with her friends and especially with Anne, who seemed to possess helpful insight into the workings of a young man's mind, or the lack of it working properly, but she refrained.

She hoped Zach would eventually cease to be upset with her and realize she was also an innocent, injured party in the whole disastrous mess.

Part of her couldn't help but think wounded pride was at the root of Zach's problem, but surely that wouldn't keep him away if he truly cared for her. Perhaps she'd wrongly interpreted his affections. Maybe she was merely someone he thought to trifle with before a more interesting prospect came along. Even as the thoughts trickled through her mind, Lorna knew they weren't true.

Zach cared about her. Cared deeply. Which was why his absence hurt her so.

Part of her wondered if her father had been meddling, but he'd promised he'd done nothing more than talk with the manager of the engine house about Zach.

The more she thought about Zach, Gordon, and her father, the more distressed she'd become. However, today was meant to be a day of fun and jollity, and she was determined to make it a delightful memory for her friends.

Lorna grabbed Ellery's hand as the train rolled to a stop, then led the way off the train car when a porter appeared at the door, offering a hand as they descended.

"The only time I've been in Baker City was the day I switched trains to go to Holiday. You ladies will have to lead the way," Lorna said, smiling at them. "I've heard nice things about the dress shop in town, and Cora Lee suggested a place to have lunch. Do we want to shop together or break into groups?"

Anne took one look at the twins, who could hardly stand still for their excitement. "Mariah and

Mercy will come with me. I have a long list of shopping to see to, and they can help."

"I guess that leaves the three of us to explore on our own," Lorna said, looping her arm around Ellery's and then Jenny's. "Shall we visit the dress shop first?"

"Yes, please!" Jenny smiled and pointed to the street where the shop was located. "Cora Lee's wedding dress came from this dress shop. Mrs. MacGregor's fashions are well known in the area."

Lorna followed Jenny and Ellery inside a dress shop that appeared every bit as elegant as any she'd ever seen. Gowns in holiday hues of green, burgundy, cream, and red hung on racks and filled the broad display window.

At the sound of the tinkling bell on the door, a beautiful young woman walked out of a back room to greet them. "Welcome to MacGregor's Boutique," she said with a welcoming smile. "How may I be of assistance to you today?"

Lorna studied the girl who had to be closer to Burt's age than hers. She had beautiful, lush hair that was an unusual shade between blonde and brown and lovely brown eyes that made Lorna think of rich molasses syrup. The young woman possessed a rare beauty, and from the genuine kindness in her gaze, she seemed to be beautiful inside too.

"We're just looking around. It's my first time to visit Baker City," Lorna said, taking a step forward. "I'm Miss Lorna Lennox. This is Mrs. Jenny Coleman and Miss Ellery Milton, all from Holiday. We came to town to do a little Christmas shopping."

"Welcome to town and to our shop. I hope you enjoy visiting both. I'm Miss Danielle MacGregor. If you find something you'd like to try on or have any questions, please let me know."

"Thank you," Lorna said, smiling at Miss MacGregor, then turning to look at a display of gowns. One of them featured the finest lace she'd ever seen. "The lace is so delicate and superbly made."

Danielle nodded and pulled out a dress with a lace placket down the front. "A friend of our family makes it. My mother said she's never seen lace as fine as what Mrs. Amick creates."

"I haven't either." Lorna continued to glance through the gowns, then moved on to the selection of hats. Ellery was busy choosing a pair of gloves, while Jenny stared in awe at a dress the color of sapphires. A double peplum fell from a belted waist while thick ecru lace edged the sleeves and neck.

Lorna bumped Ellery with her elbow and tipped her head toward Jenny.

"Try it on, Jenny, just for fun," Ellery said, abandoning the gloves to go stand by their friend.

"Oh, I couldn't," Jenny said, but she reached out and fingered the soft fabric of the gown.

"You can't hurt anything just trying it on," Danielle said, lifting the dress and carrying it toward a dressing room. "I'll help you."

Jenny hesitated only a moment before she hurried after Danielle.

While she tried on the dress, Lorna perused the rest of the stock in the store, coming back to the dress with the placket of fine lace down the front. The emerald hue combined with the lace gave the dress such a festive air. One Lorna found she couldn't resist.

Jenny stepped out of the dressing room with Danielle and moved to stand in front of a large mirror.

"Oh, Jenny! That color is magnificent on you," Lorna said, smiling at Jenny's reflection in the mirror.

"You look positively lovely," Ellery said, moving so she could study the front of the dress. "Noah's eyeballs will pop right out of his head."

"Oh, I'm not going to purchase it. With Christmas and … well, I don't think it's an expense I should make right now." Jenny studied her image with a look of longing, then turned to step back into the dressing room.

Before she could, the door swung open and a handsome, older couple breezed inside.

"Lass, we brought you a treat," the man said, smiling at Danielle.

Immediately, Lorna could see the resemblance between the young woman and the older one who'd just stepped inside the store. The man's voice held the hint of an accent. Lorna pondered if he might be Scottish.

"Mama, Daddy, this is Mrs. Jenny Coleman, Miss Ellery Milton, and Miss Lorna Lennox, all from Holiday." Danielle hurried over to the older couple. The man kissed her cheek and handed her what appeared to be a bakery box. "These are my parents, Ian and Maggie MacGregor."

"It's so lovely to make your acquaintance," Lorna said, taking a step closer to the couple. "You have a marvelous shop."

"My Maggie and our girls, make the finest gowns this side of the Mississippi," Ian MacGregor boasted.

"Ian, you do go on," Maggie said, offering her husband an indulgent smile. "I'm so pleased you all stopped in today. Mrs. Coleman, that gown looks like it was made just for you."

"We were just trying to talk her into purchasing it, Mrs. MacGregor," Lorna said, glancing from Jenny to Maggie.

"Call me Maggie, please." The woman removed her hat and coat, tossing them onto a glass case, then turned and kissed Ian on the lips. "I'll see you this afternoon."

"Yes, you will," he said, stealing another kiss, tipping his hat to them all, and disappearing out the door.

"Mama, must you and Daddy do that?" Danielle asked, rolling her eyes.

Maggie gave her a playful swat on the backside of her skirt. "I must. What else is a woman to do when she's in love?"

They all laughed, then turned their attention back to the clothes in the shop.

"Is your mother Anne Milton?" Maggie asked Ellery.

"Yes, she is," Ellery said with a nod.

"You look so much like your lovely mother. I remember the first time she and her friend, Cora Lee, came into my shop. Like you girls, they were

Christmas shopping and enjoying a fun day. They tried on dresses, but couldn't afford to purchase them. Mr. Coleman came in and bought one for each of them." Maggie turned to Jenny. "Might I assume you are married to one of their sons?"

Jenny nodded her head. "I am. Cora Lee still has that dress. She said it's the prettiest gown she's ever owned."

"Oh, I'm so happy to hear that," Maggie said, motioning for Danielle to take the dress Jenny had tried on to the front counter rather than returning it to the display. "Now, what else are you girls looking for today?"

While Danielle helped Ellery choose gloves and Jenny find stockings, Lorna tried on the dress with the lace placket and fell in love with it the moment she glanced in the mirror.

"It's perfect for you," Maggie said, adjusting the right sleeve and smoothing down the skirt.

"I'll take it, and I'll need a hat, gloves, and perhaps a sapphire blue gown to go with it." She gave Maggie a conspiring wink.

The woman nodded. "I'll wrap it up, and she'll never know it's with your purchases. In fact, I can have whatever you purchase delivered to the depot so you don't have to pack it around with you."

"That would be much appreciated. Thank you."

Lorna and Jenny couldn't talk Ellery into trying on anything, other than a hat. Jenny bought two pairs of stockings and wistfully looked toward the empty display where the sapphire gown had hung.

Maggie offered Lorna a sly smile as she paid for her purchases, which included an embroidered shawl for Cora Lee. She quietly asked Maggie to add the hat Ellery liked to the total and knew it would be among the boxed and wrapped items Maggie offered to send directly to the depot.

"I'm so happy to have met you, Maggie, and your beautiful daughter. The next time I need a gown, I'll certainly be back."

"Excellent," Maggie said, walking with them to the door. "We're so happy you girls stopped in today. Don't be strangers."

Excited about the gifts for her friends, Lorna followed as Ellery and Jenny led the way down the street. They stopped in a book store, and a crystal shop, visited the local saddle shop, and even stopped by a photographer's studio where Lorna felt inspired with a gift idea for the Milton family. She made arrangements for the man to travel to Holiday to take a photo of the family once the winter weather cleared. After that, they headed to the Hotel Warshauer dining room, where they'd arranged to meet Anne and the twins for lunch.

"What a beautiful place," Lorna mused as they stepped inside the opulent lobby.

"I see Mum," Ellery said, tugging on Lorna's hand as they crossed the lobby to where Anne, Mercy, and Mariah waited by the door to the dining room.

"Is anyone hungry?" Lorna assumed they were all hungry from a morning of shopping.

"Yes. I wanted to go to the bakery, but Mum said we had to wait. As Burt would say, I'm as empty as a hollow log," Mercy said, grinning at Lorna as they followed the host to a table for six.

"Lunch is my treat, so please order whatever you like," Lorna said as she lifted the menu.

"No, Lorna. I would like to buy lunch today," Anne said, settling a hand on her arm.

"Please, Anne, allow me to do this tiny little thing. You and your family have been so kind to me, welcoming me into your home and lives and making me feel like part of the community. The very least I can do is treat you to lunch. Please?" Lorna gave Anne a look of such pleading, much like a pouting child might deliver, Anne finally laughed aloud.

"Have it your way, dear girl." Anne kissed her cheek, then picked up the menu.

Content and happy for the first time in nearly two weeks, Lorna listened as the twins debated what to order. Jenny and Ellery appeared undecided, and Anne had set her menu aside a moment after she'd opened it.

Finally, Anne looked to Lorna. "Would you like to order for us, Lorna? You've no doubt dined in many fine establishments and would have a better idea of what to choose."

Lorna glanced from Anne to Jenny, then Ellery. At their nods, she smiled. "I'd be happy to do that. Is there anything any of you don't like?"

"Liver."

"Asparagus."

"Slimy vegetables."

Lorna laughed. "I think we can avoid all that."

When the waiter came, she placed the order, then sat back and glanced around the dining room. It really was quite something to see, yet unexpected to find such a grand hotel in Eastern Oregon.

"Did you know the elevator here was one of only three located in the West for a number of years?" Jenny asked.

"Really?" Lorna asked, taking a sip of the water the waiter had poured.

Jenny nodded. "Noah said it's an Otis birdcage elevator."

"I want to ride in it," Mercy said.

"Me too!" Mariah added.

"We'll see how much time we have after lunch, girls," Anne said with an indulgent smile.

Lorna continued to study their surroundings, taking in the festive touches of garlands and ribbons that adorned the dining room. Several tables featured centerpieces with greens and holly in gilded urns. The dining room was something she would have expected to see back East, not in a town known for mining.

"Your first course, our special winter soup," the waiter said as he arrived with a large tray. He set cups of soup in front of them, then left with a nod.

"It's just potato and leek soup," Lorna whispered when Mariah and Mercy held their spoons poised but seemed reluctant to give it a try.

"Mmm, that's delightful," Jenny said, trying a bite.

The girls were more adventurous with the next course of sweet potato croquettes. The main course of chicken in a cream sauce served over a bed of mashed potatoes accompanied by a celery salad and tender yeast rolls seemed to please them all.

Ellery's eyes were nearly as wide as those of

the twins when the waiter carried out dessert. Lorna had ordered a cranberry floating island. The impressive dessert was made of gelatin, cranberries, and meringue spooned into a mold, then covered in a boiling custard. Coconut macaroons marched around the base of it, along with a few fresh cranberries.

"It's spectacular!" Mercy declared, leaning closer to get a better look at the towering creation.

"How lovely!" Anne declared as the waiter served each of them a helping of the sweet yet tart dish.

The moment he left the table, they all took a bite.

"Delicious!" Lorna declared, pleased with the quality of the food and the service of the establishment. She would recommend it to her father. She knew as he journeyed from Holiday to other places, he would often pass through Baker City. The food and the atmosphere of the hotel would both suit him well.

After the meal, Anne told Mercy and Mariah they could ride in the elevator, and Ellery went along to make sure they didn't get into any mischief.

Lorna paid for the meal and made arrangements for the hotel to have the various packages they'd carried in from their shopping excursion taken to the depot; then they ventured outside. A gust of frigid air made her glad she'd remembered her warmest scarf. She tugged it up higher beneath her chin and glanced at her friends.

"We still have time before we need to head to

the depot. Is there anywhere else you'd like to go?"

"The mercantile," Anne said, looking across the street. "They sell a few things we don't have available in Holiday."

"The mercantile it is," Lorna said, following as Anne led the way.

The store was busy and smelled of kerosene, leather, and bayberry as they stepped inside. Although not as large as some stores she'd shopped in, the business appeared to carry a variety of merchandise.

"You girls look around. I have a list to attend to," Anne said, then hurried toward the back of the store.

Lorna and Ellery wandered past displays with jewelry and perfume. Jenny stopped to look at men's gloves, while Mariah and Mercy headed straight for the spools of hair ribbons.

Ellery stopped to look at a display of books, while Lorna continued meandering along. She happened upon several Christmas items, and one, in particular, caught her interest. An idea for a gift to the town of Holiday entered her thoughts. Lorna grabbed the box in question and rushed up to the front of the store.

Discreetly, she inquired how fast a dozen or so boxes could be acquired, and if the order could be shipped directly to her in Holiday.

"Of course, Miss Lennox. I'll send a telegram today, and your order should arrive in about four days."

"Perfect," she said, paying for the order and returning the box she'd carried up to the counter to the shelf where she found it. Lorna picked up a basket and filled it with little gifts and trinkets for her friends. She'd already purchased a gift for her father, as well as Dodi, Maude, and Marcus. And she'd ordered a gift for Zach that should arrive soon.

She just hoped he'd get over what was bothering him and return to being her friend before Christmas.

Lorna glanced outside as the store clerk totaled her purchases and packed them into a box. Large, fluffy flakes fell in a flurry. She hoped it wouldn't hamper their trip home. She knew the railroad crew worked hard to keep the track cleared.

Zach had shown her the powerful snowplow that took two engines to push, but he said it cleared the track faster and better than anything else they'd tried.

"Oh, it's snowing again," Jenny said as she carried several items to the front counter.

"Again," Ellery said as she stepped next to Jenny with a few purchases.

"Do you mind walking to the depot, or would you rather I hire a ride?" Lorna asked, looking at the women.

"It's not far. We'll walk," Anne said, then glanced back to where the twins held up bolts of fabric and teased each other.

It didn't take long for them to be on their way. At the depot, Lorna made arrangements to have their purchases loaded onto her father's private car.

"The train from Holiday just arrived a few moments ago. We'll have your car ready for you to board soon."

"Thank you," she said, nodding to the stationmaster. She glanced outside the depot office to see her father speaking with someone, realizing it was Gordon.

"I'll be right back," she said to Ellery, then rushed outside.

"Papa?" She hurried over to him.

"Oh, sweetheart, I'm so glad I caught you. It's terrible news. Terrible." Her father didn't wear a hat, and his hair looked as though he'd forked his fingers through it many times. His collar was askew, and he had ink stains on his fingers, like he'd been writing letters or working on his books. Two young men hovered nearby, as though awaiting his instruction.

"Hook my car to the train heading for Omaha," he said to the young men, then turned to her. "I have to head to New York for a little while, Lorna. Due to the horrid war overseas, our stocks have plummeted. I need to see what can be done, and I can't do that from here." Her father pulled her into a tight embrace, something he rarely did in public. "I apologize for leaving so close to Christmas, but I will do everything in my power to be back by Christmas morning."

"Don't fret, Papa. I understand," she said, saddened her father was leaving so soon. She hoped, though, that Gordon's presence meant he'd given up on talking her into marrying him.

"I'm taking the train car you ladies rode in this morning. I hate to leave you without other accommodations, but there is no help for it. Will you mind terribly if you have to ride in the passenger car back to Holiday?"

"Not at all, Papa. It will be an adventure, but I believe they already loaded our purchases on your car."

Her father snapped his fingers, and another young man appeared. After accepting a coin from George, he rushed off to transfer the women's purchases from the private car to the train heading for Holiday.

"You'll need to purchase tickets for everyone. Do you need money?" her father started to dig into his pocket.

"No, Papa, I still have plenty left."

"Good. You have a safe trip home." He hugged her again, then stepped back. "Enjoy these days leading up to Christmas. Spend time with your friends and rejoice in the season. No matter what happens, darling girl, remember I love you."

"I love you, too, Papa. Now, enough of this depressing talk. Might I embrace a giddy anticipation of Gordon returning with you?" Lorna looked at the man who had annoyed and irritated her beyond endurance. She'd known Gordon her entire life. Her father and his had been close friends for years and years. Everyone had assumed when the time came, she and Gordon would wed, but Lorna had known since she was old enough to notice boys were different than girls that she would not become Gordon's wife. They had nothing in common and, if the truth were told, she didn't like him. He was pampered, spoiled, unkind, and often selfish. Gordon raised himself to a level above everyone else that she found both absurd and disturbing. Her father knew all that, which is why he'd never pushed a union between the two of them. Her father had explained that Gordon had insisted on coming to see her, sure a few months in the "wilderness" of Oregon would have changed her mind about marrying him, but it hadn't made his odious presence any easier to bear.

"You've made it quite clear you still haven't come to your senses, and I refuse to spend my holiday in this detestable place." Gordon sniffed and raised his pointy chin in the air.

"Safe travels to you." Lorna felt like cheering instead of offering a civil comment. Overjoyed to at last have Gordon leaving, she also felt overwhelmed with sadness that her father would be gone so close to Christmas. She hated the thought of him traveling all the way to New York alone.

"Would you like me to accompany you, Papa?" she asked.

"No, Lorna. You stay in Holiday with your friends and enjoy the season. I promise I'll do my best to be home as quickly as I can. In the meantime, I'd appreciate your prayers."

"Of course, Papa." Lorna gave him another warm hug and kissed his cheek.

"You may board, sir," a young man said as he ran up to her father, his cap askew and grease on one cheek, like he'd been laboring beneath one of the train cars. She wondered if he was one of the switchmen who worked to hook up the various cars.

"Thank you." Her father tossed him a coin, gave Lorna an encouraging smile, then strode off to the other side of the platform with Gordon jogging to keep up with him.

Lorna waved to her father as he boarded his private car, then returned inside the depot office. She purchased tickets, then went to stand next to Anne, needing the older woman's comfort as she settled an arm around her shoulders and gave her a hug.

"Your father is leaving again?" Anne asked quietly.

Lorna nodded and brushed at an errant tear that rolled down her cheek. "He has urgent business in New York. He said he'd try to be back for Christmas."

"I'm so sorry, Lorna. I'm sure it must be hard to have him gone so often." Anne patted her back.

"At least he took Gordon with him," Ellery said, offering Lorna a bright smile.

"There is a silver lining, after all," Jenny quipped, adding a bit of levity that lightened Lorna's mood.

"Father is taking the car we rode in. I'm so sorry, but we'll have to ride in the passenger car on the way back."

"Don't apologize, Lorna. It's still a fine adventure for us all," Anne said, looking to the others for agreement.

Had Lorna known how the day would unfold, she would have delayed the trip a few days so they could have taken her father's other private car. It had been in the shop, having the interior woodwork refinished, and the lacquer had not yet dried. That was the reason her father hadn't taken the second car instead of appropriating the one she'd borrowed.

Thoughts of her father missing Christmas made an ache settle in her heart. It was bad enough Zach continued to avoid her, but now she wouldn't even have her papa's presence to cheer her.

When the conductor gave the boarding call, she followed her friends on board the passenger car where their purchases had been loaded. Lorna had purchased two extra seats just so they had somewhere for the boxes and paper-wrapped parcels to travel. She could have had them loaded in the freight car, but she didn't want the Milton girls or Jenny to stand around in the cold waiting as the freight was sorted out at Holiday. This way, they could take their purchases and be on their way as soon as they arrived.

The car was packed full of people as they prepared to leave the station, and a woman with three young children tried to corral them all on her lap. Ellery volunteered to sit in one of the seats with the parcels, to make more room so the poor woman could have the children sit next to her.

Lorna found herself seated next to an elderly gentleman a few rows behind the others. Once she settled her skirts around her, she turned and looked into blue eyes that seemed to twinkle with mirth and joy. The older man had a white beard and hair, rosy cheeks, and the jolliest appearance she could ever recall encountering. He wore dark trousers with a forest green coat, a red brocade vest, and a crisp white shirt.

When he tipped his hat to her and smiled, Lorna felt her earlier concern and worry swirling away, like a strong breeze chasing after snowflakes.

"Hello," the man said in a mellow, deep tone.

"Hello." Lorna studied him a moment, feeling happiness seep into her. She had no idea how or why she felt that way, but was vaguely aware of a lightness settling into her soul.

"Do you live in Holiday, or are you just visiting?" he asked, then shook his head. "I suppose it's rude to ask questions of you without a proper introduction. I'm Nick."

Lorna was surprised he didn't offer his last name. "Lorna Lennox," she said with a smile. "To answer your question, I live in Holiday. We moved there a few months ago."

"We? Are you married? Have a family?" he glanced around the car, as though checking to see if she'd become separated from loved ones.

"No. Goodness no. My father built a new house in Holiday, and I moved there with the staff in October."

Nick's brow wrinkled in a slight frown. "Your father isn't there with you?"

Lorna glanced out the window, then back at the man beside her. "Frequently, he travels on business. It's the way he's always been, but after my mother passed two years ago, he is gone even more. We moved to Holiday to get away from the memories that plagued us in Philadelphia."

"I'm so sorry for your loss, Miss Lorna." The older gent sat back in his seat, settling in more comfortably as the train left the station.

"What about you Mister … Nick? Do you live in Holiday, or are you just visiting?"

"Oh, I'm merely visiting, but I've been there before. It's a thriving, growing place these days, isn't it?"

Lorna nodded. "It is, at least from what my friends have shared."

"Friends? So, you aren't completely alone when your father is gone?" Nick gave her a studying glance, one that made Lorna wonder what he saw when he looked at her, beyond a spoiled rich girl.

"I do have friends. Wonderful, kind friends who have opened their homes and hearts to me and made me feel welcome. I came with five of them today for a shopping excursion. They're sitting up there." Lorna tipped her head toward the seats where Jenny and Anne sat behind Mercy and Mariah and Ellery.

"That's grand. Did you find everything for which you were shopping?"

"For the most part." Lorna had no idea why she seemed incapable of holding her tongue, but words began to tumble out before she could stop them. "I was looking for a gift for someone special, at least he was special. When I first arrived in Holiday, I went exploring and was nearly run over by a wagon. Zach saw what was about to happen and rescued me. I've been in love with him ever since. Not because he rescued me, but because he's funny and smart, kind and caring."

"Is he handsome?" Nick asked with a teasing gleam in his eye.

"Well, there is that too."

Nick chuckled. "Tell me more about Zach. I

sense something has happened between the two of you."

A weary sigh escaped her. "I thought Zach cared for me as much as I loved him. We went to a delightful play one evening, and when he saw me home, well … he … I … that's to say …" Lorna huffed and cleared her throat. "My father had just arrived that evening and stepped outside along with a man who won't accept my refusal of marriage. I hadn't mentioned Gordon or his insistence on our nuptials to Zach. He was caught by surprise when Gordon announced his plans for us to wed. But they were Gordon's plans, not mine. I was so taken aback by his untimely arrival, I didn't say anything to defend Zach when Gordon made disparaging comments about him. My father also said some things that were unkind. Zach accused me of lying to him and won't even speak to me. My father didn't help matters when he went to Zach's place of employment and pried into things there."

"How terrible." Nick crossed his fingers over his round belly and rocked in his seat to the rhythm of the train. "Was Zach correct in calling you a liar?" he finally asked.

"No! I'm not a liar. I didn't feel the need to say anything about Gordon because I thought I'd made it clear to him I would never, ever marry him when I left Philadelphia. His father and Papa are the best of friends, which has made the situation rather complicated."

"Yes, yes. I can see how that would muddy the waters a bit."

Lorna relaxed into her seat, surprised at the

comfort they provided. She'd expected them to be hard and uncomfortable, but for a short trip, they were acceptable.

When she remained silent, Nick glanced over at her again. "Do you think your father spoke with Zach? Asked him to stay away from you?"

That thought had not crossed her mind, but it wouldn't surprise her in the least. Her father tended to distrust everyone, especially any men who showed interest in her. Railroad tycoon George Lennox assumed if a man came to see Lorna his only interest was in gaining access to the Lennox fortune. It stung that her father thought she had so little to offer a man, but she supposed he was probably correct. Some of the men who'd attempted to call on her were so blatant in their interest, even a child could have discerned the real reason for their interest in her.

She directed her thoughts back to Nick's question. "It's possible, sir, but I don't know anything for a fact."

"Facts are useful things, aren't they?" he asked, then gave her a cryptic look, one she found impossible to decipher. "Perhaps Zach thinks it is a fact that you were engaged while trifling with his affections."

"But I didn't, and I wasn't." Lorna wanted to shout that she'd done nothing wrong, but she could see how Gordon dogging her every step while he'd been in town might allude otherwise. The Milton family knew how much she detested Gordon. Surely Andy or Burt, or even Ellery, would have said something to Zach. Then again, Zach might have been so upset he didn't want to hear what anyone had to say about the matter.

"I wouldn't give up on Zach just yet. There are few things more bothersome than a young man nursing his wounded pride."

Lorna hoped Zach wouldn't nurse his for too long, if that was, indeed, the problem.

"Will your father be home for Christmas?" Nick asked, abruptly changing the subject.

"He just left today. In fact, I feel quite fortunate I ran into him at the depot. He hopes to be back for Christmas, but given the length of his previous absences, I'm not going to get my hopes up."

Nick offered her a sympathetic nod. "I'm sorry to hear that, Miss Lorna. Hope is the one thing we should never let go of."

Lorna considered his comment for a while before she looked at him again. "Perhaps instead of dwelling on my disappointment, I could think of ways to make the holiday happy for others."

A bright smile settled on Nick's face. The smile held such warmth, it made her feel as though sunlight flooded through her.

"Now that's the ticket!" Nick said, nodding his head approvingly. "What do you propose?"

"A party," Lorna said, before she had time to think about it. "A grand Christmas party, for anyone and everyone who wants to come. There could be gifts for the children and food and games. An event the entire community could enjoy."

"Splendid, my dear! That sounds splendid." Nick rubbed his hands together, as though he was excited.

Suddenly, Lorna felt giddy with anticipation. "I could fill baskets for the needy families and enlist my friends to help deliver them."

"A spectacular idea!" Nick looked at her with a great deal of pride.

The notion that he was proud of her warmed her heart. "Thank you."

"Of course, Miss Lorna." Nick glanced out the window, then back at her. "There is nothing grander than bringing joy to others. I'm so pleased you want to do that for Christmas."

"I do," Lorna said, already making lists in her head for the party. "And I will, Nick. Even if my Christmas doesn't turn out exactly like I want, I'll do my best to help others have a happy holiday."

"I know you will. Now, tell me, if you could wish for one thing for Christmas, only one thing, what would it be?"

"Zach," she said without a second of hesitation. "I want him to have a long, happy life, but I don't mind telling you I'd be thrilled if I could be part of it."

Nick grinned and reached out, patting her hand in a comforting gesture. "Grab onto that wish and hold it close in your heart. Believe it will come true, without any doubt or worry, and you might be surprised what will happen. All you need is hope blended with prayers and patience, and a pinch of perseverance never hurt either. Have faith, Miss Lorna, and you'll be amazed by the wondrous things that transpire."

She smiled, thinking Nick sounded whimsical and silly, even as she clung to every word he said.

"Oh, look. We're here already," she said, glancing out the window.

"Merry Christmas, Lorna," he said.

She smiled at him over her shoulder, only to find his seat empty. Ignoring the squeal of the brakes and the motion of the car as it rocked to a stop, she stood, braced a hand on the back of the seat in front of her, and looked around the car, wondering how Nick had so quickly disappeared.

As soon as the other passengers began to rise, she rushed over to Jenny and Anne. "Did you see the man sitting next to me?"

"No, Lorna. We didn't turn around once you said you were going to sit a few rows back." Jenny looked to Anne.

"What about you, Ellery? Or the twins?"

"I fell asleep," Ellery admitted as she repositioned her hat and straightened her gloves.

"I was reading, and Mariah was doodling," Mercy said with a shrug. "Was he handsome?"

The old gent had probably been quite dashing in his younger days. Something about him, something she couldn't begin to describe, seemed to draw people to him. And convince them to confess their secrets, Lorna thought as she helped gather their packages and leave the train.

"I had the best time," Jenny said, giving her a one-armed hug. "Thank you for inviting me, and for a fabulous day I'll long remember."

"My pleasure, Jenny. Do you need a ride home?" Lorna asked, glancing around to see if Noah or even Jace waited for her.

"No. Noah's coming to get me. He should be

here any moment," Jenny said, turning, then waving as Noah strode across the platform. He pulled her to him, kissing her quite ardently, then swinging her around as he gave her a hug.

Mariah and Mercy both held dreamy looks on their faces. "Wouldn't it be divine to be loved like that?" Mercy asked.

Anne gave the girls a nudge along with an indulgent grin. "You two need to stop thinking about love and romance and focus on finishing your schooling. The way you bob along with your heads in the clouds, it's a wonder your feet don't float right out from under you."

"But, Mum …" Mercy whined.

Ellery rolled her eyes at Lorna, making them both work to subdue their laughter.

"I trust you ladies had a nice time," Noah said, smiling at each of them. "Thank you for including my Jenny."

"Our pleasure," Lorna said, meaning it. Jenny had proven to be a good friend as well as someone she enjoyed being around.

Noah looked at the pile of purchases near Jenny's feet. "Did you buy out the whole town?"

"Only part of it," Jenny said with a saucy smile. "Now, you can pack it all home."

With a feigned grunt, he lifted her purchases, held out his arm to his wife, and tipped his head to them. "Thanks again."

They watched Noah kiss Jenny's cheek as they made their way down the platform steps. Lorna agreed with Mercy. It would be divine to be loved like that. To be so loved and cherished by a good-looking, good-hearted man.

"Oh, there's Andy," Ellery said, pointing to the big sleigh her brother stopped at the end of the platform. "Would you like a ride home, Lorna?"

"I see Marcus coming up the street," Lorna said, giving her friend a parting hug. "Thank you all for such a lovely day."

"We are the ones who are most grateful to you, Lorna, for a beautiful adventure." Anne kissed her cheek and gave her a hug before Andy bounded up the steps and helped his mother and sisters with their purchases. He tipped his hat to Lorna and held his arm out to Anne; then they left just as Marcus reached Lorna.

"Did you have a good day, Miss?" he asked, stacking two crates of her purchases and carrying them toward the sleigh.

"I did, Marcus. A good day with sweet friends." Lorna glanced back over her shoulder once, wondering if she'd somehow imagined Nick and her conversation with him. Surely not. Surely someone had to have noticed him.

But without time to question every passenger on the train, she followed Marcus to the sleigh. One thing was certain, though. She had a week to pull together the best Christmas party the town of Holiday had ever seen.

Chapter Ten

"You have to come, Zach. Please?" Ellery gave him an imploring look, one of such genuine pleading, he almost agreed to her request.

Almost.

"No. I have no interest in attending some fancy-pants party at *her* house."

Ellery, a young woman who was generally as calm and unruffled as any he'd ever encountered, looked like she could spit nails directly at him as her pretty face flushed with frustration. She fisted her gloved hands at her sides and marched right up to him as he stood at the workbench wiping off his tools, waggling a finger in his face.

"Zachariah Coleman! You are being a mulish, obstinate lunkhead! Lorna never lied to you. She thought Mr. Pemberly understood she had no interest in marrying him. Why do you continue to blame her for his actions when she's done nothing wrong?"

Zach shrugged, unwilling to tell her how much it had hurt him to see Lorna with that bothersome Pemberly. The man looked like a strong wind would fell him, and he was at least three inches shorter than Lorna. Pemberly had followed her around town like a besotted pup, trailing her every step until Zach wanted to pound something in frustration. So, he had. He'd pounded iron in Uncle R.C.'s blacksmith shop. When that didn't relieve his pent-up tension, he'd chopped enough wood at home to last for a year. He'd cleaned the barn, twice, and even volunteered to stay late and take care of additional work at the engine house.

The fact that he was working for George Lennox wasn't entirely lost on him, but he preferred not to think about his pompous employer.

He'd been such a dunce to think Lorna could love him, that they had a chance at building a life together. He was a nobody, as Mr. Lennox had bluntly pointed out. The man had made it clear he thought Zach had no business pursuing someone so far out of his reach.

Foolishly, he'd thought love would be enough to overcome any obstacles he and Lorna might face, but, apparently, the word of George Lennox meant more to Lorna than the feelings in her heart.

Neither he nor Lorna had confessed their love, but it was there. It was in the way she said his name. The way her eyes softened and grew dreamy when she saw him across the room. It was in the way she smiled at him; like he alone was her reason to experience joy.

And he felt the same about her. Despite everything, he still loved her. Still wanted her.

That was the reason he planned to stay far away from Lorna and her Christmas shindig.

He'd heard all about her last-minute plans to throw the biggest party Holiday had ever seen. She'd invited the whole community to come for lunch and partake in games and frivolity. The entire Milton family wouldn't stop talking about it. The girls had been enlisted to help with the planning. Andy and Burt had both been coerced into assisting with any number of projects, from fetching Christmas trees to delivering invitations around town.

In fact, Zach heard from his sister-in-law that Lorna had hired a whole group of women to cook for the party and a dozen more to help serve. Mike Milton had told him she'd hired him to install electricity in the gazebo at the park, of all places. Zach still hadn't figured out what she had planned there, and he didn't care.

Nope. He was perfectly fine acting as though Miss Lorna Lennox hadn't breezed into his life, turned his world upside down, and then left him with a broken heart.

Admittedly, she had tried to explain about Pemberly the morning after the nitwit had arrived, but Zach hadn't been in a mood to listen. He supposed it was now up to him to make a move, but he was still smarting from the verbal dressing down George Lennox had delivered that same day.

"I won't stand by and watch my daughter fall for your money-grubbing schemes. I won't have it, I tell you. Stay away from Lorna!" the man had shouted at him, then stormed off in his sleigh.

Zach sighed. The last thing he'd do is put Lorna in a position to choose between him or her father. If they continued seeing each other, he knew that would eventually happen. Lorna spoke of her beloved papa with such fondness and affection; Zach knew she loved her father deeply, especially now that her mother was gone. He refused to be the reason there was discord between the two of them.

He couldn't spend time around Lorna, pretending his heart didn't ache with every beat, yearning for her. In the three weeks that had passed since the play at the Opera House, he'd hardly slept a wink since Lorna haunted his dreams. He'd settle into his bed only to be taunted by her smile. He'd toss and turn, listening to the whisper of her voice or tasting her sweet kisses.

"Zach?" Ellery placed a hand on his arm, drawing him from his musings back to the moment. "Please? She'd be so happy if you were there."

"I can't go, Ellery. Besides, her father said …" Zach cut himself off. No one needed to know what that ostentatious old goat had told him.

Ellery fisted a hand on her hip. "What did Mr. Lennox say?"

"It doesn't matter." Zach glanced up at the big clock on the wall above the doors where the engines rolled into the workshop. "You'd best be going. Aren't you meeting Tom for supper at the hotel's dining room?"

"I am, but, Zach, please reconsider. It would mean the world to Lorna if you were there tomorrow."

He looked at Ellery, a girl he'd considered a sister, and saw the tears in her eyes, knowing her concern for him and for Lorna had put them there.

"I'll think about it."

She smiled and started to give him a hug, but he stepped back.

"Don't get too close, or you'll end up with grease all over you. Now, go on. Tom will be anxious if you don't head over there soon."

"I hope to see you tomorrow, Zach." Ellery waved at him, then rushed outside, leaving Zach alone in the quiet building. Corliss, Henry, and the others had already left for the day. Zach had promised Henry he'd take care of closing the shop for the night.

He made sure the tools were all cleaned and put away, banked the fire in the engine they'd use in the morning, and made certain everything was in its proper place before he locked the door and stepped outside. The cold air made him glad he had a warm scarf wrapped around his neck and ears. He tugged his hat down, shoved his hands in his pockets, and hastened toward his uncle's livery where he'd left his horse. Uncle R.C. kept a stall for him to use when he rode Buckley into town instead of his motorcycle, which was pretty much from the time the first snow fell until the mud dried up in the spring. Not that Zach minded. Spending as much time as he did in town with his job, he sometimes missed being on the ranch, chasing cows, and working alongside his dad and Noah as well as the cowboys they hired to keep the ranch running smoothly.

"Hey, did Ellery get you to change your mind?" Burt asked the moment Zach set foot inside the blacksmith shop.

He'd planned to cut through it to reach the livery. Burt had spent every extra minute he had working on his snow car. The one-of-a-kind machine was nearly finished, although none of them, including Burt, were sure if it would work. The engine ran, but whether the car would travel in the snow like Burt planned was a whole other matter. Zach thought Burt planned to take the car out the following day for a test drive.

"Your sister let me have an earful, but I wouldn't say it changed my mind." Zach tossed a flippant grin at Burt as he passed through the blacksmith shop. "About finished?"

"Almost. I just need to fasten the track on the back wheels. I think I've got it figured out. Dad said he'd lend me a hand after supper."

"That's great. I look forward to seeing you out driving it soon."

"Me too," Burt said, returning to his work as Zach left and walked into the livery. He soon had Buckley saddled and led him outside where it had started snowing again.

Zach couldn't ever remember having this much snow before Christmas. Tomorrow, he'd ride into town early to help shovel walkways before he went to work. He and several other men in town went around with shovels, doing their best to keep the main paths clear. The city had a snowplow pulled behind a big team that helped clear the streets, even though it left huge piles of snow scattered about that took up part of the walkways. The children in town didn't seem to mind. It made for many sledding opportunities. Timothy Milton, according to Andy, had come home two days ago with a black eye from hitting a rock when he flew off his sled.

Zach swung onto Buckley, turned up the collar of his coat against the cold, and headed toward home. There were days he knew he should probably stay in town, and he always had a place at Aunt Anne's table, but he enjoyed the peacefulness of Elk Creek Ranch. He also liked the opportunity to let his thoughts wander on the ride home.

Enveloped by the darkness and frigid air, he was grateful the snow was light and he could see well enough to stay on the road to the ranch. He kept an electric bicycle lamp in his saddlebag in case he needed it, but with the snow and a tiny sliver of moon trying to peek through the clouds, he had no trouble finding his way.

Chilled and starving by the time he reached the ranch, he rode Buckley to the barn and took care of him before heading inside the house. He was stamping his feet on the mat outside the kitchen when the door swung open and light spilled out, surrounding his mother in the amber glow as she gave him a look filled with relief.

"I'm so glad you made it home. I was beginning to worry."

Zach stepped inside and closed the door behind him, then leaned over and kissed his mother's cheek. "You always worry, Mamie."

Playfully, she swatted him with the dish towel in her hands. "Only because you and your brothers are a worrisome bunch of hooligans."

"And yet, you love us anyway." Zach gave her a teasing grin as he removed his hat, scarf, coat, and gloves. He toed off his boots and gratefully pulled on the slippers his mother had thoughtfully set by the kitchen stove so they'd be warm.

After he washed his hands and face, he set the table while Cora Lee dished up the food. She'd just placed a bowl of sauerkraut on the table when his father rushed inside, letting in a blast of icy air.

"I think it's dropped ten degrees in the last hour," Jace said, hanging up his things, then washing his hands at the sink.

"I'm glad you both are in for the evening. It's too cold to be out tonight." Cora Lee set her hand on Jace's back as he dried his hands on a dish towel.

"It's a good night to sit by the fire and read or maybe even work on a Christmas present."

Cora Lee moved over to the table and took a seat when Jace pulled out her chair. "You mean to tell me you aren't finished with your gifts? Tomorrow is the twenty-third. You're running out of time."

"I'm well aware of what day it is, wife of mine. I just have a few things to finish up." Jace looked to Zach. "Will you ask the blessing tonight, son?"

Zach bowed his head and offered a prayer. He realized then he should have been praying about the situation with Lorna all along instead of letting his head and heart try to control matters.

With a sigh, he passed his father the platter of schnitzel and listened to his parents discuss things they'd heard or done that day. Eventually, their conversation circled around to Lorna and her party tomorrow.

"Zach, I know you're upset with Lorna, but I

don't think it's right or fair of you to continue to ignore that sweet girl. She had no idea that wretched Mr. Pemberly would come all this way to try to force her into marriage. I can't begin to fathom why her father would allow him to do such a thing," Cora Lee said, her voice sounding agitated as she spoke. "Anyone could see Lorna had no interest in that uppity young man. I'm so glad he left last week, although it is a shame Mr. Lennox felt the need to travel so close to Christmas."

Uncertain what his mother wanted him to say, Zach remained silent.

"Lorna is a wonderful girl, Zach," Jace said as he buttered a slice of bread. "If you ask me, she's one worth keeping."

"You can't keep what you never had," Zach mumbled to himself.

"What was that, son?" Jace asked, stopping in the midst of spreading berry jam over the bread to stare at him.

"Nothing, sir." Zach shoved in a big bite of meat so he couldn't talk, then listened as his parents began discussing Lorna's party.

"You'll be there." Cora Lee looked across the table at him. From the look in her eye and the stubborn tilt of her chin, Zach knew she meant the words as a directive, not a question.

"Mamie, I'm not going." Zach set down his fork and knife and looked from his mother to his father. "Lorna may not have lied to me like I thought at first, but maybe this all happened for a reason. Her father has made it clear he wants me to stay away from her, and I have. Someday, it would come down to Lorna being forced to choose between me or her father, and I won't put her in that position."

"What did Lennox say to you, Zach?" Jace asked, his jaw hardening.

Zach sighed. "It's not important, Dad. But he was very distinct in expressing his wishes that I leave her alone." His pride still stung as he thought of the lecture he'd received from George Lennox. The man seemed to operate under the opinion that anyone with fewer funds than he possessed was lacking intelligence and civility. At least that was the point he'd relayed to Zach.

"I have a feeling whatever he said is important, but I won't push you, son. You're a grown man and can make your own choices, but before you do something you'll regret the rest of your life, talk to Lorna. Share your thoughts and concerns with her, then let her decide how she'd like to proceed." Jace looked at Cora Lee, then lifted her hand and kissed the back of her fingers. "I kinda had the idea you were falling in love with her. If that's true, you both deserve a chance to make things work."

Zach studied his parents, who still seemed so in love even after thirty years together. That's what he wanted. Someone who would love him for a lifetime, no matter what came their way.

He hadn't exactly given Lorna an opportunity to speak with him. In fact, the one time she'd tried, he'd all but kicked her out of the engine house. Although he still didn't fancy the notion of attending her Christmas party, he'd at least give it some thought.

Right now, though, he had no desire to continue talking about it or how he'd bungled things with the woman he loved. He picked up his fork and smiled sweetly at his mother.

"Tell me again how you and Dad fell in love, Mamie."

Chapter Eleven

Despite the turmoil churning inside him, Zach managed to get a few hours of sleep and rose early. After building a fire in the kitchen stove, he filled the kettle and set it on to heat. While the water warmed, he carried in enough wood to fill the box by the cookstove and the one by the fireplace in the living room. When he finished that chore, he made a cup of strong tea. In the time it took for it to steep, he slid meat left from last night's supper between slices of bread, grabbed an apple and a handful of cookies, and set them in his lunch pail. Slowly stirring a generous spoon of honey into the tea, he sipped it while eating the last piece of the cinnamon breakfast cake his mother had baked the day before yesterday.

Quickly rinsing his dishes and drying them when he finished his simple meal, Zach picked up his lunch pail as he headed out the door, then stopped. He hurried back to his room, grabbed a change of clothes, and rolled them into a bundle, then wrapped them in a rain slicker to keep the snow off them.

If he changed his mind and decided to go to Lorna's party, he at least wanted to have clean clothes to wear. Before his parents awakened, he rushed out the door, saddled Buckley, and headed into town.

The livery was quiet when he opened the door and led Buckley inside. Zach flicked on the electric lights his uncle had recently had Mike install. He led Buckley to his stall, then fed and watered all the stock. He left his clothes tied to the back of his saddle, along with his lunch pail. Zach walked into the blacksmith shop and over to the forge that always seemed to be warm. He stoked the fire, knowing R.C. would be in to do it soon anyway. Zach let his frozen toes and feet thaw a few minutes before he picked up a broad, flat shovel, then went outside. He'd only shoveled about ten yards in front of the livery when he heard the sound of someone else working and glanced up to see Andy and Burt shoveling their way toward him from the corner of the blacksmith shop.

"Morning!" he called to his friends.

They waved and returned to work.

Before thirty minutes had passed, a dozen young men joined their efforts, including Tom Stewart. By the time the hint of dawn appeared on the horizon, pathways had been shoveled along Main Street, down to the doctor's office and the hospital, and up Milton Road all the way to the lane to Lennox Manor.

Tom had even shoveled a pathway through the park to the gazebo. His friend didn't elaborate on the reason why, but Zach thought it probably had something to do with Lorna.

Cold and hungry by the time he finished, Zach returned to the blacksmith shop, left the shovel where he'd found it, and spent a few minutes warming himself by the forge.

"You boys did good out there this morning," R.C. said as he walked inside. "If you're hungry, Anne will have something to warm you up."

"Thanks, Uncle R.C. I brought something. I needed to thaw a bit before I head to work." Zach flexed his fingers, tugged on his gloves, and walked toward the livery door. He looked around, noticing Burt's car was absent. "Did Burt get his project finished?"

R.C. chuckled. "He sure did. Took it for a drive around town last night. That thing runs even better than I expected. Who would have thought all that junk you boys found would turn into a car that runs on snow?"

Zach thought of the old bar stools that were converted to seats, the boat engine James had acquired somewhere as his contribution to the cause, and the body of the car made from pieces of scrap metal and iron they'd scrounged here and there. Of course, R.C. had donated whatever supplies they needed, including the can of green paint Burt had used to paint the car.

"I can't wait to see it." Zach grinned at his uncle. "I suppose Molly Turner will be his first passenger of the day."

"I reckon she will be, if Burt can convince her to climb in that thing." R.C. shook his head as he chuckled again. "At least he had Ellery help him cover those old stools so the seats are more comfortable."

"He did a good job. The way Burt's mind works is a wonder. I think he's destined for great things."

R.C. swelled up with pride. "He does have a unique way of seeing things, and he's always tinkering with some new idea. He's been working on surprises for everyone for Christmas. It will be fun to see what that mind of his has created."

"It will be. Have a good day, Uncle R.C." Zach edged toward the door.

"You, too." His uncle gave him a knowing look but refrained from mentioning the party.

Before he could, Zach escaped into the livery, snatched his lunch pail off his saddle horn where he'd left it, and headed off to work. When he reached the engine house, Henry was already there, and a pot of coffee bubbled on the back of the stove.

Zach poured a cup and held it with both hands, savoring the warmth as well as the rich fragrance of the brew. After a few sips, he ate his sandwiches and apple. All but one of the cookies he gave to Corliss, who always seemed to be hungry. Then again, Zach thought he'd probably been the same way when he was that age.

"You boys did good with your shoveling this morning," Henry said as he held a coffee cup in one hand and climbed aboard an engine that was ready to hook to the morning train.

"I would be perfectly happy if it didn't snow again until next December," Tom commented as he opened the main doors so the engine could be driven outside.

"Now, where's the fun in that? It wouldn't seem like Christmas without a little snow," Henry teased.

"A little is fine, but you could lose a yardstick out there," Corliss added as he brushed cookie crumbs from his hands.

"That you could, my boy," Henry said with a grin. "Come on. Let's quit yammering and get to work. Last I heard, there's a party today, and we're all invited. It won't hurt to shut down the engine house for an hour."

"I can stay," Zach offered, refusing to look at Tom or Henry.

"That's good of you to offer, son, but I do believe you need to go to the party."

Zach didn't bother to ask what made Henry assume he should go. Instead, he focused on his work.

At half-past eleven, Henry began shooing them out. "If you boys want to clean up a bit, get to it. I'll lock the doors and meet you at the Lennox place."

"Are you sure you don't need me to stay here, Henry? I don't mind."

Henry shook his head, then thumped Zach on the shoulder. "Nope. You go on ahead, Zach. I think there's one pretty lil' gal who'll be overjoyed to see you."

Zach wasn't sure Lorna would welcome him at all, after he'd spent three weeks ignoring her existence. The possibility existed that she might slam the door in his face, not that he could blame her. He'd been wrong not to listen to what she had to say. Regardless, it didn't change the fact that her father disliked him and didn't want him around. How could he pursue a future with Lorna when her father would always come between them?

Filled with questions for which he had no answers, Zach jogged through town to the livery. He retrieved his clothes, then used the rooms above the livery to clean up, change his clothes, and even comb his hair. He left off a hat, since he hadn't brought along his nice one, shrugged into his coat, and walked to Lennox Manor.

People arrived on foot, in sleighs, and heavy wagons. It seemed as if Lorna had opened her home to the entire town. Even the schoolchildren marched in file down the street toward the front walk. Zach knew today was the last day of school and had heard from Timothy the teachers had decided to release all the students after the party instead of making them return to class for an hour or two before the holiday break.

As he stood at the end of the walk watching Lorna greet each and every person who entered her home with a warm smile, a loud noise drew his gaze to the street.

Burt turned the corner and appeared in his snow car with Molly Turner sitting beside him. Andy, Ellery, and Tom rode in the back.

"What on earth is that thing?" Zach heard Marshal Durant ask as he craned his neck to look at Burt's latest invention.

"A snow car," Zach said, watching as Burt turned the wheel and stopped the car at the end of the walk, where everyone could see it. "Burt made it from scraps."

The marshal removed his cowboy hat and slapped it against his leg with a laugh. "I swear that boy could make anything."

"I think he can, sir," Zach said, joining the other men who crowded around to get a better look at the car. Using a Model T car as a starting point for his design, Burt had built the body from scratch and scraps. Instead of tires on the front, it had two skis that attached to the axle. The back had two sets of wheels on each side, encased in a wide track made of steel plates. It was unlike anything Zach had ever seen, and he was sure others were just as impressed.

"Hey, Burt! How much do you want for this thing?" Doctor Holt asked above the noise of the people crowded around the car.

"Sorry, Doc. It's not for sale." Burt grinned and offered Molly a rascally wink, causing her to blush and the group to laugh. "But I might be able to make you one."

"Let's discuss those possibilities after Christmas." The doctor nodded at Burt, then escorted his wife up the steps.

Zach looked back at the house and saw Lorna greet them. He waited until those who'd been admiring the car made their way inside to fall in step with Andy and head up the walk.

"Have you seen inside of this place?" Andy asked quietly at the bottom of the front steps.

"A few of the rooms. Why?" Zach wondered when his friend had been inside, then recalled Jenny saying something about the Milton brothers being enlisted to help with the party.

"It is something else. I heard Lorna tell Mum it was more than fifteen thousand square feet. Can you imagine? No wonder they have so many staff employed here. Susie Benton said her sister got a job as a housemaid and enjoys it."

With renewed clarity, Zach understood why he and Lorna would never work as a couple. She lived in a mansion with servants to see to her every need. He lived on a ranch in a house that was years older than the town. He would never be comfortable living in such splendor, and she'd never adjust to living a simple life. Zach would never be wealthy, not when he was already doing what he loved, working on trains. If, by some miracle, Lorna agreed to marry him, would her father expect him to turn into a businessman like him?

The thought made him feel ill.

"Go on in, Andy. I forgot something," he said, backing away from the steps.

"Zach, don't turn into a coward now," Andy warned.

"Go on. I'll catch up." Zach turned and strode down the walk and past the vehicles that were parked in front of the house. He walked all the way to the livery before he realized he might never again have the opportunity to see how Lorna really lived. Once more, he made his way to Lennox Manor.

By the time he reached the door, it had been closed against the cold. It seemed everyone who was coming had already arrived.

Silently, Zach stepped into the entry, hung his coat on one of the many racks that had been left there, then moved into the grand foyer. Marble floors glistened beneath sparkling chandeliers while the scent of pine hung heavy in the air. Garlands with red satin ribbons wound along the stair banisters with towering trees flanking each side of the marble steps. Pots of red flowers decorated tabletops, and the sound of laughter drifted to him from down the hall.

Before he joined the other guests, he wandered upstairs. He remembered the night he and Tom had arrived to escort Lorna and Ellery to the play. The two girls had each walked down a branch of the steps before stopping at the landing and making their way to the bottom of the steps. Zach had thought Lorna couldn't look any lovelier than she had that night, but even from a distance, she appeared even prettier today.

Zach stood at the top of the stairs, looking along a hallway that opened on one side to let in light. He took a few steps and glanced down at the stairs he'd just walked up before he turned and peeked through an open door. A large desk sat in the room with neat stacks of papers on top. There was a telephone on the desk and a peaceful painting on the wall behind it. Two upholstered chairs sat in front of the desk. From the hint of fragrance in the air, he knew Lorna used this room. A few holiday decorations sat on one corner of the desk, along with a framed photograph. Unable to stop himself, he picked up the frame and studied the image of a younger Lorna with a woman who looked remarkably like her. Lorna and the woman sat on wicker chairs outdoors while George Lennox stood behind them, his hand resting on the woman's shoulder. Instead of the scowl Zach had seen on his face, the man wore a happy smile.

Perhaps the death of Lorna's mother had left George so bereft in grief, he'd lost the ability to feel joy. Zach tried to imagine what his father would do if something happened to Mamie, and couldn't form a picture in his mind. It seemed too impossible to consider.

Zach returned the frame to the desk, then continued down the hall, feeling like an intruder as he glanced in open doors. There were multiple bedrooms, all with private bathing rooms. At the corner where the hallway swept around to meet up with the hallway that led from the other side of the stairs, he walked into a bedroom drenched in sunlight.

Unlike the darker colors of the other rooms, this room was done in white and pale blue. An evergreen wreath adorned with pine cones and white ribbons hung on a hook above the large cherry wood sleigh bed. Without looking around, he knew this was Lorna's room. Her scent lingered there, one that carried a hint of flowers, along with a fragrance he found entirely tantalizing.

Lest he do something idiotic, like lift a pillow from the bed and bury his nose in it, he left the room. He continued along the hallway and stopped in a sitting room to stare outside the window at the nearby mountain. With snow capping it and the trees around it, the view was spectacular.

He turned down a corridor, discovered more bedrooms, and happened upon the servants' staircase. He followed it down to the first floor, going through a door that opened into a narrow hallway near the kitchen. The voices of women talking and laughing as they worked spurred him to hastily head back toward the main section of the house. He passed the dining room, where a table held a tall, festive arrangement made of greens and red flowers. A Christmas tree stood at the end of the china cupboard, and garlands graced the fireplace.

At the music room, he stopped and lingered in the doorway, watching as members of the Holiday Community Band performed a variety of Christmas songs. Mrs. Kipling plucked the strings of a gilded harp while Mrs. Mahon played a grand piano. Three Christmas trees twinkled with strings of electric Christmas lights. Zach had read about them but had never seen them operating. The shimmering colors of red, green, and blue added to the already festive atmosphere.

He listened as the group played two more songs before the clear notes of a bell ringing echoed through the house. Others wandered into an open doorway down the broad hall, so he joined them, finding himself in a ballroom. More Christmas trees festooned the corners of the room, while garlands were draped seemingly everywhere.

Long tables at the back of the room groaned beneath the weight of the food placed on them. The mouth-watering aromas of roasted meats mingled with the fragrance of bayberry from the candles he'd seen burning in various rooms and the scent of pine and fir originating from the various trees and garlands.

The house smelled like home and Christmas with a little bit of magic tossed in for good measure.

Annoyed with himself for his fanciful thoughts, Zach moved to what he hoped would be an unobtrusive spot as Lorna stood on a small stage, crystal bell in hand, as she motioned for Pastor Ryan to join her.

Children, hungry and full of excitement, tried hard to stand still, although several of them kept turning to look at the vast array of food awaiting them.

"Thank you for being here today. Someone mentioned to me the other day the best way to celebrate this glorious season is with others. From the bottom of my heart, I am so grateful to each one of you for making time to be here. Merry Christmas, Holiday! Now, before we partake of what I know will be a delicious meal, Pastor Ryan has agreed to ask a blessing. Pastor?"

Lorna stepped aside and the pastor took center stage. After the simple, heartfelt prayer, amens echoed throughout the room.

"Perhaps the eldest among us would like to begin the line," Lorna suggested, then nodded to an older couple who both used canes to walk.

Zach thought they were beyond ancient when he was a little boy and would see them at church on Sundays. Now, they looked wizened by their years.

He wasn't surprised when his mother and the pastor's wife stepped forward to help them fill their plates, then seated them at a table.

Tables of every shape and size filled the room, while chairs that appeared to have come from anywhere Lorna could acquire the seats were pulled up to them. However, every table was covered with a white cloth, and in the center of each was a small centerpiece of greens.

Honestly, Zach had never seen anything like this house that seemed to ooze not only wealth but also Christmas cheer and friendship, as well as warmth and a genuine welcome.

As people began filling their plates and taking seats at the tables, Lorna wandered among them, making them feel like cherished guests.

"Are you going to stand there staring at her all day or go talk to her?"

Zach turned to scowl at Noah, wondering how his brother had snuck up beside him, especially since he held Tilly.

"Hi!" she said, holding out her hands to him.

Zach lifted his niece in his arms and kissed her rosy cheek. "What do you think, Tilly? Do you suppose Saint Nicholas lives here?"

Her eyes widened, and she gaped around the room, as though she expected the jolly old elf to appear.

"Thanks, Zach. Thanks a lot. She'll be looking around every corner, trying to find him."

Zach smirked at Noah. "You're welcome."

Noah bumped him with his elbow and tipped his head toward Lorna as she helped a young mother settle her two rambunctious children at a table. "Just wait until you have little ones, brother. I'll be sure to ply them with candy, then send them home to you."

"Thanks for the tip. I'll make sure Hayes and

Tilly get extra treats today." Zach chuckled as his brother scowled at him.

"You don't have to be so ornery. If you'd go talk to Lorna and make up with her, maybe you'd be a whole lot better company for the rest of us." Noah took Tilly from him and headed to where Jenny seated Hayes between Ava and Grant.

Zach had been so focused on Lorna he hadn't even noticed the arrival of his grandparents. He filled his plate and found a table far away from his family and friends, knowing they'd only tease him about Lorna. He sat with a family new to the area. Somehow, he managed to answer their questions and ask a few about them while eating and keeping his eyes on Lorna.

Not once did she sit down the entire time her guests ate. She continued to mingle among the tables, pouring coffee and sharing smiles.

When the meal ended, Lorna announced the schoolchildren would perform.

Zach enjoyed the skit and laughed at all the appropriate places. When the applause faded away, the community band moved to the stage, with the exception of Mrs. Kipling, since the harp remained in the music room. There was, however, a smaller piano tucked at the base of the stage, where Mrs. Mahon took a seat and launched into a lively version of *Jingle Bells*. Marlin Freemont, the band leader, invited everyone to sing along to carols both familiar and new.

Zach didn't sing, but he enjoyed listening to the songs of the season. Lorna had taken a seat next to Ellery and joined her voice to the others.

The band had just finished the last song when the sound of sleigh bells rang throughout the room. All heads turned to the doorway where a man dressed in a red velvet robe with a long white beard shook a string of bells in one hand, while he carried a large black bag in the other.

"It's Santa!" children chanted, scrambling out of their chairs and running over to him as he settled into a plush chair next to a towering tree. Beneath it, dozens of packages wrapped in foil paper reflected the electric lights.

The two children seated at Zach's table looked with longing toward Santa.

"Go on. Don't be shy," Zach said, offering them an encouraging grin.

The little girls waited for a nod from their parents before scampering across the room to join the other children.

Zach had no idea who played Santa Claus, but he did portray the fabled man in style as he called out the children's names and handed each one of them a gift. He couldn't begin to fathom how Lorna had accomplished so much in a week, including buying gifts for every child in attendance, but she somehow had. He knew she'd had many helpers, but he had an idea Lorna had been involved in every aspect of the party, except maybe baking treats. She'd told him not long after they met, she had little to no skill in the kitchen, not that it mattered.

Tilly squealed with delight when she opened her present to find one of the new Kewpie dolls that were popular with adults and children alike.

"A baby. I gots a baby!" Tilly exclaimed,

holding the doll to her chest and squeezing it tight.

Zach excused himself from the table where he sat and hurried over to where Noah helped Hayes wind the key on a toy train engine that was a close match to the town's favored Hope engine.

"That's quite a gift, Hayes," Zach said as he knelt by his nephew.

"It's from Santa!" Hayes looked up at him with bright eyes. "Watch it go, Uncle Zach."

"I'm watching," Zach said, grinning at his nephew, then catching Tilly as she launched herself at him, pushing the doll into his face.

Although he couldn't figure out the fascination in the naked baby-faced dolls, his niece appeared quite taken with it. He noticed several other girls received the same gift.

"What are you gonna name your baby?" Zach asked as he settled Tilly on his arm and she lavished kisses on her toy.

"Mabel." Tilly held the doll up for him to kiss. Despite feeling like an idiot, Zach kissed the doll's cheek, then tickled his niece.

The ringing of the crystal bell from the stage silenced everyone and drew their attention to where Pastor Ryan stood by Lorna.

"Everyone is welcome to linger as long as you like, but for those who need to return to work, this concludes the activities today. Miss Lennox extends an invitation to everyone to join her tomorrow evening at dusk at the gazebo. And don't forget the Christmas Day service at ten that morning. Now, if you'll all join me in a brief prayer ..."

Zach bowed his head and listened to Pastor

Ryan's prayer, wondering what Lorna had planned at the gazebo. He assumed it had something to do with the electric power Mike had installed out there.

Several people left the ballroom, returning to businesses they'd closed for the event. Others seemed inclined to tarry.

Zach wanted to say something to Lorna, to thank her for her kindness and generosity, but he headed for the door. Before he reached it, a hand on his arm drew him to a stop. He glanced back to see his mother and Jenny looking at him with disappointment on their faces.

"Don't leave without talking to her, Zach. Give her a chance," Cora Lee said, her tone pleading.

"Please, Zach. She has missed you so these last few weeks. If you just talk to her, I think you'd be surprised by any number of things." Jenny took a step closer to him and the look on her face, one that nearly made him rush back into the ballroom to find Lorna, caused him to ponder how Noah ever resisted anything Jenny suggested.

"I have to get back to work, but I will talk to her."

Jenny looked at Cora Lee; then they both turned to him. "You promise?"

Zach nodded as he edged toward the entry where people were collecting coats and hats. Cold air wafted into the foyer each time the door opened. "I promise. I will talk to Lorna when there aren't quite so many people around."

"We'll hold you to that," his mother said before she and Jenny spun around and rushed back to the ballroom.

Zach grabbed his things and rammed his arms in his coat sleeves as he jogged down the steps.

He hurried to the livery, changed into his work clothes, then made his way back to the engine house. On the way, he stopped at the park and glanced at the gazebo for a moment. He couldn't tell that anything looked different about it, other than someone had set up a large Christmas tree next to it. Without time to give it a more thorough study, he returned to the engine house as the whistle from the approaching train blew.

That evening, Zach left work, returned to the livery, where he once again changed his clothes and washed up, then made his way to Lennox Manor. He thought about taking Lorna a gift but had no idea what to take. What could he possibly give her that she didn't already have? He had nothing but himself, and he wasn't ready to turn his heart into her keeping. Not just yet. Not until they talked.

Mindful that Mr. Lennox might have arrived home unbeknownst to him, Zach walked around to the entrance where deliveries were made and stepped inside. A plaque on the wall by a telephone instructed him to pick up the earpiece and push the black button. When he did, the phone rang twice; then a woman answered it.

"Lennox Manor. Do you have a delivery?" she asked.

"No. This is Zach Coleman. I'd very much like to speak with Miss Lennox. Please?"

"A moment, please."

Zach waited what seemed like half an eternity before the woman returned to the line. "You may see her. Go down the hall, take a left to the stairs, follow them up one floor and you'll come out by the kitchen. I will meet you there."

"Thank you."

Zach hung up the earpiece and followed the woman's directions. When he walked out of the stairwell, he recognized Dodi Truman, Lorna's former nanny. The woman gave him a pinch-lipped glare before spinning around and marching down the hall.

"Well, don't dawdle. Step right along, Mr. Coleman," she said over her shoulder.

He followed her as she turned into another hallway, then a third, before opening an oak-paneled door and motioning for him to enter the room.

He stepped inside, and Mrs. Truman shut the door behind him without uttering a word. Startled by her abrupt departure, he looked around what appeared to be a library. Books and pieces of art filled the shelves that lined the room. A huge fireplace cast off a warm, welcoming light. A Christmas tree in the corner opposite the fireplace filled the room with a pleasant scent. And in an overstuffed chair in front of the fire, Lorna sat with her chin propped on her hand on the arm of the chair, asleep.

Quietly, he moved further into the room until he stood beside the chair. Lorna had kicked off her shoes and had her feet tucked under her. A woman's magazine was open on her lap. He turned his head to see it wasn't an article about the latest fashions that caught her interest, but one about gifts any woman could make at home.

Were there more gifts she wanted to give after she'd done so much for the community?

He moved so he was in her line of sight, wanting to study her. Long lashes fanned her cheeks, and her mouth was open slightly as she breathed evenly. The firelight set her hair aflame and bathed her in a glorious golden light that made her skin fairly glow.

Even with her hair mussed and her expensive emerald gown wrinkled from the day's activities, he thought she'd never looked lovelier.

The proper and polite thing for him to do would have been to leave without awakening her and come back tomorrow. But Zach couldn't make his feet move. Instead, he removed his coat, took a seat on the hearth, and watched Lorna for several minutes, drinking in the sight of her.

Until that moment, he hadn't realized how fully, how deeply, he'd missed her, nor how completely he loved her.

He loved Lorna. Not for her money or stature or the empire she stood to inherit.

He loved her because she dressed like a scarecrow so she could attend a party without people knowing she was the daughter of the local railroad tycoon. He loved her because she cared about the people of Holiday, evidenced by the event she'd hosted and the gifts she'd given to every child there. Tom had told him Ellery said she'd asked the teachers at school for a list of names of all the children, then acquired the names of those too young to attend, and purchased a gift for each one, even those who couldn't attend the party. Burt and Timothy had helped her deliver them that afternoon.

This incredible, sweet woman had earned his respect and love because of her tender heart, her sense of humor, her need for adventure, and her intelligence.

George Lennox might have millions of dollars to his name, but his most priceless treasure was Lorna. Zach could understand why he'd want to protect her from someone who didn't have Lorna's best interests at heart.

But Zach did.

He only wanted Lorna to be happy, even if it meant her happiness didn't include him.

Unable to keep from touching her, Zach scooted closer to her chair and carefully slid the magazine from her lap, setting it on a nearby table. Then he took the hand that rested on her lap in his, brought it to his lips, and pressed a kiss to her palm. "I love you, Lorna."

"Mmm. That's nice, Zach," she mumbled in her sleep, making him smile.

Pleased she thought of him in her dream-like state, he kissed her palm again, then pressed his lips to her wrist. Slowly, with great intention, he worked his way from her wrist up the inside of her arm, caressing her soft skin with his kisses.

"If you keep doing that," Lorna whispered in a languid tone, "there might be a shotgun wedding in your future."

He drew back and watched as Lorna lazily opened her eyes and gave him a saucy smile, too stunned by her words to take her up on the offer and send for Pastor Ryan.

"How long have you been awake?"

"Who said I was asleep?" she asked, tossing a flirtatious wink at him before stretching her arms over her head, then swinging her legs around until her feet rested on the floor.

Zach sat on his hands to keep from sweeping her into his arms and lavishing her with kisses.

"What are you doing here?" Lorna straightened in the chair and pushed in loosened hairpins. "Did you enjoy the party?"

Zach nodded. "I did enjoy it, Lorna. It was such a nice thing of you to do for Holiday. The children, especially, loved it. So did the people who have no family in town. You made them feel welcome."

"It was fun." She blew out a breath and fixed her gaze on his. "Why didn't you at least say hello? I was so hoping you'd be here today. Ellery wasn't sure you'd come."

"I know, and I'm sorry. I wanted to talk to you earlier, but there were so many people around, it just seemed better to wait. I do apologize for intruding unannounced, though. You're probably exhausted. I'll come back another time." He started to rise, but Lorna reached out and placed her hand on his arm.

"Stay, Zach. Please. Have you eaten supper?"

"No. I came here right after work."

"Then you should stay. We're eating leftovers from the party. We can eat in here or with the others."

"Others?" Zach asked, unaware Lorna had guests staying at the house. He hoped to goodness

Pemberly hadn't returned.

"Maude and Marcus and Dodi. When my father is gone, they join me in the breakfast room for dinner."

"That sounds nice. I'd be happy to join you, but before we leave this room, I'd like to say a few things."

Lorna's expression went from pleased to blank as she assumed a perfect, stiff posture. "Go on."

Zach stood and paced back and forth in front of the fireplace. "I know you had nothing to do with that idiot Pemberly coming here. Since you assumed you'd never see him again, there wasn't a reason for you to mention him. I shouldn't have called you a liar, and I'm sorry I've avoided you these past few weeks."

"Avoided me?" she asked, crossing her arms over her chest and scowling at him. "Here I thought you were offering Tilly and Hayes lessons in how to sulk and pout," she said sarcastically.

Slightly affronted by her words, even if there was a bit of truth in them when it came to his skills at sulking, he chose to ignore them. "Lorna, I'm trying to say I was wrong, and I'm sorry. Would it be too much to ask for your forgiveness?"

"No, I suppose not." She lifted her chin and gave him an imperial look. "As long as you promise it won't happen again."

He stopped pacing, placed a hand over his heart, and held her gaze. "I promise I will not sulk or pout. In the future, if there is a problem, I will discuss it with you right away."

"Very well, then. You are forgiven." Lorna

relaxed her stiff posture and held out a hand to him.

He took it in his, bringing it to his mouth and kissing her fingers. "I missed you, Lorna."

"And I missed you, you big dolt. It's been horrible, thinking you were mad and never again going to speak to me."

"I apologize, Lorna. It's just …" Zach stopped before he said too much.

"Just what?" she asked, rising from the chair and moving so she stood toe to toe with him. The firelight flickered in her pale green eyes, pulling him into their fantastical depths.

"Nothing, Lorna. Nothing at all." He'd merely meant to apologize to her and leave. Not become so entangled in her gaze, so entranced by the sound of her voice, that he never wanted to be away from her again.

She pulled her hand from his and stepped beyond his reach. "Let's play a guessing game."

The time hardly seemed right for game-playing, but this spontaneous side of Lorna was something he adored about her.

"What's the game?"

"I have ten chances to find out something you know. You only have to respond if the statement or question I ask is correct."

That sounded easy enough. Odds were good she wouldn't think to ask about her father. "Go ahead."

Lorna gave him a long, thorough look, as though she could see all the way into his soul. Unsettled by the intensity of her gaze, he leaned with an arm propped against the fireplace mantel.

"My father said something to upset you, beyond being so rude to you the night of the play. Correct?"

Lorna was far more perceptive than he'd realized. He'd promised to answer her, so he would, even if he didn't want to. "Yes."

"Papa accused you of consorting with me for both nefarious reasons and financial gain."

Zach gaped at her. How could she possibly know that? He didn't want to say anything to make her upset with her father, but he wouldn't withhold the truth. "He mentioned something along those lines."

Lorna thrust her chin in the air, pushed her lips out like a bulldog, and crossed her arms in front of her in a pose that looked exactly like George Lennox. "I bet he said something like, 'I won't stand by and watch my daughter fall for your money-grubbing schemes. I won't have it. Stay away from her!' And then he probably stormed off. Right?"

Amazed by how well she could imitate her father, both in posture and voice, Zach mutely nodded his head.

"Papa gives that same speech to everyone. Don't take it to heart. He means well, but it makes him seem like an overbearing scrooge. Up until now, I haven't minded him running off potential suitors. If part of the reason you've stayed away is because you're worried you'll come between me and my father, you shouldn't be concerned."

"I know you love him, and he obviously cares for you. It would be wrong of me to do anything that comes between you two."

Rather than looking pleased by his selfless act, Lorna picked a cushion off the chair closest to her and whacked his arm with it.

"What was that for?" he asked, taking a long step out of her reach.

"For being a stupid, stupid man!" She advanced and whacked him again, then glared at him, fury staining her cheeks pink and adding a fiery spark to her eyes.

Entranced, Zach couldn't move, let alone gather his scattered wits enough to form a reply. She'd called him stupid, hadn't she?

"Oh!" Lorna tossed the pillow back on the chair, then stamped both feet before turning to him with her fists at her sides. "I will tell you, just like I've told my father, it's not up to either one of you to decide whom I love or who I will marry. That choice resides with me. The two of you had better grow accustomed to the idea."

Uncertain what she was getting at, since his brain seemed mired on the thought of how entirely tempting she looked when she was furious, Zach finally found his tongue. "Why do we both need to warm up to the idea, Lorna? What are you saying?"

"Well, I … um … I assumed, at least I'd hoped …"

Zach laughed and pulled her to his chest. With his index finger, he tipped her chin up until she looked into his eyes, and their gazes tangled. A smile curved her delectable lips, ones he'd been dreaming of for weeks.

"Let's start over, Lorna. How do you do, Miss

Lennox? I'm Zach Coleman. I work for your father, have no plans to do anything other than repair trains, and I love you."

"I love you, too, Zach. You could be a chimney sweep or drive a peddler's cart, and I wouldn't care. I just know I love you."

"That's all I need to hear," he said in a husky voice before his lips claimed hers in a tender kiss. Zach tightened his arms around Lorna, lifting her up as their kiss deepened and grew in passion.

A throat clearing from the doorway made them jump. Zach set her down and turned a sheepish look to Dodi as she stood just inside the room, giving him a warning glare.

"Dinner is served, Miss Lorna. I shall accompany you both, if Mr. Coleman is staying."

"He is, Dodi, and thank you." Lorna looped her arm around Zach's and winked at him as they followed Dodi down the hall to the breakfast room.

"We'll talk more tomorrow," Zach whispered in her ear when he held out her chair for her at the table.

The look she gave him, full of love and yearning, kept him warm even on his frigid ride home.

Chapter Twelve

"At such time when a young woman has found the attention from her suitor quite agreeable, she may, in an unspoken, careful manner, indicate her interest in a proposal of marriage. Under no circumstance, would a lady offer a blatant encouragement to her gentleman."

Miss Mulberry's Advice for Today's Young Woman

"Happy Christmas Eve!" Lorna proclaimed as she breezed into the kitchen, startling Maude so badly, the pan of cookies she'd just removed from the oven flew into the air, sending gingersnaps scuttling to every corner of the kitchen.

"My lands, child, you scared me half to death," Maude chided as she set the baking pan down with a clang. Two of the kitchen maids scurried to pick up the cookies and started to toss them away.

"Save those, please. I have an idea of something to do with them." Lorna grabbed an empty tin and the girls dropped in the cookies. "Thank you." She turned to Maude and gave her a placating look. "I'm sorry, Maude. I didn't mean to catch you unawares, but isn't it a glorious day?"

"Glorious? It's still so dark you can't see a thing outside, and if I'm not mistaken, it's snowing again," Maude groused.

"Oh, but Maude, none of that matters to Miss Lorna today," Dodi said as she walked into the room with a stack of clean linens in her hands. She set them on a shelf in the pantry, then returned to give Lorna a hug. "There's snow on the ground, Christmas filling every corner, surprises beneath the tree, love all around, and romance in the air, isn't that right?"

Lorna nodded. "That is exactly right. I have a feeling it's going to be a splendid, splendid holiday here in Holiday!"

Everyone laughed, and Lorna snatched a piece of broken sugar cookie from where a tray of them cooled on the counter.

"Breakfast will be ready in thirty minutes, Miss Lorna. Now, scoot out of my kitchen." Maude waggled a wooden spoon toward the doorway.

"I'm going," Lorna said with a laugh, then pecked Maude's wrinkled cheek. "Will you still be able to make hot chocolate and cookies for this evening?"

"Yes, dearie. Why do you think I've been up baking dozens of cookies already this morning?"

Lorna frowned. "I didn't mean to make more work for you, Maude, or the girls. I'm sorry."

Maude wiped her flour-dusted hands on her apron, then pulled her into a hug. "I'm happy to do it, darling girl. It's a lovely thing you have planned, and we're all so pleased to be part of it. Besides, you've given us the rest of the day and all of tomorrow off to enjoy ourselves, and that is a precious gift we all appreciate."

"Well, you all deserve it. Should Papa arrive home, he can go along with my plans, or eat bread and cold meat for his dinner."

"Now that would be a first," Maude said under her breath as she moved away from Lorna and returned to her work.

Lorna practically skipped through the house in a most childish manner as she checked all the decorations one final time, made sure the gifts she'd purchased were either beneath the tree in the small parlor where she'd planned to welcome Christmas morning with her father, if he made it home, or packed into boxes to deliver to her friends.

After he'd stayed for dinner last night and charmed both Maude and Dodi until the two older women were practically tittering in his presence, she'd walked Zach to the door. He'd kissed her cheek and told her he loved her and would see her tomorrow at the park.

Lorna could hardly wait to share the surprise she'd planned. She'd hired Mike Milton to run electricity to the gazebo. The dozens of strands of lights she'd ordered had arrived on last night's train. As soon as she finished breakfast, she intended to enlist the help of some of the Milton family to help her string the lights around the gazebo. If enough were left over, she intended to decorate the large tree she'd asked Andy Milton to set up next to it.

She'd sought out the mayor to ask his

permission, but the man had taken his family to Portland to visit relatives through the end of the year. With no one to tell her no, she assumed it would be far easier to ask forgiveness for overstepping if anyone was upset by her plans. She couldn't imagine who would be, though.

Filled with anticipation for the day ahead, Lorna ate breakfast, donned her warmest coat, slipped on gloves and a scarf, then asked Marcus to take the crate of lights to the gazebo after leaving her at the Milton home.

She'd barely raised her hand to knock when the door swung open and Ellery pulled her inside.

"Happy Christmas Eve, Lorna!" Ellery nearly shouted to be heard above the chaos flowing out the door.

Mercy banged on the piano, playing Christmas carols with far more enthusiasm than "Silent Night" was ever intended to be performed. Timothy and Mariah strung popcorn and cranberries on thread to decorate the tree. A handful of little ones who belonged to Charlie and Rance ran through the house, giggling as they chased each other. A toddler with one sock on and the other nowhere to be seen burst into tears when he couldn't keep up with the rest. Ellery scooped him up, kissed his chubby cheeks, then set him back on his feet.

"What brings you to our loud, chaotic corner of the world?" Ellery asked with a grin as she motioned for Lorna to follow her toward the kitchen.

"I was going to see if you had time to help with a project, but it appears you have more than enough to keep you busy here.”

“Oh, I’d love a few minutes to escape. How much help do you need?” Ellery asked as they walked into the kitchen where Anne and three of her daughters-in-law worked.

“The more hands the better. I don’t suppose Burt or Andy are available, are they?”

“Andy is working this morning, but Burt is around somewhere, probably tinkering on his car. Maybe he’ll give us a ride.”

“I saw it yesterday. Truly, he is quite clever. He ought to patent some of his inventions.”

“That’s what Mum and Dad tell him. Burt just thinks it’s all fun.” Ellery walked over to where Anne rolled out dough for pie crust. “Mum, I’m going to go with Lorna for a bit. I won’t be missed, will I?”

“Yes, you will, but have fun.” Anne smiled at them both, then rubbed at her cheek, smearing flour across it.

Ellery wiped it away, then kissed the spot. “Thanks, Mum!” She grabbed her coat and led Lorna out the back door. They walked along the road to the feed store, cutting across the loading dock behind it and entered the blacksmith shop. The sound of a hammer striking metal made it known someone was hard at work.

“Burt!” Ellery hollered above the racket.

He stopped, hammer in mid-air and looked at them, nodded in acknowledgment, then finished pounding a piece of hot metal. He used tongs to dip it into a bucket of water before setting it on the anvil to cool, then turned to them.

"Hi, Lorna! What brings you by this morning?" Burt yanked off his gloves and grinned at her. "That was quite a party yesterday. Thank you."

"Thank you for coming. I'm glad you all enjoyed it. And I'm so grateful for your help in preparing for it." Lorna smiled at Burt. "I don't suppose you'd have time to help with one final Christmas project, would you?"

"Maybe, but I might need something in return."

"Burt Milton! You are not bargaining with Lorna," Ellery said, sounding appalled at her brother.

Lorna elbowed her friend, then nodded to Burt. "What can I do in exchange for your assistance?"

"Tell me if you think Molly will like this." Burt walked over to the workbench and lifted the cloth covering a silver box. He'd somehow fashioned scrolls and vines into the metal, giving it a unique, beautiful design.

Lorna ran her hand over the surface, then lifted the heavy lid. Inside, it was covered in deep burgundy velvet, with three separate compartments.

"Oh, Burt, it's incredible!" Lorna smiled at him. Molly was indeed a very fortunate girl. "She'll love it."

"Should I get a few ribbons to tuck inside?" he asked, sounding uncertain.

"I don't think that is necessary. This is a gift any girl would treasure." Lorna looked to Ellery.

She studied the box, then wrapped an arm around her brother's shoulders. "You are amazing, Burt. It's perfect."

"Oh, good. I'm glad you think so." He removed

the leather apron he wore, then looked at Lorna. "So, what can I do for you?"

"I need help with a secret project. It shouldn't take long and will be something everyone can enjoy later today."

"Let's get to it," Burt said, looping an arm around both Lorna's and Ellery's shoulders. Together, the three of them walked to the park, where Marcus was unloading the crates of lights from the sleigh.

"I should have thought about a ladder," Lorna said as she looked at the gazebo.

"What are we doing?" Burt asked, prying the lid off a crate and lifting out a box of the lights.

"I thought it would be something special to hang electric lights on the gazebo and this tree. Tonight, at dusk, when people meet here, we'll have hot chocolate and cookies and sing carols.

"What a marvelous idea, Lorna. Everyone will be so surprised!" Ellery smiled at her, then lifted a box of lights. "Where do we start?"

After plugging in a string of lights and determining that both the lights and the power worked, Burt hopped up on the gazebo railing and began hanging the lights by using the hooks that held the garland that Lorna had enlisted Andy and Tom to help her and Ellery drape there earlier in the week.

While he did that, Marcus pried off crate lids and took lights out of boxes. Lorna plugged in the strings to make sure they worked before handing them to Ellery, who fed them to Burt. In no time at all, lights encircled the top of the gazebo and wound around the pillars. One crate of lights remained, so they strung them around the tree.

"Oh, this is going to be wonderful!" Ellery proclaimed clapping her hands together. Lorna hoped it would be so.

"Thank you all for your help. I have a few errands to attend to, but I hope to see you back here at dusk," she said, smiling at the others.

"We'll be here, Lorna. Thank you for adding so much cheer to Christmas this year." Ellery gave her a hug, and Burt nodded in agreement. The two of them hurried off toward home.

"May I drive you somewhere, Miss Lorna?" Marcus asked as he picked up the empty crates and tucked them into the sleigh.

"Thank you, Marcus, but I'll be fine walking. Please let Maude know I'll be back in time for lunch."

"I'll do that, Miss Lorna. If you need me, just have someone ring the house."

"I will, and thank you." Lorna waved to him as he drove off, then hurried across the street to the mercantile. She purchased spools of red ribbon, a pair of scissors, eight boxes of peppermint sticks, and six boxes of French chocolates.

"More decorating to see to, Miss Lennox?" Helen Rogers asked as Lorna carried her purchases to the counter.

"Yes, ma'am. Are you and Mr. Rogers ready for Christmas to arrive?"

Helen smiled. "We are. I'm looking forward to whatever you have planned in the park this evening and, of course, the church service tomorrow. It's such a lovely time of year."

"It is," Lorna agreed, paying for her purchases, including the basket in which she'd gathered the items. "Enjoy your day, Mrs. Rogers."

"You do the same, Lorna."

Lorna hurried back to the park. She tied big, fluffy bows of red ribbon and hung them from the pillars of the gazebo, then used what was left to drape around the tree.

When she finished, she stepped back, holding her thumbs and index fingers together to create a frame. She continued backing up and closed one eye to get a better vision of how the gazebo and tree would look aglow with lights that evening.

She'd just taken one more step back when she bumped into something solid. A scent that haunted her dreams, one that was rugged and thoroughly captivating, filled her nose while warmth enveloped her.

She spun around and looked up at Zach as he smiled at her, his heart shining in his beautiful blue eyes.

"This seems oddly familiar. Are you going to make a habit of backing into busy streets? If so, I'm not sure I can leave you unattended," he teased, placing a hand on her waist.

The intimacy of that simple touch, one that Dodi would declare demanded a slap to his face, warmed Lorna from the inside out. "If you're volunteering to keep an eye on me, I wouldn't mind," she said, offering him an impish grin.

"Is that right?" An eyebrow lifted as he gave her a studying look. "Are you trifling with me, Miss

Lennox?"

"I would never do such a thing, Mr. Coleman," she said, in mock seriousness, wondering how a girl was supposed to behave with decorum when a handsome man like Zach had captured her affections. All she wanted at that moment was to kiss his tempting lips and lean into his strength.

Before she surrendered to the desire, she moved back, aware that anyone passing by might think their behavior too forward for a couple that hadn't professed to be even courting, let alone engaged.

Zach tipped his head toward the gazebo. "What are you doing out here?"

"Just added a few festive touches." She wouldn't spoil the surprise of the lights and show them to him now. Not when she knew he'd enjoy seeing them aglow. After all, she'd noticed him admiring the lights on the trees at the house. Even if he'd acted aloof, she'd been fully aware of his presence. According to one of the housemaids, he'd even given himself a tour upstairs, not that Lorna cared. She'd shown a few people who had remained after most of the others had left through the house. The large home was a bit of a talking point for the people of Holiday, but everyone had been so kind and seemed to appreciate the party. Perhaps it might even become a tradition to host an event each year. At the very least, she wanted the lights in the gazebo to become something the town looked forward to annually.

"Are you all set, or do you need help?" he asked, as she walked over to collect the basket she'd left sitting on a bench.

"I'm finished and was just about to head home. Are you working today?"

"I am. Henry sent me to Uncle R.C.'s shop to pick up a part. I just happened to notice you about to repeat the circumstances that led to our initial meeting." Zach leaned closer to her with a mischievous look on his face. "I wouldn't mind sweeping you off your feet again. I'm sure the snow would be a much softer cushion than the bare ground was."

Lorna feigned offense as one of the older women in town walked by, listening to their conversation. "Sir, I shall not put up with such talk. It's positively …" She looked around to make sure the woman couldn't hear, "true."

Zach winked at her, took the basket from her hand, and motioned to the shoveled pathway that led to down the street. "May I walk you home, Miss Lennox?"

"You may walk me as far as the blacksmith shop." Lorna glanced at him. "I don't want to take up too much of your time, but I do hope I'll see you later this afternoon."

"Don't worry. I'll be at the park later. Are you certain I can't help you with anything?"

"I'm quite sure, but thank you for offering."

At the corner across from the livery, Lorna glanced to make sure no one was watching, then pressed a quick kiss to Zach's cheek. "Stay out of trouble, and I'll see you later."

"That you can count on, Lorna." Zach waved to her as she hurried toward home.

At four that afternoon, Lorna bundled into her warmest coat, tugged on her boots, and helped Marcus load the big sleigh with cookies and hot chocolate. Burt and Andy volunteered to set up makeshift tables with sawhorses and wood planks.

After Marcus delivered the treats, he returned to the house. Dodi packed a box of linens in the sleigh; then she, Maude, and Lorna climbed inside.

People were already beginning to gather at the park when they arrived. Several of those there came over to help set up the refreshments.

Lorna had sworn Ellery and Burt to secrecy, but the entire Milton family was there, looking on with eager anticipation as the sun dipped closer to the horizon.

Pastor Ryan and his family appeared. Lorna had asked if he would lead the impromptu service by offering a prayer.

Just before she was set to begin, she glanced across the park and saw Zach standing with her father. Flabbergasted to see the two men she loved most in the world standing together, she had to take a moment to yank the threads of her unraveled composure together before she stepped into the gazebo with Pastor Ryan.

"Good evening, folks," the pastor said in a loud voice that carried over the park. People who had just arrived hurried across the shoveled paths to reach them. Others sat in sleighs and wagons parked on the street, waiting to see what would transpire. "Miss Lennox thought it would be a nice way to welcome this special Christmas Eve to have everyone gather here in our town park. Let's bow our heads and offer a prayer to start things off."

When the pastor finished his prayer, Lorna motioned for Timothy Milton to come forward. He stood by the electrical outlet, grinning at her as he waited for her signal to plug in the lights. The boy had been thrilled when she'd asked him to help.

"Happy Christmas Eve, my friends. Thank you for being here with us this evening to join in something I hope will become a tradition we all look forward to each year. For those who may not have seen them before, there are strings of lights that run on electricity. We've hung them around the gazebo and the big tree here. If you'll help me count down from five, young Timothy will do the honors of bringing light to our festivities."

Together, the crowd counted backward from five. "Four, three, two, one!"

Timothy plugged in the lights, and the gazebo was illuminated in globes of red, blue, and green.

"Oh, my!"

"Look at the lights."

"It's like a fairyland."

The members of the community who'd gathered oohed over the lights.

"Shall we sing a few carols?" the pastor asked. Mrs. Felton, who led the singing at church, moved to the front of the crowd, and began the opening notes for "Away in a Manger."

After a dozen carols were sung, Lorna thanked everyone for coming, then encouraged everyone to enjoy the hot chocolate and cookies.

Several people grabbed cookies on their way out of the park, in a rush to go home to their own festivities. Some lingered, admiring the lights and thanking Lorna for such an innovative idea.

Finally, she made her way to where her father stood talking to Jace and Grant Coleman. Jace was telling a story about being caught in a blizzard and having to push the engine through drifts a few feet at a time.

"It's a great thing you've got the snowplow now," Jace said. "I've seen it in action and it cuts through the snow in no time at all."

"It has been a handy thing to have," George Lennox agreed, appearing far more jovial than Lorna had seen him in a long time. When he noticed her approach, he opened his arms wide. "Daughter! Merry Christmas to you!"

Lorna stepped into his embrace, giving him a warm hug, then kissing his cheek. "You look happy, Papa."

"I am, sweet girl. I am. I have much to say to you, but I'll see you back at the house. You and Zach don't stay out too long. It's far too cold to linger with your feet in the snow." With that, he waved off Marcus' offer to drive him home and strolled down the street, whistling "God Rest Ye Merry Gentlemen."

Lorna gaped after his departing form; wondering what in the world had gotten into her father. When she looked at Zach for an explanation, he shrugged, then jumped in to help clean up the refreshments. Lorna packed all the leftover cookies into tins and set them into a large box full of gifts for a family in need.

Maude, Dodi, and Marcus all looked like

doting parents as she encouraged them to go home and enjoy their evening; then she hugged the Coleman family members. "I'm so looking forward to coming out to Elk Creek Ranch tomorrow. Thank you for inviting us."

"Of course. We're so happy you'll come and thrilled your father is home, Lorna. What a special surprise," Cora Lee said, giving Lorna a delighted smile.

"It is quite a surprise," she said, still curious about the change in her father. Perhaps he'd met a woman on his trip. Or maybe he'd decided to move somewhere else. The thought of leaving Holiday made her chest ache. If her father decided to move again, she definitely planned to stay right where she was. Holiday was not only her home, it was where her heart longed to set down roots.

"We'll see you at Aunt Anne's in a bit," Zach said, urging his family to leave them alone.

"What's all that about?" Lorna asked as Zach waved to his parents and grandparents, then turned and took her elbow in his hand, guiding her back to the gazebo.

Inside, when she sat on a bench and he slid next to her, she released the breath she felt like she'd been holding in all evening. Being with Zach felt so right. Being together in the quiet peacefulness of a magical December night.

"After our talk last night, I checked with Marcus to see if he knew when your father was due back. He'd just received a telegram saying your father was on his way. When Mr. Lennox stepped off the train, I asked him for a moment of his time.

Much to my surprise, he agreed."

Lorna placed her hand on Zach's as it rested on his leg. "And? What did you two discuss? Papa looks as happy as I've seen him in years."

Zach nodded. "I explained to your father I was not interested in you because of your name, social standing, or his wealth. I told him I loved you because you're just Lorna."

She frowned. "Just Lorna. What does that mean?"

"It means that I love you because you're full of fun and life, and you make me want to be a better person. You're one of the most generous, genuine people I've ever met. In these uncertain, trying times when it seems the world is full of hate and anger, we could use more caring, amazing people like you. It means you're beautiful and smart, and your smile fills me up with light. And it means I asked your father a very important question. One he surprisingly agreed to."

Uncertain what Zach alluded to, but hoping it meant he'd shared her Christmas wish, she tightened her hold on his hand. "And what question might that be?"

"Oh, a simple one, really. I asked if he'd give his blessing if I asked you to marry me."

"And Papa agreed?" she asked, shocked that her father would be in favor of her marrying a man of her own choosing.

"He did, with stipulations. Before I say more about that, I need you to know, Lorna, my love, that I will spend my life courting you, wooing you, loving you, and doing my best to bring happiness to you every day of our lives together. I have nothing to give you but my heart, and if you'll accept it, accept the little I have to offer, I would like nothing better than to be your husband. Will you marry me, Lorna?"

Tears stung her eyes, and emotion clogged her throat, but she nodded her head and threw her arms around Zach. He kissed her cheek, then her temple, and held her close, his breath warm on her neck.

"I love you so much," he said, giving her a quick kiss before pulling back and taking a ring from his pocket and sliding it onto her finger. "This ring belonged to Mamie's grandmother. I thought you might like to have it. It's nothing fancy, but it's something cherished in our family."

"Oh, it's beautiful," Lorna said, holding out her finger to study the lovely gold ring.

"You sure you like it? I could buy you a new one, if you'd rather."

"No, this ring is perfect. The only thing I want for Christmas is you, Zach. Your love. The gift of your heart is the best one I've ever received. Thank you for loving me, for wanting to spend your life with me." She snuggled against him as they watched the snow begin to fall and the lights glow in the darkness.

Unable to hold back her questions, she turned her head and looked up at Zach. "What are Papa's stipulations?"

"That we'll live at Lennox Manor and allow him to fill the role of doting grandfather to our children."

"That's it? He didn't demand you accept a

different job or anything like that?"

"Nope. I made it clear to him I enjoyed my work and had no desire to do anything different. He said he could accept that if I could get used to living in luxury." Zach grinned at her. "That's gonna take a little adjustment on my part, but I'd do anything to be with you, Lorna. Honestly, your father could have made a long list of demands, and I would have given him whatever he asked because all that matters to me is you."

"I don't deserve you, Zach, but I love you. I have since the moment you saved me from being smashed by that lumber wagon. I can't wait to begin a future together—just your heart and mine."

"Entangled forever," he said, giving her a kiss full of promises and passion.

Later that evening, after they'd delivered food and gifts to young Willie and his family and joined the Milton family for dinner, Lorna stood in the foyer at Lennox Manor, not wanting to say goodnight to Zach, but knowing she had to.

Her father had given them five unsupervised minutes to say good night.

"Will you come out to the ranch right after church services tomorrow?" Zach asked, caressing her cheek with his work-roughened hand.

She knew he had grease embedded in his skin that might always be there from the work he did, and she didn't mind it at all. Zach was a hardworking, honest, good man. One who had captured her heart completely.

"I'll be there as soon as I can get Papa out the door."

"I'm glad he made it home for Christmas, Lorna. I know how much you miss him when he's gone."

She wrapped her arms around him and rested her cheek against his chest, listening to the steady beat of his heart. A heart that now belonged to her. "I do miss Papa, but I'd miss you more if you ever went away. In fact, I dread the thought of you leaving now."

"It's just for tonight. Would you like me to ride in and check on you early in the morning?"

"No, you don't need to do that." Lorna traced the line of Zach's strong jaw with her finger and gazed up at him, seeing the love she felt reflected in his eyes. "I was thinking, rather than give Papa time to plan an elaborate wedding, what would you say to a wedding the day after Christmas?"

Zach's face lit with a huge smile. "I'd say I'll talk to Pastor Ryan on my way home." He picked her up off her feet and swung her in a circle, barely missing one of the Christmas trees. "Do you mean it, Lorna? Would you really marry me the day after tomorrow?"

"I would and I will. I can't wait to be your wife, Zach. This truly has been the best Christmas."

"A Christmas from the heart." He set her down and kissed her again before he lifted his head just enough to touch his forehead to hers.

"Stop slobbering all over my daughter and go home, you insolent young pup," her father bellowed from down the hall.

Lorna giggled, and Zach rolled his eyes. He gave her one more sweet kiss, then hurried out the door.

At eleven in the morning on the twenty-sixth day of December, Lorna walked down the aisle at the church on her father's arm. He looked so proud, she wondered if the buttons might pop right off his shirt.

Zach stood at the front of the church next to Pastor Ryan, with Andy and Noah beside him. Ellery and Jenny had both agreed to stand up with her.

She had no idea how he'd acquired them, but Zach had sent a large bouquet of red hothouse roses to her this morning, and she carried them down the aisle.

Everything had happened so quickly and seemed like such a dream, but so, so perfect too. Lorna had spent a considerable amount of time speaking to her father on Christmas Eve. She discovered he'd liked Zach all along but wanted him to prove that he loved Lorna enough to fight for her. And Zach had.

When she and her father reached Zach, her papa placed her hand on top of Zach's then leaned forward and whispered, "You be good to my little girl or I'll bury you so deep in the ground, no one will ever find you."

"Papa!" Lorna hissed, giving him a warning glare, then turned to see her father wink at Zach.

Everyone close enough to hear the threat released a relieved sigh to know he was teasing; then the service began. Cora Lee and Anne both shed tears of joy along with Maude and Dodi, who had jumped in to help Lorna with preparations. The new dress she'd purchased in Maggie MacGregor's shop had worked perfectly as a wedding gown, and Jenny proudly wore the dress Lorna had purchased for her Christmas gift.

When it came time for their first kiss as husband and wife, Zach cupped Lorna's face and shared such a tender kiss, she could hear Mercy and Mariah sighing from their seats in the second row.

"That's how I want to be loved," she heard the girls whisper as she and Zach walked down the aisle.

After enjoying a luncheon with their guests at Lennox Manor, Zach nudged Lorna toward the door. He pulled an expensive pocket watch from his vest, rubbed his finger over the steam engine embossed on the case, and opened it.

"Look at that. Time for us to go." He grinned at her. "Thank you for my watch. It's a dandy."

"Like my handsome husband," Lorna said, casting a saucy grin his way.

Before anyone could stop them, he settled a cloak over her shoulders, swept her into his arms, and kissed her until she was breathless.

"I'm so happy you married me, Mrs. Coleman," Zach whispered before he carried her outside.

"I'm so happy you asked," Lorna said, glancing over his shoulder and waving to everyone who stood outside in the bright winter sunshine, watching them leave.

"Are you sorry you married a simple cowboy who works on train engines?" he asked as he headed toward the sleigh that would carry them to the depot. Marcus hurried ahead of them, ready to drive them there.

The wedding gift from Lorna's father was a two-week trip in his private train car. Zach had thought it would be nice to go someplace warm, so they were planning to head south. Lorna had never been to California and liked the idea of an adventure there. Truthfully, though, where they went didn't matter to her, as long as she was with the man she loved.

"I will never be sorry I married you, Zach. In fact, the gift of your heart is the most precious thing I've ever been given." Lorna brushed her lips over his as he settled her in the sleigh and climbed in beside her. "I can't think of any gift I'd like any better."

He offered her that lopsided smirk she loved so much as he tucked a heavy robe over her lap after he slid onto the seat beside her. "And I can't think of anything better than spending forever loving you, Lorna."

Lorna waved one last time to their family and friends as the sleigh started down the street. "It seems both appropriate and wonderful the engine that will pull our car to Baker City is the one your father used to drive."

Zach pulled her closer against his side. "Dad was so pleased when your father asked if he'd like to be the one driving Hope today."

"They both seem rather excited," Lorna remarked as Marcus stopped the sleigh at the station and Zach hopped out, waving to Jace and George as they both stood inside the engine car.

"Is Mr. Lennox sure he wants to ride up there the whole trip?"

Lorna grinned as Zach lifted her to the ground, keeping her hands on his shoulders as they both turned to look at their fathers. "Papa said it had been far too long since he'd experienced the thrill of riding with the engineer. It will be good for him."

Zach kissed her cheek, then took her hand in his, leading her up the steps to the private car. They waved to Marcus; then Zach opened the door and waited for her to walk inside before he stepped into the opulent warmth of the car. Someone had already built a fire in the stove in the sitting room, creating a cozy welcome.

Before Lorna could do more than look around, Zach removed her cloak, tossed his coat aside, and pulled her into his arms.

"Thank you for giving me your heart, Lorna. I'll cherish it always," he whispered before his lips captured hers in a kiss brimming with promises.

"Always," she echoed, feeling blessed beyond anything she'd dared to hope or imagine, to be in love and be loved by the man of her dreams.

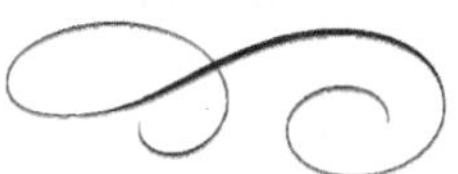

I hope you enjoyed watching another
generation of Coleman men fall in love!
Keep reading for an excerpt from
Holiday Home,
the third book in the Holiday Express series!

Cranberry Coffee Cake

This is a modern take on the cranberry cake Maude made for Lorna to give to Zach as a peace offering. While sweet enough to serve as a dessert, it is yummy on a cold winter morning, enjoyed with a cup of tea or coffee.

Cranberry Coffee Cake
Cake
2 eggs
1 cup sugar
2 teaspoons vanilla extract
1 cup all-purpose flour
¼ teaspoon baking soda
½ teaspoon baking powder
1 teaspoon ground ginger
½ cup melted butter
½ cup sour cream
¾ cup white chocolate chips
¾ cup dried cranberries
Frosting
8 ounces cream cheese, softened
1 cup powdered sugar
1 teaspoon vanilla extract
Topping
½ cup white chocolate chips melted
⅔ cups dried cranberries
1 teaspoon orange zest (optional)

Preheat oven to 350 degrees F.
Spray a 9-inch square baking pan with

nonstick spray, line with parchment (leaving edges to hang over), then spray parchment.

For the cake:

Soak the cranberries in warm water for about twenty minutes. Drain, pat dry and set aside.

In a large bowl, combine eggs, sugar, and vanilla. Add flour, baking soda, and baking powder along with ginger, mixing until just incorporated. Stir in melted butter and sour cream until blended, then fold in cranberries and white chocolate chips.

Pour the batter into the prepared pan, spread evenly, and bake for about 35 minutes, until a toothpick inserted into the center comes out clean. Remove from oven and cool.

Once cool, it's easy to remove from the pan by lifting out parchment and placing on a cutting board.

For the frosting:

Mix together cream cheese, powdered sugar, and vanilla extract. Spread over the top of the cake.

For the topping:

Melt the white chocolate chips in the microwave for about 30 seconds (use 10-second intervals) stirring until smooth and melted. Transfer to a resealable sandwich bag and snip off one corner of the bag.

Sprinkle cranberries and orange zest on top of frosting, then drizzle with melted white chocolate

Allow to set for about an hour, then cut and serve.

NOTE: If desired, you could also add sliced almonds to the batter and topping.

Author's Note

I'm so grateful you chose to read *Holiday Heart.* Zach and Lorna were such a neat couple to create and I hope their journey to love brought you joy.

The first time I wrote about the town of Holiday was in Valentine Bride, part of the *Holiday Brides* series. I didn't get too particular about the exact setting of the fictional town, just placing it between Baker City and Pendleton in Eastern Oregon.

When I started writing the *Holiday Express* series, I needed a defined location, mostly because the train had to run to and from somewhere! I started looking at old ghost towns that were once located within an hour of Baker City. The town of Cornucopia snagged my attention.

Located east and a little north of Baker City, Cornucopia was hastily constructed when gold was discovered in the area in 1884. A famous and highly profitable mine, Cornucopia, led to the name of the town when it was platted in 1886. Millions of dollars in gold came from this area where steep mountains and deep canyons are honeycombed with miles of subterranean shafts.

It is unique among Oregon gold camps in that the location is a rugged mountain valley that resembles some of the alpine camps in the Rocky Mountains. The winters there were harsh, with homes and buildings regularly buried beneath many feet of snow.

Despite the frigid winters and remote location, by 1902, the population was up to 700 residents. At the time, it was one of the largest mining operations in the entire United States. Eventually, a railroad connected the town to the rest of the region, and growth continued. The decline came after the stock market crash in 1929. By the 1940s, the mines shut down for good and the town never recovered. Today a lodge with modern cabins serves as a base to explorers of the Eagle Cap Wilderness, the Wallowa Mountains, and Hells Canyon.

Cornucopia inspired the location and many details about the town of Holiday in my stories about its early years. At one time, Cornucopia boasted two general stores, a hotel, a post office, two saloons, and a school with sixty-five pupils.

Another source of inspiration for this story comes from the mansion that inspired Lennox Manor. A beautifully restored home known as the Pittock Mansion is located near the Portland Zoo. The first time we toured it, I was in love with the story, the architecture – everything!

The Pittock Mansion story begins with a young man named Henry. Henry Pittock was born in London, but grew up in Pittsburgh, Pennsylvania. In 1853, when he was 19, he headed west on the Oregon Trail to seek his fortune. He arrived in Portland, a frontier "stumptown" at the time, and found work as a typesetter at *The Oregonian* newspaper. It was a risky, competitive time to be in the newspaper business with more than thirty newspapers launched in Portland during this period. Henry met and married Georgiana Burton, who came with her family from Missouri. In 1860, five months after they wed, he was given ownership of the newspaper in exchange for back wages. Henry went on to transform the publication into a successful daily newspaper that continues to thrive today.

Henry might be best known for his successful newspaper endeavors, but he also built a financial empire by investing in real estate, banking, railroads, steamboats, sheep ranching, silver mining, and the paper industry. He was known as an avid outdoorsman and was among the first people to climb Mount Hood.

Georgiana was fundamental in founding several charity organizations and fundraising for others including the Ladies Relief Society, Women's Union, and the Martha Washington Home which provided residences for single, self-supporting women.

It wasn't until the early 1900s that Henry began to think about building a grand home on the hill on a piece of property that offered panoramic views of Portland, the Willamette River, and the Cascade Mountains in the distance. Construction began in 1912 and the family moved into the mansion in 1914. The couple only lived there for roughly four years before they died. The last resident, a grandson, moved out in 1958 and put the mansion up for sale.

For years, the mansion remained empty, then it was pummeled by the Columbus Day Storm in October 1962.

Hurricane-force winds damaged the roof and windows, which allowed water to seep into the mansion. By 1964, a home that had once been among the finest in the Northwest was in danger of being torn down due to its derelict condition. Dedicated citizens rallied to save the mansion and helped raise funds for the city to purchase the home.

It took fifteen months to restore the mansion and transform it from a private residence to a public space before it opened as a historic home museum. In 1968, the Pittock Mansion Society was formed to take on the responsibility of furnishing the home, maintaining the collection, and providing educational activities. The society took over the day-to-day museum operations from Portland Parks & Recreation in 2007, and has been operating it ever since.

Today, the Pittock Mansion offers a glimpse of the grandeur of a time long past. If you ever have a chance to visit it, go. It's definitely worth the time! Be sure to check out the 3-D model of the house that allows you to experience it up close and personal.

Anyway, the Pittock Mansion is the inspiration behind Lennox Manor. I loved being able to go online and look through photos and the 3-D tours to get ideas for the home Lorna shares with Dodi, Marcus, and Maude. I could just picture Zach wandering through the house, or Lorna curled by the fire.

You might wonder why I incorporated the Halloween costume contest. It was inspired purely by some photos I happened across from vintage costumes of that era. Oh, my goodness! Some of them were so incredibly creepy! And others were so fun. There really was a man who won a contest dressed as a side of bacon.

The game the girls went into the closet to play, to see if they could peel an apple in one long peel (something my mom could do but I have not yet possessed the patience required to victoriously complete the task!) then look into a mirror and see their one true love is one I found in a book of holiday traditions and games from the Victorian and Edwardian eras. Another game that was included was baking the different items into the cake. Personally, I prefer my baked goods without hidden potentially tooth-cracking items in them, even if it is all in fun!

Wasn't Lorna a lucky girl to get a brand-new car from her father? I was flipping through a history of the auto book and a note about the first Dodge caught my eye. On November 14, 1914, the very first Dodge car rolled off the assembly line. It cost less than $800, had a 110-inch wheelbase, and set itself apart with an all-steel construction. Positioned to be a direct competitor to Henry Ford's Model T, only 249 Dodge Model 30s were produced that first year. The car Lorna received is described just like a photo I found of one of the cars. It was a beaut!

While I'm mentioning cars, I have to tell you about Burt's snow car. The inspiration for it is a combination of two actual wonders in automotive history.

The first: A man named Virgil White filed a patent in 1913 for a snowmobile conversion kit for Model Ts, but it wasn't until 1922, after he "perfected" every detail that he offered it on the market. Henry Ford took notice and allowed White to sell the kit exclusively through Ford dealers for $400. The kit, much like Burt's car, converted the front tires to skis and added tracks to dual rear wheels.

The second: One day Captain Cavedweller was watching a program about old cars and the mention of one built from junk drew me back into the room. Apparently, a love-struck young man named Bobby Sheldon decided to impress a girl by building a car. In 1905, Bobby set out to build an automobile, even though he'd never seen a real car before. He used bar stools, a two-cycle marine engine, wood, tin, and his own buggy wheels to create a two-seat runabout. He didn't win the woman's heart, but he did create Alaska's first car.

It was easy to picture Burt building his "snow car" after I'd seen images of these two vehicles.

The mention of Tilly being excited about a Kewpie doll came from an exhibit we saw in an old railway museum. They had set up a display for Christmas and it was full of Kewpie dolls as well as old advertisements. I thought it would be a fun gift for a little girl back in 1914!

You may have noticed Miss Mulberry's Advice for Today's Young Woman that starts each chapter written from Lorna's point of view. It isn't a real book, nor is Miss

Mulberry a real person, but the instructions were inspired by a publication called "Things a Woman Wants to Know," written for Edwardian-era housewives. Some of the advice just made me giggle, and inspired me to write my own advice for Lorna's benefit!

When I was browsing through pictures of gazebos for the Holiday gazebo, I knew I'd found *the* one the moment I set eyes on it. Located in the Fellows Riverside Gardens at Mill Creek Park, Youngstown, Ohio, the gazebo's roofline makes me think of a petticoat swirling at a ball. Any of you who've seen it in person, I'd love to hear more about it.

I chose for Lorna and Zach to attend a performance of *Snow White and the Seven Dwarfs* because I found a reference to the play having been performed at the Opera House in Sumpter, Oregon (located west of Baker City) around the same time frame and thought it was a fun tidbit to include in the story.

The Coleman family and the Milton bunch have just captured my heart and I hope you are enjoying meeting them, too.

The reason I gave Zach the job of a train mechanic is because when we visited the Nevada Northern Railway Museum, I was fascinated with the pits that ran beneath the trains so the mechanics could work on them. It made me think about a character who works in the engine house. Then I thought it would be fun if the girl he meets is the daughter of the man who owns the railroad and the engine house.

Lorna is such a free-spirited character, but one with a huge, giving heart. It's going to be fun to see what's in store for her and Zach in the future!

Thank you for coming along on this journey with me, and for your readership.

And special thanks to Katrina, Allison, Alice, Linda, and all my Hopeless Romantics for your assistance with this book. I greatly appreciate you. Also, thanks to Josephine Blake for the amazing covers for this series!

Wishing you a holiday season rich with love and blessings!

Shanna

Thank You

Thank you for reading *Holiday Heart*! I hope Zach and Lorna's sweet romance brought you joy. If you did enjoy it, I'd be so appreciative if you'd consider leaving a review so other readers might discover the book, too.

Holiday Express
Four generations discover the wonder of the
season and the magic of one very special train
in these sweet holiday romances.
Find them on all Amazon

Also, if you haven't yet signed up for my newsletter, won't you consider subscribing? I send it out when I have new releases, sales, or news of freebies to share. Each month, you can enter a contest, get a new recipe to try, and discover details about upcoming events. When you sign up, you'll receive a free digital book. Don't wait. Sign up today!

Holiday Home Excerpt

Widow Britta Webster can hardly remember life before her village was overrun with German soldiers during World War II. All she wants is to live a peaceful existence and raise her child. But she will do anything to protect Joshua, even if it means begging a stranger to take her to America where her son will have a safe place to call home.

Honor, grace, and duty are the driving forces behind Bryce Coleman's approach to life, even as he strives to survive in war-torn France. Severely wounded, he's left by his comrade in the cellar of a woman who clearly wants nothing to do with him. When she pleads with him for her son's future, Bryce feels bound by an obligation to the widow for saving his life.

Will a burdensome agreement turn to love when hearts come home to Holiday? Find out in this sweet historical romance packed with vintage charm, nostalgia, and the wonder of Christmas.

August 1944

A fly tormented his ear, but Bryce Coleman was too exhausted to swat it away. Unless a tank drove through the tent where he rested or a bomb threat drove him to seek cover, he intended to catch a few minutes of much-needed sleep. Nothing as meaningless as a pesky insect was going to keep him from it.

The ability to sleep anywhere, anytime, was a skill he'd gained during his involvement in a war that seemed endless. He never knew when he'd be able to rest, so he took advantage of any opportunity to grab a few winks.

He breathed deeply, inhaling the scent of the food being prepared for lunch in the mess hall. The aroma mingled with cigarette smoke, the lingering odor of sweaty men, and gunpowder.

Bryce released the breath and listened to the sounds of a busy base camp. Vehicles running, men talking, equipment creaking, and footsteps marching. Somewhere in the background, a scratched record played Kay Kyser's version of "Praise the Lord and Pass the Ammunition," adding to the cacophony around him. A marching band could have performed a rousing tune two feet from his head and he wouldn't have cared. All he wanted was his sleep.

With a final deep breath, he dozed off. He had no idea how long he slept, but he awakened with a start when someone swatted the soles of his boots. Bryce jerked and almost tipped over the chair he sat in at Colonel Lee Thompson's desk.

Granted, he'd balanced the chair on the back two legs and settled his boots on top of the desk, which he probably shouldn't have done, but it felt so good to elevate his feet and rest for a few minutes.

"You are an insolent pup, Coleman," the colonel groused, glowering at him as he set the stack of files he'd used to smack Bryce on the corner of the desk.

"Like father, like son," Bryce said, sliding his boots off the desk, rising to his feet, and grinning at the officer as he offered a snappy salute.

The colonel rolled his eyes, then returned Bryce's grin. "You are definitely like your father, although I would have shot Zach if I'd found him asleep with his feet on my desk."

"Back then, you didn't have your own tent or desk," Bryce said, stretching his arms over his head, then twisting from side to side to loosen his tight muscles. His father had served with Colonel Thompson in World War I. At that time, Lee had been a lieutenant.

"True, but if it hadn't been for Zach, I wouldn't be standing here today," Lee said, shaking his head in wonderment. "I still have no idea how your dad managed to carry me to safety when he was so gravely injured."

Bryce shrugged. "Dad always says it was strength beyond his own that made it possible."

The colonel nodded in agreement, then took a seat in the chair Bryce had vacated.

When Bryce had arrived at this base camp in France four days ago, he'd been thrilled to discover a man not only familiar to him but one he considered a close family friend. His father and Lee had exchanged many letters since they returned from the Great War. The Coleman and Thompson families had even made trips to visit each other half a dozen times over the years.

Due to the nature of his work, Bryce was frequently moved from one place to another. He'd spent less than thirty minutes with Colonel Thompson upon his arrival before Bryce had been sent out with a group of engineers and railroad soldiers. He'd only returned to the camp two hours ago. Colonel Thompson had been busy when Bryce had sought him out, but he'd motioned to the tent he used as an office.

More than happy to have a quiet place to rest, Bryce was grateful three sides of the tent had been rolled up, allowing air to circulate inside. The slight breeze felt wonderful in the rising heat of the summer day.

Bryce hadn't slept in the past thirty-six hours and felt ready to drop, but he'd continue doing whatever the U.S. Army needed him to do, even if he wasn't officially a member of the American military. The past two years, he'd served his country as a civilian contractor, providing much-needed assistance with trains in war zones. If it involved a track, a train car, or an engine, Bryce was the one who knew exactly how to fix it, build it, or get the most use out of it.

Since Colonel Thompson was aware of his lack of sleep, Bryce assumed the man had awakened him for an important reason. One that would likely curtail his time spent in this particular camp. He'd traveled so much the past month, he'd lost track of his exact location a week ago.

"I know you need some rest, son, but you can sleep on the way there." The colonel pulled a map out of a drawer, spreading it across the top of his desk. He pointed to a spot that looked like nothing but forest to Bryce. "They've hit a snag on a project a few hours south of here and could use your expertise. I'm sending along one of my best engineers. Between the two of you, I'm confident you can iron out the wrinkles and get things back on track, both literally and figuratively."

"I'll do my best, sir," Bryce said, studying the map. If he wasn't mistaken, the track was being installed near an area currently occupied by Germans.

"I know you will, Bryce. I wouldn't expect anything less than that from a Coleman." The colonel stood and thumped Bryce on the back. "Head over to the mess hall and fill your belly, then gather your gear. I'll make arrangements for a car. Be ready to leave in an hour."

"Yes, sir," Bryce said, saluting the colonel as a captain entered the tent.

Bryce jogged over to the mess tent and hurriedly ate a meal of overcooked meat and potatoes, a slice of flavorless bread, and a serving of canned peaches, which tasted delicious. He drained his cup of canned milk, dreaming of the glasses of cold milk he enjoyed on his family's ranch, then glanced at his watch. If he rushed, he could clean up before he had to leave.

The showers were empty when he carried his things inside. In less than ten minutes, he'd showered, shaved, and donned a fresh uniform. He rolled his dirty clothes inside the damp towel and tied them to the bottom of his knapsack, similar in color and design to the haversacks issued by the Army. Bryce had learned right away to carry whatever he needed with him because he never knew when or if he'd return to a camp once he was sent out on a project. Often, he went from one project to another, receiving his orders on the go. Everything he had in his possession was contained in his knapsack.

Bryce returned to the colonel's tent to find him and another officer studying the map on his desk.

"Bryce, this is Lieutenant David Kelly. He's one of the best engineers I've met, and he'll accompany you on the trip. If all goes well, you should be back tomorrow in time for supper." The colonel tapped his index finger on the map he'd spread out earlier. "Lieutenant Kelly has pertinent project details and can brief you on the way there."

"I thought you were going to let me sleep," Bryce teased as he shook the lieutenant's hand in greeting.

"You can sleep after the war is won," Lee said, offering Bryce a fatherly glare.

"Whatever you say, sir. Do you ..." Bryce was interrupted as a four-door Chevrolet sedan pulled up outside. The dark color, known as Volunteer Green, would blend in well with a forested area.

A young corporal jumped out of the car, saluted the colonel and lieutenant, then glanced at Bryce. Although he wore the same clothes as the lieutenant, his lacked any insignias, stripes, or other identifying emblems.

"Ask Lieutenant Kelly if you have questions," Lee said, leading the way to the car. After the men saluted him, he handed Bryce a pistol and two boxes of ammunition.

Bryce raised an eyebrow in question, but Lee almost imperceptibly winked at him. "I already have a pistol."

"I know, but it never hurts to be prepared," the colonel said, then waited as the lieutenant and Bryce slid into the back of the car. "Be careful and stay safe. Your dad would never forgive me if I sent you off and let you get yourself killed."

Bryce grinned as he rolled down the car's window. "It's my mother you should fear, sir."

The colonel laughed as Bryce shut the door, then tapped the top of the car, letting the corporal know he could leave.

The car started forward as Bryce set his bag between his feet, tucked the pistol and ammo inside, then settled back against the seat, fighting the urge to sleep.

"Go ahead and snooze while you can," David said, setting the duffel bag he carried at his feet. "I'll wake you in an hour."

"Thanks," Bryce said, tugging his hat down to cover his face. In less than a minute, he was asleep.

"Coleman! Wake up," a voice said near his ear as a hand shook his arm. "Coleman!"

Bryce pushed his hat back on his head, yawned, and opened his eyes. "That hour sure flew by in a hurry."

David smirked and opened a file he held in his left hand. "Come on, sleeping beauty, we need to go over this information before we get there."

Bryce and David spent half an hour going over the project details and making notes for improvements as well as discussing how to handle the problem that had been relayed to the colonel.

"That should do it," David said, tucking the papers back into his duffel and zipping it shut. He glanced over at Bryce. "The colonel didn't give us time for much of an introduction. Where are you from?"

"A little town in Eastern Oregon named Holiday. My family has lived there since before it was a town. My great-granddad was one of the first to settle the area."

"Really? What is the nearest bigger town? Any name I might recognize?"

Bryce shook his head. "There isn't a town in the whole eastern half of the state with a name anyone who didn't live there would recognize, although Pendleton has been on the map thanks to the annual rodeo."

"Pendleton? As in the Pendleton Round-Up and wild west shows and Indian encampments? That Pendleton?"

Shocked, Bryce nodded his head. "Yep. I take it you've heard of it."

"Sure have. My cousin's husband used to compete in rodeos before they wed. He mentioned riding broncs there a few times. How far is it from Holiday?"

"About two hours. Holiday is off the beaten path, on the way to nowhere, really, but there's a big lumber mill there. It used to be a top producer of gold with a variety of successful mines, including the Yellowbird, one my family owns. The mines have all been abandoned now, but they operated for almost forty years before they played out."

"Is your family still involved in mining, or is it now lumber?"

Bryce grinned. "Neither. My father's family are ranchers and have been since they moved there. My great-granddad imported Angus cattle from Scotland. Elk Creek Ranch supplies beef to restaurants and stores all along the eastern side of the state and a few in Boise, Idaho, and Portland."

"Beef, huh?" David gave him a long glance. "How'd you get so knowledgeable about trains? The colonel said you could take a train engine apart and put it back together with your eyes closed and one hand tied behind your back."

"Both sides of my family have been involved in the railroad. My father spent many years as the head mechanic at our local engine house. Grandpa Coleman was an engineer and worked every job you could think of except conductor to get there. He and my dad taught me everything they know about repairing and running trains." Bryce glanced out the window as they drove into what appeared to be an ancient forest. "My mother's father also had ties to the railroad."

"What kind of ties?" David asked when Bryce fell silent.

He'd always been cautious when sharing about his grandfather Lennox because his name was well known. His family had worried someone might hold him for ransom if they realized Bryce was related to George Lennox.

Bryce glanced over at David. The man appeared honest and upright. If he wasn't a good man, one who knew what he was doing, the colonel wouldn't have sent him along.

"My mother's father is George Lennox."

David's mouth dropped open. "*The* George Lennox? The railroad magnate? The man who owned a good portion of the railways in America along with a dozen other profitable enterprises?"

Slowly, Bryce nodded. "That's him."

David whistled softly. "He's worth millions, maybe billions."

"Maybe," Bryce agreed, wishing he could change the subject. It always made him uncomfortable to discuss his family's wealth. It was something he never flaunted and rarely discussed. He much preferred to be Bryce Coleman, grandson of a cattle rancher.

The Lennox fortune, or perhaps it was the way George Lennox had used it, was something his father had despised. If it had been up to Zach Coleman, he would have raised his family in a modest home, depending solely on the income he earned as a mechanic. However, his father-in-law had demanded the best for his only child—Bryce's mother—and his grandchildren, insisting they live in his mansion where he'd spoiled them with the best of everything.

Grandfather Lennox could be a hard-nosed tyrant when he wanted and had often thought throwing money at something could fix any problem, even if he had been a good grandfather, for the most part.

The Coleman family was so different from him. They were among the most hardworking, honorable people Bryce had ever encountered. Every day, he was grateful he'd been raised with his father's beliefs and morals instead of those held by his maternal grandfather.

George Lennox was the reason Bryce was not in the Army and was instead forced to do his part in the war as a contracted civilian. He'd been so angry at the man's meddling,

Bryce had refused to speak to him the last time he'd seen him. He regretted not telling his grandfather he loved him before he left for Africa two years ago, because five months later George Lennox had died of a heart attack.

"So, I guess you grew up around trains?" David finally asked.

"I did. Dad let me work on them from the time I was big enough to hold a wrench, and Grandfather Lennox took me on trips with him. I got to ride in the engine or the caboose, or wherever I wanted and asked the men working for him endless questions. Grandpa Coleman taught me how to drive a train, how to get the most out of it using the least fuel, that sort of thing. The rest I learned from studying books and in the field."

"Colonel Thompson said he'd never met anyone who knew more about trains than you. I suppose that's partly due to your family, and the rest is because you are a driven maniac."

Bryce turned his head to see if David was joking or serious.

David chuckled. "I heard how you skip sleep, meals, and whatever is necessary to get the job done right and completed as quickly as possible. You've made a reputation for yourself, Coleman."

"I hope it's not all bad," Bryce said with a grin. "Speaking of reputations, I heard the man in charge of this project can be a real donkey's derrière."

A laugh rolled out of David. "I heard the same thing, although not in words quite that polite. The second in command is a good man, though. I worked with him in Sicily. When we get there, let's report to him. If possible, we can sidestep the captain and get the job done without his interference."

"I like that plan." Bryce looked outside and breathed in the scent of forest along with the dust the car kicked up as it turned off a paved road and onto a narrow dirt lane. There weren't any road signs to mark the way, so he hoped the driver knew where he was headed. This close to the border of German-occupied France, it would be easy to inadvertently cross over into enemy territory.

Taking a firm grip on his thoughts instead of worrying

when there wasn't yet a problem, Bryce tamped down his concerns and looked back at his traveling companion. "What about you, David? Where are you from? Do you have a wife or family waiting for you?"

David leaned further back into the seat and sighed. "I grew up in Illinois. My uncle was a conductor, and that's how I got interested in trains. I was always fascinated by what made them go and wanted to learn how to make them run faster, better. The military intrigued me, and here I am. Eight years ago, my brother's wife introduced me to her cousin, and I knew I'd met the girl of my dreams. Three months later, we married. We have two kids. Ryan is six and Camille is almost four. I sure miss them. How about you? Wife? Kids? Although you seem pretty young to have any."

"I turned twenty-four in January, so not as young as some. I'm not married, although there is a girl back home who's special to me. We dated all through school and it seems like everyone expects us to wed someday, but we'll see how we both feel after the war is over and I return to Holiday."

Bryce had forced himself not to think about Katherine Kingston for a while. When he did let memories of her surface, it made him so homesick he could hardly stand it. Kate had been his sweetheart since he first noticed girls. She was friends with his oldest sister and was always at their house even before she became his girl, but something had held Bryce back from proposing to her.

Once he decided to head into the war, he was glad he'd refrained. He didn't want to leave behind a widow. In case something happened to him that left him maimed, he didn't want a woman tied to him if some other fellow came along who captured her eye.

David gave him an approving look. "That's a smart thing to do. So many young people have rushed to wed just weeks or days before the men shipped off to war. They hardly know anything about each other, and now they'll spend months, sometimes years apart. I can't imagine enduring that kind of separation and then going home to a person who is virtually a stranger."

"Me either," Bryce said, knowing David spoke the truth. He'd seen it happen time and again as young soldiers feared going off to war without leaving anyone behind and married the first girl who said "yes."

David glanced at the watch on his wrist, then leaned forward, looking out the windshield. "We ought to be there soon, I would think."

"The directions I have say it's another twelve miles up this road," the corporal said, glancing at them over the front seat.

"Okay," David said, sitting back in the seat.

"What about you, Corporal Matthews? Where are you from?"

The corporal looked at them in the rearview mirror, as though he was surprised to be included in the conversation.

"From Ohio, sir. Grew up in a town named Waverly. I'm the oldest of five. I have two sisters in high school and two brothers, who are eight and eleven. My dad owns a hardware store. I used to drive all over making deliveries for him, even before I had a license."

Bryce grinned at the corporal. "My Gramps let me drive his car when I was seven. I had to sit on his lap, but I sure thought I was grown up that day."

The corporal and David laughed.

"I was ten before my father let me touch the steering wheel," David said, then looked to the corporal. "How about you?"

"I was nine when I first got to drive, but Dad let me start driving by myself when I was twelve. I was tall for my age and could see over the steering wheel by then. One time, I accidentally hit the gas instead of the brake and ran into a stack of lumber behind the store. It didn't even scratch the grill, so I kept that to myself for a whole week before the guilt got to me and I confessed what I'd done. Instead of punishing me, my dad told me honesty was the best and only policy; then he gave me the keys and sent me out on an errand."

"He sounds like a great father," David said as the car rounded a curve.

One minute they were driving along the dirt road in the peaceful forest. The next, a hail of bullets hit the car.

"Drive, drive!" David shouted to the corporal, but the boy made a gurgling sound then slumped over the wheel, his foot buried heavily on the gas pedal.

Bryce started to scramble over the front seat, but the vehicle veered wildly to the left, hit a stump, and came to a stop with the front of the car nosed upward in a tree and the driver's side pinned against another towering deciduous giant.

Although he wasn't sure when it had happened, Bryce had been tossed out the open window of the car before he could reach Corporal Matthews. By a miracle, the car hadn't crushed him to death, although he felt as though every bone had been jarred loose. Shots rang around him as he waited for the air to return to his lungs. When it did, he hopped up into a crouched position and zig-zagged his way to the car. He felt a sting, then another, but kept going, focused on reaching the two men in the automobile resting at an unnatural angle.

"David?" He yelled as he took in the precarious position of the car. Something in the undercarriage seemed to be caught on a limb, and that looked to be all that was holding it upright. He feared one false move might send it crashing backward to the ground. He climbed over a tree stump and started to climb up the massive trunk. He raised his left hand to grab onto a branch and pull himself higher just as the exhaust pipe fell off the car and seared his arm as it toppled to the ground.

Bryce winced but kept working his way up to the passenger side door.

"David?" he called again.

"I'm here," a voice replied, sounding groggy. It grew stronger when he spoke again. "I'm here, Coleman!"

"I'm coming to you. How's the corporal?"

He heard rustling and the car groaned. Suddenly, a gush of boiling water washed over him as the radiator cracked open, scalding his left side from shoulder to hip. Ignoring the pain that rendered him lightheaded, he managed to climb up and wrench the back passenger door partway open. David remained pinned in place by the front seat that had been shoved backward onto his right leg.

"Is anything broken?" Bryce asked as he cautiously worked his way into the car.

"I can't tell," David said, tugging on his leg but unable to work it free. He ducked as more shots echoed around them, shattering what few pieces of window glass hadn't already cracked and fallen out. "I'm thinking the corporal might have taken a wrong turn somewhere."

"Probably. How is he? Has he said anything?" Bryce asked, carefully leaning over the front seat. At a glance, he could see the corporal was gone due to two bullets to his head, but he felt for a pulse to make sure. He edged back and shook his head at David.

David closed his eyes, as though saying a prayer for the young man's soul, while Bryce frantically worked to free the lieutenant's trapped leg. With strength borne of desperation, he turned so his back was against the front seat and pushed while David yanked upward. The second David's leg was free, Bryce grabbed his arm and tugged him toward the door. Before he slid out of the car, he handed David's haversack to him, then snagged his knapsack that had been wedged beneath the seat and slipped the straps over his shoulders. The feel of it against his burned flesh nearly made him pass out, but he forced himself to remain focused on escaping.

David was bleeding from a head wound and holding his left arm like it was broken. Bryce somehow managed to help him out of the car, then half-carried him down to the ground.

"Can you walk?" he asked as random bullets continued to knock bark off the trees around them. Either the shooters had terrible aim or they were far enough away they couldn't see their targets well through the trees.

"I'm not sure," David said, tentatively putting his weight on his right foot. It held him so he took another step, then dropped to the ground as a volley of gunfire popped around them. Bryce flopped onto his belly and crawled several yards on his elbows until he was hidden behind the trunk of an enormous tree. He looked back to make sure David had followed him.

"We can't stay here," he said, rising to a sitting position and glancing around the tree that offered protection from the shooters. "I think we should blow the car."

"Blow the car? Make it explode?" David asked, eyes wide as blood continued to trickle down his forehead and along the side of his face.

"Yes. I don't know what official papers or maps are

inside it, and I'm not crawling back up there to find out. I would like to give the corporal a proper burial, but it's more important the Germans not get their hands on him or the car."

David nodded in agreement. "We've got our bags and papers. Unless the explosion draws the whole German army down on us, it's probably the best plan to get rid of the car and anything we don't want them to find."

"Can you move on your own?" Bryce asked, slowly working his way back around the trunk of the tree.

"I think so." David pushed himself up. He took a few wobbly steps, then looked back at Bryce. "What are you going to do?"

"If you can run, now would be a good time to start." Bryce didn't wait for David's answer. Instead, he pulled a pistol from his bag, aimed for the gas tank, and hit it with his first shot. He took cover behind the tree as pieces of metal went flying in every direction; then he sprinted after David, who was now racing in earnest through the trees.

Bryce caught up with him and they kept on running until they could no longer smell the smoke from the explosion. They came to a stream, crossed it, then stopped to rest on the other side.

Up until that moment, Bryce had been fueled by pure adrenaline. But after he bent down to wash the blood from his hands and drink the cool water, he found himself unable to regain his feet.

David's wounds appeared to be mostly superficial since water washed away a good portion of the blood that had been covering him. However, his arm still dangled at an odd angle.

"Let me see that," Bryce said, pointing to his arm. David moved so he sat facing him. Bryce felt along David's arm and shoulder, then his collar bone. "What did you say your wife's name is?"

"Natalie," David said.

"Picture Natalie on your wedding day. Recall her fragrance. Think of how you felt right in that moment," Bryce said trying to give David something pleasant to focus on. Before the man had a chance to speak, he braced David's arm and gave it a hard jerk, pulling the dislocated shoulder back into place.

David didn't utter a sound, but when Bryce finished, he rolled his shoulder and nodded in appreciation.

"Better?" Bryce asked.

"Much," David answered, then motioned to Bryce. "You look worse. Why didn't you mention you'd been shot?" he asked as he ripped the sleeve of his shirt and tied it around Bryce's left thigh. Two bullet wounds bled in his thigh, a lump on his shin made him think his leg was broken, and burns embedded with scraps of his uniform throbbed on his left arm, side, and upper leg.

"I hadn't actually noticed the bullet wounds with everything else that hurts," Bryce said, biting his lip as David tried to pull a piece of what had been his shirt from a burn on his arm. "Just leave it. It's going to take more medical care than either of us has the time or ability to deliver. If you can splint my leg, we'll keep going."

"Keep going?" David stood and glared at him like he'd lost his mind. "You can't walk on that leg. And with all those burns, you shouldn't even be moving. Are you delirious?"

"Not yet, but I reckon that'll come sooner rather than later. We need to find shelter; then you can leave me and go for help. I figure the corporal took a wrong turn on this road. If we keep heading west, we'll eventually find a road or someone who will help us instead of shoot at us."

"For the record, I think this is a terrible idea." David gathered a few long sticks then wrapped them around Bryce's leg using strips torn from the dirty shirt Bryce had changed out of earlier. When he finished, David picked up the haversack he'd set down near the bank of the stream and settled the strap over his head so the bag rested against his back.

Bryce reached out his right hand and David reluctantly took it, pulling him upright. He started to slide an arm around Bryce to support him, then stopped when he realized no matter where he touched him, it would inflict pain.

"Can you find a stick I can lean on? It might be easier," Bryce suggested, closing his eyes and drawing in deep breaths to keep from being violently ill. His stomach roiled and bile surged upward, but he swallowed it down.

David disappeared into the thick trees and soon returned carrying a sturdy branch. "Will this do?" He held the stick out to Bryce.

Bryce pulled a sock from his pack, slipped it over his left hand, blocked the pain it caused his burned hand to hold onto the stick, then took a step forward. Fire shot both up and down his leg, but he forced himself to take another step, then another.

"Let's go. Maybe by the time I pass out, we'll be somewhere safe."

David scowled as he hovered next to him. "Aren't you just a bucket of merry sunshine?"

Bryce tried to grin, even though he was sure it looked more like a grimace. "I do what I can. Tell me more about Natalie and your kids."

If he was going to survive walking on a leg he was sure was broken, he needed something, anything, to take his mind off the overwhelming agony flooding through his body.

Bryce didn't know how long they walked, but by the time they came out of the trees in a little clearing, he knew David's daughter's favorite bedtime story and even the names of all her dolls.

"What do you think?" David asked as they stood in the safety of the trees and looked at an ancient farmhouse made of stone, surrounded by a wooden fence that had seen better days. A big barn, also made of stone, stood about ten yards behind the house. The fenced pasture was empty, and a few outbuildings appeared to be on the verge of collapse.

The place looked forsaken, but it also appeared no Germans were there. They stood and watched for a quarter of an hour, but nothing stirred, not even the breeze.

"Want to give it a try?" Bryce finally asked, taking a slow step forward.

"What's the worst that can happen?" David asked. "Someone might shoot us and put us out of our misery."

Bryce chuckled at the man's attempt at humor. The effort at laughing caused sharp pain in his side. He wondered if he had a few cracked ribs to go along with the rest of his injuries.

They made their way across the clearing and had just stepped past a weathered gate into the yard when the door to the house swung open. A woman rushed out with a rifle in her hands.

She uttered a warning in German as she held the gun, poised to shoot.

David looked quizzically at Bryce.

"She said to stop or she'll shoot," Bryce whispered without taking his eyes from the woman. Her hair was fashioned in two braids, like a little girl would wear, making him question her age. She could have been thirteen or thirty, but he had no idea which was more accurate. She had on a loose worn shirt and an equally worn pair of trousers with a hole in the right knee. Her feet were bare. If they'd been back in the states, Bryce might have called her a hillbilly based on her appearance. Behind her scowl and wary eyes, he couldn't tell much else about her.

"You speak German?" David asked, sounding awed by Bryce's knowledge of the language.

"German, thanks to my grandmother, and French due to my mother's insistence I have a well-rounded education." Bryce kept his voice low as he conversed with David, then turned to the woman and smiled. He raised the hand not holding the walking stick in the air in a gesture of surrender and spoke to her in German. "We mean no harm, miss. We only seek a place to rest this evening."

"You speak German?" she asked in English.

"And French, and a little Italian," Bryce said, his smile widening. "We really don't mean any harm. Our car ran off the road and crashed. We need to get back to our base, but we aren't exactly sure where we are."

The woman sighed and lowered the gun slightly, although she still kept it pointed at them. "There's an American camp about twelve miles that way," she motioned to the west, "but you can't walk straight there. The river must be crossed at the bridge, and it's half a day's walk to the south."

"Are we currently in Germany or France?" David asked, taking a small step forward.

"At the moment, Germany, but I hope by the end of the war, this land will revert once again to France."

Bryce could hear the woman and David speaking, but they sounded far away. His vision grew cloudy and he felt like he was being sucked underwater as the world around him began to darken and waver.

David grabbed his good arm and kept him from falling over. "Please, miss, my friend here is in bad shape. May we please have shelter for the night? I promise we'll not cause any trouble."

"How do I know you aren't pretending to be injured?"

David frowned and pointed to the blood caked on Bryce's leg. "Does this look fake to you?"

The woman sighed a second time and set the gun inside the door of her house. She motioned to them, flapping her hand forward. "Come on, but just so you know, I don't have much to offer."

"As long as you have clean water and a spot on the floor where we can rest, that's all we ask," Bryce said, aware his words sounded slurred.

"You better hurry before he faints," she said, reaching out to help Bryce over the threshold and into her home. He drew in a breath, inhaling a faint fragrance that smelled soft and feminine. Something about it reminded him of his grandmother, Cora Lee.

Three steps inside the door, his leg gave out on him and pain swept over him with such force, he crumpled to the floor. The last thing he remembered was looking into a pair of bright blue eyes framed with a halo of golden curls.

Perhaps the woman in the farmhouse was really an angel in disguise.

Available now!

About the Author

PHOTO BY SHANA BAILEY PHOTOGRAPHY

USA Today bestselling author Shanna Hatfield is a farm girl who loves to write. Her sweet historical and contemporary romances are filled with sarcasm, humor, hope, and hunky heroes.

When Shanna isn't dreaming up unforgettable characters, twisting plots, or covertly seeking dark, decadent chocolate, she hangs out with her beloved husband, Captain Cavedweller, at their home in the Pacific Northwest.

Shanna loves to hear from readers. Connect with her online:

Blog: shannahatfield.com
Facebook: Shanna Hatfield's Page
Shanna Hatfield's Hopeless Romantics Group
Pinterest: Shanna Hatfield
Email: shanna@shannahatfield.com